MISS FORTUNE SERIES INFORMATION

If you've never read a Miss Fortune mystery, you can start with LOUISIANA LONGSHOT, the first book in the series. If you prefer to start with this book, here are a few things you need to know.

Fortune Redding – a CIA assassin with a price on her head from one of the world's most deadly arms dealers. Because her boss suspects that a leak at the CIA blew her cover, he sends her to hide out in Sinful, Louisiana, posing as his niece, a librarian and ex–beauty queen named Sandy-Sue Morrow. The situation was resolved in Change of Fortune and Fortune is now a full-time resident of Sinful and has opened her own detective agency.

Ida Belle and Gertie – served in the military in Vietnam as spies, but no one in the town is aware of that fact except Fortune and Deputy LeBlanc.

Sinful Ladies Society – local group founded by Ida Belle, Gertie, and deceased member Marge. In order to gain membership, women must never have married or if widowed, their husband must have been deceased for at least ten years.

Sinful Ladies Cough Syrup – sold as an herbal medicine in Sinful, which is dry, but it's actually moonshine manufactured by the Sinful Ladies Society.

SWAMP SNIPER

JANA DELEON

CHAPTER ONE

"FORTUNE." GERTIE'S VOICE SOUNDED LIKE IT WAS COMING from a mile away, even though she stood right next to me.

I turned to look, figuring maybe I could read her lips, when someone turned on a microphone on the makeshift platform in the middle of Main Street, and the screech made my ears throb. If someone had told me this many people lived in Sinful, Louisiana, I would have called them a liar. In the two weeks I'd lived in the tiny bayou town, I'd come across only a handful of residents in the General Store and Francine's Café and one small subdivision of perfectly manicured homes, but apparently, the swamps held families I didn't even know existed.

Now I couldn't move a foot without bumping into someone, and for an introvert and someone who was used to working in complete silence and alone, it was a huge stretch. I wasn't certain I had the patience to last the rest of the day. In fact, I'd bet on it.

Gertie's mouth moved, but the screeching microphone eliminated any possibility of understanding her words. I shook my head, pointing to my ears. She sighed and shoved a box of promo items at me, then waved to the crowd, apparently indicating I should hand them out to random people. I looked down at the contents of the box and my eyebrows involuntarily shot up. At that second, the microphone clicked off and I took advantage of the momentary lull to speak.

"Should we be handing out SLS cough syrup for promo?" I asked. The sample bottles were small—like airplane drink size—but even at small doses, the stuff was potent.

Gertie looked confused. "Sure. Why not?"

Apparently the fact that the Sinful Ladies Society "cough syrup" was actually code for moonshine in a bottle had become so commonly known that Gertie no longer thought it would be a problem.

"What if someone doesn't know and gives it to a kid?" I asked, pointing at a group of screaming hellions, running through the crowd and shooting them with water pistols.

A burst of water hit Gertie square in the forehead. "What's the downside?"

I thought about it for a second, but couldn't come up with one. Being arrested for contributing to the delinquency of a minor would guarantee at least a night in jail...the very quiet, very empty jail.

I started working my way through the crowd, carefully picking people to give my cough syrup to. If a screaming kid yelled "Mom" and a woman responded, she got a bottle. If a woman looked harried and disoriented, I assumed she had kids, and she got a bottle. I slipped two into my pocket for myself. If this fiasco ever ended, I was going to need them.

"Vote Ida Belle for mayor," I said as I handed out my wares.

Every woman I handed a bottle to had the same response. "Absolutely."

When I was down to my last bottle, I ditched the cardboard tray in a trash can, then climbed on top of a picnic table and scouted the street for Gertie.

"I see you're still in the middle of things left well enough alone."

His voice sounded behind me and I flinched, which pissed me off. Then I reminded myself that I was in the middle of a noisy festival and decided to cut myself some slack for not hearing him walk up behind me. I turned around and jumped off the picnic table, landing a foot in front of Deputy Carter LeBlanc.

"It's a small-town election," I said. "How bad can it be?"

He grimaced. "With Ida Belle running...you have to ask?"

I shook my head. "Ida Belle's not trouble. In fact, it seems to me that she fixes a lot of this town's problems, including some of yours."

He frowned as I picked at a sore point. Ida Belle and company, myself included, had foiled more than one criminal lately and Carter caught an infinite amount of flak for it. Because he insisted on maintaining his aggrieved and slightly agitated stance about the whole thing, I couldn't resist poking at him when he gave me an opportunity.

"Did it ever occur to you," he said, "that if you had stayed out of my investigations, the only position the three of you would have been in was knitting at Gertie's house or waxing Ida Belle's prize Corvette? Instead, all of you have come close to a permanent residence in Sinful Cemetery."

"And you're saying all that is Ida Belle's fault?"

"I'm saying that if you insist on looking for trouble, you're likely to find it."

He wasn't entirely wrong, and I understood how he probably felt that Ida Belle had stolen his thunder. Maybe if we'd stayed out of police matters, he would have solved the cases and no good people would have died or gone to prison. But it wasn't a risk Ida Belle and Gertie had been willing to take, and God forgive me, I'd allowed myself to be dragged into their drama.

"I should have known I'd find you hitting on the hottest girl in town."

The man's voice sounded behind me and I turned in time to

see a good-looking, muscular man cross the street, giving me the once-over as he approached.

Midthirties, six foot four, two hundred pounds and most of it muscle, looked like he knew his way around a fight. Threat level medium.

The man stepped right up in front of Carter, grinning like he'd just heard the best joke in the world. Carter didn't look nearly as enthused. I felt the testosterone level increase by a hundred percent.

"How are you, Bobby?" Carter said and stuck out his hand.

Bobby shook Carter's hand and inclined his head toward me. "Clearly, not doing as well as you."

Carter sighed. "I'm wearing a uniform. I was talking to Miss Morrow about a police matter."

Bobby glanced over at me and raised his eyebrows. "You going to arrest her for being too hot for this town? 'Cause that's the only thing I can think of her being guilty of."

Given that my current "hotness" consisted of shorts, tank top, tennis shoes, lip balm, and hair in a ponytail, I wasn't convinced of Bobby's sincerity. But despite my inclination to hurl at his clumsy attempt to gain my interest, Carter's obvious dismay was too good to pass up on.

"See," I said. "Someone appreciates what I have to offer this town."

"Darling," Bobby said, "any time you feel unappreciated, you give me a call. I'm always happy to show one of Carter's girls what they're missing. Bobby Morel. Anyone can tell you where to find me." He winked at me and walked away, giving Carter a wave over his shoulder.

I watched him walk away then turned back to Carter and smiled. "I guess now you're going to tell me Bobby is trouble, too?"

Carter tore his gaze from the retreating Bobby and looked back at me. "No, not really. I mean, he can be a hothead and I don't think he's ever read a book outside of school, but he's not a bad guy. He was Army Special Forces until last week. His mom told me he was coming home after discharge."

Special Forces? The threat level ticked up a notch.

"Can't be much work in Sinful for you ex-military types," I said, "unless you figure he's going to give you a run for your job."

Carter laughed. "Not a chance. Starting in middle school, Bobby counted the days until he was getting out of this town. I imagine he'll stay long enough to figure out what he wants to do next, and then he'll head to some city where 'things happen.' He always said things never happened in Sinful."

"He should have been around the last couple of weeks."

"Hmmm." Carter looked thoughtful for a moment, then focused in on me again. "According to the girls in high school, he'll show you a good time. I just wouldn't get attached if I were you. My guess is he's just stopping by."

"Do I look like the kind of 'girl' who gets attached?"

"No. Which only makes you more fascinating." He grinned at me and headed across the street toward some kids who were climbing up a light pole.

I felt a blush start on my chest and creep up my neck, then I whirled around and stalked off in the other direction, happy that Carter hadn't stuck around long enough to see my girly reaction. I would have never lived that one down.

I hated to admit it, but despite his annoying insistence on following the rules, something about Carter LeBlanc attracted me in a way I'd never been to another man. Not that I was some shrinking-violet virgin, destined to be the agoraphobic cat lady, but I'd never had a relationship that I considered serious. I'd certainly never met a guy who'd made me flush.

And wasn't pleased that I finally had.

Even more disturbing was that I was pretty sure Carter knew exactly what effect he had on me and enjoying poking at the chink in my armor.

"You going to just stand there lollygagging or are you going to come hear me speak?" Ida Belle's voice boomed right beside me.

I held in a sigh that yet another person had managed, in broad daylight, to sneak up on me. If I ever got out of Louisiana and back to the CIA, I was going to need serious retraining time before I would be suitable for a mission.

"Is it time already?" I asked, but what I was really thinking was "thank God it's finally time." As soon as the speeches were over, I would haul butt to a quiet, empty house as fast as my Jeep would carry me.

"It's time," Ida Belle said. "Did you give out all your cough syrup?"

"I have one left," I said, holding out my hand with the bottle and not bothering to mention the two in my shorts pockets. It was the least Ida Belle owed me after this crap.

Ida Belle plucked the bottle out of my hand. "I'm going to need this later."

I nodded and hurried behind her as we made our way through the crowd to the makeshift platform at the end of Main Street. Ida Belle slipped around the side and onto the stage while I pushed my way through the mass of sweaty people to stand up front next to Gertie.

As the election coordinator talked to the two candidates, I got my first opportunity to make a good assessment of Ida Belle's competition.

Midfifties, five foot ten, one hundred eighty pounds—twenty of it potbelly.

No threat to me, but I had no idea what kind of threat he represented to Ida Belle. "What's the story on the other guy?" I asked Gertie.

Gertie looked at the man and frowned. "Theodore 'Call-Me-Ted' Williams. Not much to know, really. He moved here about two years ago from somewhere up north. He's never come out and said so, but the rumor is that he inherited his money from a family business—some sort of manufacturing. They sold out, he packed up his entirely-too-young-for-him wife and moved from New England to Sinful."

"Really? That seems rather odd. How did he even know about Sinful?"

"He said he'd been here before years ago with old James Parker, who lived in Mudbug and had apparently brought Ted fishing at several of the area bayou towns."

"*Lived* in Mudbug. Past tense?"

"Yeah. He died fifteen years ago or so, but apparently Ted remembered the area fondly and when he got control of his money, he had a real estate agent look for a house in the area. The Adams family had just moved to New Orleans, so we were the lucky winners who acquired Ted."

I smiled. "The Adams family?"

Gertie grinned. "I know. I can barely hold in a chuckle every time I say it. You're really catching up on regular society, Fortune."

I nodded. "I've been spending a lot of time watching TV and on the Internet. I never realized the world was so big, interesting, boring, and odd, all at the same time."

"That pretty much sums it up."

"So is this Ted going to be any competition? I figure with him not being here very long and being a Yankee on top of it..."

Gertie frowned. "You wouldn't think, but he's managed to ingratiate himself pretty well in town."

"By ingratiate, you mean throw money around?"

"Of course. Money's the only thing that's always scarce in Sinful. It doesn't take much to impress this bunch of yahoos, or to buy loyalty. My guess is most of the men are going to vote for Ted —because of the man thing and because he hands out fishing equipment like business cards."

"And the women?"

"Except for Celia's group, I think most of the women will swing Ida Belle's way."

I shook my head. Celia Arceneaux was the leader of the Catholic-based women's group who called themselves the GWs, short for God's Wives. Ida Belle referred to them as "Got No Lives" and based on what I'd seen in my short stint in Sinful, I was leaning toward agreeing with Ida Belle, despite the fact that it seemed kinda rude.

Ida Belle ran the Sinful Ladies Society, the other women's group in town, which was completely comprised of old maids and women who had been widowed for at least ten years. The Sinful Ladies believed that having men around tended to dull a woman's natural superior abilities, so no women with men in tow were allowed. This set of rules tended to infuriate Celia's group and a long-standing feud had ensued, mostly over banana pudding.

"You don't think Celia will vote for Ida Belle," I asked, "even after we found out who killed Pansy?"

The prior week, Celia's daughter had been the victim of a most sordid murder. Ida Belle, Gertie, and I had managed to "out" the killer, almost getting me killed in the process. I'd assumed—apparently incorrectly—that our success would have paved the way for a better relationship between the two groups.

Gertie sighed. "You'd think it would be that simple, wouldn't you? But the reality is, if Celia tells her ladies to vote for Ida Belle, then she's breaking down the fabric of their thirty-year existence. It wouldn't surprise me if Celia herself voted for Ida Belle, but she'd never admit to it."

I shook my head. "It seems like such a waste of energy."

"I couldn't agree more." Gertie pointed at the stage and clapped. "They're about to get started."

The election coordinator, an enormous woman named Cindy-Lou, stepped up to the microphone and I cringed, waiting for the screech, then smiled when only her nasally Southern accent blasted through the speakers.

"Quiet down, y'all," she said, waving at the crowd. "We're about to get started with the debate. As Sinful is a Southern town with manners, we're forgoing the coin toss and Ida Belle will speak first because she's a lady."

I heard someone mumble "that's debatable," but when I scanned the crowd behind me, no one stood out as the guilty culprit. It was just as well. The last thing I needed to do was hand Carter an excuse to arrest me and dig further into my background. So far, I'd narrowly escaped harsh scrutiny from the deputy, and I wasn't certain my cover would hold if he took a hard look.

The noise level fell to practically nothing as Ida Belle stepped up to the microphone and started her speech. It was a good one, I guess. As I'd just started watching regular television the past week, I really had no basis for comparison. And the last thing I'd watch was politicians. Given half an opportunity, they meddled enough with the CIA and often made it difficult for us to do our job. So I didn't spend any more time listening to them than was absolutely required.

Ida Belle finished up her speech and the female half of the crowd cheered. Then Ted stepped up to the microphone and the men hooted.

A shrill voice a couple of people down from us yelled, "Get those votes, baby!"

I leaned forward and gave the woman a quick once-over.

Midthirties, one hundred and forty pounds—ten of it fake breasts, nails so long she couldn't pick up a weapon, much less fire one. Puppies were a bigger threat.

The rest of the package was just as disturbing. Skintight pants, a top cut so low that it bordered on porn, poufy auburn hair, and more makeup than all of the women attending the rally combined.

"The wife?" I asked.

Gertie glanced over and rolled her eyes. "Yeah. She blends so well."

"She's a good twenty years younger than him. Why would a woman like that want to live in a place like Sinful?"

"Age-old story is my guess—daddy issues. Plus, Ted's got money, and Paulette doesn't seem like the brightest tool in the shed."

I shook my head, amazed at how much women would lower their standards simply to avoid getting a job. The general population was a confusing and contradictory lot.

Ted started his speech, and immediately, I flashed back to the last time I had to buy a car. Yep, that was it. The broad, fake smile, the nod...Ted had that used-car salesman rap down pat. What was even more irritating is that the men in the crowd seemed to buy it. Or maybe it was as Gertie said, and they just liked the free stuff he handed out.

It seemed like forever before the old gasbag wrapped up, and I prayed that was the end of it, but then CindyLou placed another microphone on the stage and Ida Belle and Ted took their places in front of them.

"There's a debate?" I asked. Given my knowledge of Sinful, I couldn't begin to fathom how that would play out.

"Not a debate," Gertie said. "Just their promises."

I frowned, not really understanding, when Ida Belle cleared her throat and said, "I promise to add lights to the playground."

All the women cheered.

Ted gave her a nod and said, "I promise to resurface the public dock."

All the men cheered.

"I get it now," I said. "Can they actually do all those things, though? I mean, don't they need the money?"

Gertie waved a hand in dismissal. "They can't do any of it, truth be known. Hasn't been extra in the Sinful till in a hundred years. But people like to know what would happen if Sinful hit the equivalent of the lottery."

I shook my head. So the crux of Sinful's battle for mayor rested on who could produce the best fiction that impressed the most residents. I mean, if a politician's mouth was open, they were probably spouting fiction, but in this case, they weren't even trying to hide it.

"I promise to make alcohol legal in the city limits," Ted said.

An uneasy lull fell over the crowd and Gertie broke into a huge smile. "He screwed the pooch," she whispered to me.

I frowned. I could see why the women didn't want legalized alcohol in town. That meant bars, which meant the potential of husbands behaving badly, and besides, they all had the Sinful Ladies cough syrup. But I didn't get why the men were oddly silent.

"Why wouldn't the men want alcohol legalized?" I asked.

Gertie snorted. "You think they want their bad behavior advertised right here in the middle of town? They all head to the Swamp Bar or to New Orleans to act like children. That way, their wives can pretend they don't know about it, and as long as it doesn't happen in front of Sinful residents, everyone else goes along with the lie."

"Ah." It made sense in a Sinful, Louisiana, sort of way.

Ida Belle leaned closer to the microphone, grinning from ear to ear, and clearly moving in for the kill. "I promise to create a town bond to pay for the installation of an additional cooler at Francine's. That way, everyone in Sinful can enjoy a serving of banana pudding on Sunday."

The crowd went ballistic and Gertie lifted her hand for a high five. "Kill shot," she said.

I slapped her hand and laughed. Only in Sinful could someone win a mayoral election on the strength of a banana pudding cooler.

IT WAS ALMOST DARK BY THE TIME I DRAGGED MYSELF OUT OF my Jeep and into the shower. Gertie left Main Street a couple of minutes before I did, and Ida Belle was still sitting on the stage, having a chat with her competition. His wife, Paulette, had long since abandoned her supportive role, claiming her hair spray couldn't hold up to the humidity. Most of the town residents had wandered off home, leaving a big cleanup for tomorrow—something I was certain I'd get roped into and wasn't looking forward to in the least, especially not in this heat.

I stood under the spray of water until my skin shriveled, then called myself done. I'd grabbed the occasional finger food during the rally but hadn't had what I'd call a decent meal since breakfast. When I stepped out of the shower, my stomach launched a full protest. I pulled my long extensions back in the standard ponytail they'd grown to expect, threw on shorts and a T-shirt, and headed downstairs to rustle up a sandwich, chips, and the latest dessert concoction my friend Ally had asked me to test for potential sale in the bakery she wanted to open.

It didn't take me twenty minutes to polish off the roast beef sandwich, chips, and something heavenly that Ally referred to as a summer tart, and then I headed back upstairs where I fell into bed and managed to go right to sleep without even putting on my noise-canceling headphones.

Banging on my front door woke me and I bolted straight out of bed, grabbing my pistol as I leaped. I landed in firing position, aiming at the door. It took a second for my mind to catch up to my body, and I realized the banging sound was downstairs at the front door and not an intruder.

One glance outside at the still-pitch-black sky and I knew this couldn't be good. Still clutching my pistol, I hurried downstairs, trying not to remember that the last time I'd been awakened at an indecent hour, I'd been accused of murder.

I eased the door open and the momentary relief when I realized it wasn't Carter standing there disappeared in an instant when I saw the look on Gertie's face.

"What's wrong?" I asked as I motioned her inside.

She clutched the bottom of her sweater, twisting it into a knot, and I noticed that her hands shook as she twisted. In the short time I'd known Gertie, we'd been in some hairy situations, but I'd never seen her this worried. And that scared the crap out of me.

"Gertie, tell me what's wrong."

"Marie called me. She lives catty-corner to the Williamses. I don't have all the facts, but the paramedics showed up about an hour ago and carried out a body bag."

I sucked in a breath. "Which one?"

"Marie says Paulette ran out of the house and threw herself over the gurney, screaming and crying. The paramedics sedated her and put her in the ambulance with the body before they took off."

I absorbed everything Gertie told me, trying to figure out what part of this story had her so vexed. So far, it seemed straightforward. "So Ted died. Why all the worry?"

"Carter sealed the house. Marie walked outside and heard him calling a forensics lab. He was holding a Baggie with a bottle in it."

"He overdosed?" I asked, still not certain why Gertie was so stressed. "The coroner should be able to determine that."

Gertie shook her head. "Marie said it was one of our cough syrup bottles in the Baggie. Marie said Paulette screamed 'she killed him' right before the paramedics dosed her."

A flashback of Ida Belle, taking my last bottle of cough syrup...Ida Belle sitting on the makeshift stage, joking with Ted after everyone had left the rally...cycled through my mind on fast forward, and an enormous feeling of dread washed over me.

"Where did he get the bottle?"

Gertie's lower lip trembled. "I'm afraid he got it from Ida Belle. She was holding one when I left."

I nodded. "I gave it to her. It was my last one."

I didn't think it possible for Gertie to look even more depressed, but she managed it anyway. "I was hoping for another explanation, even though I figured that's what you were going to say."

"Did you call Ida Belle and warn her?"

"I called, but she didn't answer, so I drove by but Carter's truck was already parked outside her house. I knocked, but he wouldn't let me in the house. Told me to go home and mind my own business."

Gertie's face flushed with anger. "Ida Belle is my oldest and dearest friend. Since when is she not my business?"

I patted Gertie's arm in an awkward attempt to comfort her. This sort of thing was definitely outside my skill set. "Carter's in cop mode right now. I'm sure he didn't mean to imply that you had no stake in things."

"Maybe," Gertie said, refusing to be mollified, "but this isn't some big city where we're all strangers. Carter has known Ida Belle his entire life. You and I both know from experience that Ida Belle's capable of killing someone, but Carter doesn't know that side of her. And we know she wouldn't move to lethal unless someone was creating a life-threatening situation. We were soldiers, not sociopaths."

"I know." And then it clicked with me that those two simple words I'd uttered, I meant 100 percent. Despite the fact that I'd known Ida Belle for less than two weeks, I was absolutely certain that she hadn't killed Ted. I would have bet my cover on it.

One look at Gertie's agonized expression, and I wondered if it might come down to that.

CHAPTER TWO

I LEFT GERTIE WITH A CUP OF COFFEE AND A BOTTLE OF COUGH syrup while I threw on yoga pants, T-shirt, and tennis shoes. It took a couple cups of the mix before she'd calmed down enough to venture out. Then we headed for Ida Belle's house. Carter couldn't put us off forever, and unless Ida Belle was straight-out telling him she'd killed Ted, Carter didn't have any cause to arrest her.

Yet.

Carter's truck was still parked in front of Ida Belle's house when Gertie pulled her ancient Cadillac to the curb. All up and down the block, I saw blinds and curtains move from nosy neighbors trying to figure out what was going on.

As Gertie and I made our way up the sidewalk, Carter stepped out of the house and gave us a frowning nod before continuing past to his truck. He climbed inside and shut the door, and without uttering a single word, pulled away from the curb and down the street. We both stood in front of the porch steps, watching him drive away. I don't know what was running through Gertie's mind, but I wasn't feeling overly confident as we walked up the steps and knocked on the door.

Ida Belle, hair in curlers and still wearing her robe, flung open the door and glared. When she realized it was me and Gertie and not Carter, her expression went from exasperated to relieved and she waved us inside.

"Hurry up about it," she said, rushing us to the kitchen. "Damn man wouldn't let me brew a pot of coffee. Like anyone is alert at three a.m. It's not like I'm old people or something with one of those bladders that's all worn out and gets you up at ungodly hours."

I looked over at Gertie, who gave me a slight shake of her head. Clearly, when Ida Belle was on a tear, Gertie thought it best to let her get it all out. I slid into a chair at the back of the kitchen table and figured I'd wait on Gertie to give me a talking cue. Gertie took the chair next to me, still silently observing.

"Then Carter stomps in here," Ida Belle continued to rant, "and starts quizzing me like he's the gestapo, and all because that idiot Ted doesn't take care of himself and dropped dead of a heart attack or something. What the hell do I have to do with his lifestyle choices? Every time I see the man, he's holding a beer and some form of red meat. Hell, that wife alone would give most people a heart attack, if only as an opportunity to get away from her."

She shoved the coffeepot under the filter basket and poked the on switch so hard the entire coffee machine scooted back a couple of inches on the counter.

"And to top it all off," Ida Belle said as she plopped into a chair across from me, "Carter wouldn't even give me a good reason for this intrusion. I've always liked the boy, but if he's going to start acting irrationally, then I'll be damned if I see him promoted to sheriff once I'm elected mayor."

I looked over at Gertie, who raised her eyebrows.

"What?" Ida Belle asked, catching Gertie's expression. "If you two know something, spill it, because I'm tired and cranky and more than a little pissed off."

Gertie took a breath and filled Ida Belle in on what Marie had witnessed.

Ida Belle's eyes widened. "Poisoned? And that fool of a wife thinks I did it? Why in the world would I waste a good murder on that idiot?"

"Got me," I said, in complete agreement.

Gertie frowned at me. "Yes, well, the three of us tend to approach human extermination from a different viewpoint than most. So while we all know it's the most ridiculous thing to even suggest, much less consider, it doesn't mean the rest of Sinful will feel the same."

Ida Belle sighed. "Which means Carter doesn't have the option to treat it as nonsense either. I get it, but I don't have to like it."

"Me either," I said.

Gertie shook her head. "I swear, sometimes it's like you two are the same person."

I grinned. "You say that like it's a bad thing."

"Under normal circumstances," Gertie said, "it could be, but given the situations we've found ourselves in lately, I suppose it's an asset."

"So what now?" Ida Belle asked.

"Given that it's a suspicious death, they'll rush the autopsy and drug tox," I said. "They should be able to screen for common poisons in a matter of hours. The rest could take longer."

Ida Belle nodded. "So maybe a couple of days of getting the squint-eye from some people and then this latest shitstorm will pass over."

I shrugged. "Probably, but in my limited experience, the passing of one shitstorm seems only to bring another."

Ida Belle sighed. "I swear, things were quiet before you got here."

"Yeah, that's what Carter keeps telling me."

Ida Belle rose from the table and grabbed the coffeepot.

"Well, I guess there's nothing else to do but have some coffee and muffins and wait."

I nodded, the smell of the coffee and the prospect of a home-made muffin improving my mood despite the complete lack of sleep I'd gotten since I'd been here. But even given my certainty that Ida Belle hadn't killed Ted, I couldn't escape that niggle in the back of my mind that said this was all far from over.

———

THE KNOCK ON IDA BELLE'S DOOR CAME SOONER THAN ANY OF us expected. I froze, coffee cup dangling in midair like an incomplete sentence. Gertie's eyes widened and she sucked in a breath as she dropped the last bite of her muffin on her plate and stared at Ida Belle.

I have to give it to her—Ida Belle remained cool as a cucumber.

"It's probably someone being nosy," Ida Belle said. "They couldn't possibly know anything already."

She rose from the table and headed to the front door.

"Do you think she's right?" Gertie asked, the hope clear in her voice.

I wanted to say she was right. Logically, what she said made sense. But somehow, that knock had sounded different—ominous, even. And I thought Ida Belle had felt it, too, even though she'd tried to mask it with optimism, most likely for Gertie's benefit.

I rose from my chair and hurried after Ida Belle, Gertie scurrying behind me, and arrived at the front door just as Ida Belle pulled it open. My worst fears were confirmed.

Carter stood on Ida Belle's front porch and his expression left no doubt where the conversation was headed. He handed Ida Belle a folded piece of paper.

"I'm really sorry about this," he said, "but that's a warrant to search your property. I'm going to have to ask you to take a seat in the kitchen. Deputy Breaux will stay with you until I've completed my search."

He looked at Gertie and me. "I'm not even going to bother telling you to leave, but if you want to stay, you have to sit in the kitchen with Ida Belle and can't move until this is over. Are we clear?"

We both gave him a nod, then followed Ida Belle to the kitchen where we slipped back into our chairs at the breakfast table. Gertie grabbed her napkin and began to pull it apart in pieces. Her face was flushed and her breathing more rapid.

"What does this mean?" she asked.

"I think it means Ted was poisoned," I said.

Ida Belle nodded. "I'm afraid she's right. Carter wouldn't have bothered Judge Aubry for a warrant without a reason. For one, he can't stand the man, and two, he would never risk his own reputation over something like this."

I heard Carter talking to someone at the front door and a couple of seconds later, a short, squatty man wearing a deputy badge walked into the kitchen.

Five feet eight, two hundred forty pounds, probably couldn't run to the kitchen counter without collapsing.

He gave us a nod as he entered the room, a blush running up his neck and onto his face as he stood awkwardly next to the counter, clearly unsure of how to handle the situation. His insecurity combined with one of those boyish, round faces was enough to generate a flicker of my sympathy. I hadn't seen someone that uncomfortable in a long time—except for myself, of course, if one took into account most of my time in Sinful.

"Well, don't just stand there lurking over us, Kyle," Ida Belle said and waved at the deputy. "There's a stool under the counter and a half a pot of coffee behind you. Cups are in the cabinet above."

Kyle froze, clearly uncertain what protocol was in this situation. "I don't know, ma'am..."

Ida Belle shrugged. "Carter could be hours. Are you really planning to stand there the whole time? First off, I don't think you're in any shape to manage it, which is something you need to address given your age. Second, what do you think we're going to do if you're sitting—make a break for the back door and head off to Mexico?"

Kyle's face turned a deeper shade of red. "No, ma'am. I just... well, I feel bad making myself comfortable given the circumstances."

"Whether you're sitting or standing, the circumstances aren't going to change."

Ida Belle turned around in her chair to face me. Deputy Kyle stared at the side of her head for a moment, then glanced back at the coffeepot. Finally, common sense, bad physical conditioning, or maybe just a slight fear of Ida Belle won out and he turned around to pour a cup of coffee.

It briefly crossed my mind to jump out of my chair and run for the back door, just to see his reaction, but I decided that was probably mean, even though I was certain the results would have been hilarious. I glanced over at Gertie, who was also casing the distance between her chair and the door, and barely held in a smile.

Great minds.

"So Kyle," I said after he hefted himself onto a stool and lifted the coffee to his lips, "I guess this means someone bumped off Ted, right?"

He sucked in a breath, which included a mouthful of hot coffee, then snorted, blowing it through his nose and across the kitchen floor.

Ida Belle sighed. "I just mopped yesterday."

I grinned. "I didn't mean to choke you up there, Kyle. But really, it doesn't take a genius to know what's going on."

Kyle grabbed a paper towel and coughed into it a couple of times before throwing it away. "I can't talk about an investigation. Deputy LeBlanc would kill me."

"Well, we can't have that," I said. "One murder a week really should be the town limit."

As the last sentence left my mouth, Carter walked through the kitchen, headed for the back door. He paused, and for a split second, I thought I had bought myself an escort to the sidewalk, but he continued on through the back door without even glancing at us.

"What do you think he's looking for?" Gertie asked.

"Household items that can be used as poison," Ida Belle said. "At least, that's my guess."

I nodded. "Which means that whatever killed Ted caused a reaction that was fairly obvious to the medical examiner. No way have they gotten tox screens back yet."

Gertie bit her lip. "What do you think it is?"

"What kind of pest control products do you have around the house?" I asked.

"The usual stuff," Ida Belle said. "Ant killer, wasps, rats...stuff for all the usual bayou suspects."

Gertie threw her hands in the air. "Hell, everyone in Sinful has that stuff."

Ida Belle frowned. "If they have enough evidence from the tox screen, can't they determine an exact match to the box of poison?"

"I don't know," I said. "I mean, I suppose they could determine the brand based on comparison."

"But if more than one person has the same brand," Gertie said, "it's not possible to say with certainty which box was used, right?"

I frowned. "Maybe, maybe not. I was reading this book on forensics and it talked about Locard's exchange principle. Basically everywhere you go you take something with you and leave something behind. So if there were hair or skin cells in the sample from Ted's, then they could look for a match."

"I always wear long gloves when I'm working with the poison," Ida Belle said.

"Then that makes it less likely," I said.

Gertie slumped back in her chair. "That's a relief. Everyone in Sinful has a storage shed full of pest control products, so that opens it wide up as far as suspects."

"Except the Spencers," Ida Belle said.

"Do the Spencers have some sort of special immunity to pests?" I asked.

"No, but they have these strange ideas about communing with nature and 'polite' ways to keep pests away. Some sort of green crap." Ida Belle waved a hand in dismissal. "They're from California. What do you expect?"

I stared at her, still confused. "So they commune with the pests?"

"They claim they ask them politely to leave and they do." Ida Belle rolled her eyes. "Can't say that I blame the pests. I'd leave too before I hung out with a bunch of weirdos."

Gertie tapped Ida Belle's arm. "Here he comes."

I looked out the back door in time to see Carter coming up the steps carrying a plastic bag in his hands. He stepped inside the kitchen and glanced at Kyle before looking at Ida Belle.

"I'm afraid I'm going to have to ask you to come down to the station," he said.

I have to give her props. If it had been me, I'd have been shitting kittens, but Ida Belle just looked up at him, cool as a cucumber. "Am I under arrest?"

"No. I just want to ask you some questions."

Ida Belle nodded. "I suppose it's all right if I change clothes?"

"Of course."

Ida Belle rose from the chair, patting Gertie on the shoulder as she passed. "Don't worry, dear. Everything is going to be fine."

Carter waited until Ida Belle had left the room before looking down at the two of us. "It's time for you to go home. I know you want to help, but there's nothing you can do. If you even think there's something you can do, remind yourself that if I catch you doing something, I'm going to arrest you both. Is that clear?"

I bristled a bit at his tone but knew this wasn't the time to challenge the good deputy. If Ted had been murdered and Ida Belle owned the poison used, this was serious business.

"How long will she be?" I asked.

"That depends," Carter replied. "I'm sure she'll call when I release her."

He left the room without so much as a glance at us, and I rose from the table. "Let's go, Gertie. We can wait at my house. I stocked up on one of everything in the General Store. It's enough to last through a hurricane, much less a little police questioning."

I hoped my light tone would perk Gertie up a little, but the woman who walked out of the house with me was a shell of the one I'd come to know.

"I think I'd just rather go home," Gertie said. "If you don't mind."

"Of course I don't mind."

As we walked down the sidewalk, Gertie clutched my arm, bringing me to a stop. "We have to get her out of there."

"It's just questioning," I said. "She'll probably be done in a couple of hours."

"And if she's not?"

"Then we'll deal with it then."

Gertie's lower lip trembled. "I've got a really bad feeling this time—one I never got with Pansy or Marie."

I felt the same way, but I wasn't about to admit it. That would only make Gertie even more anxious, and she was hovering around heart attack range already.

I patted her on the back. "You're just feeling that way because you and Ida Belle are so close."

A small sliver of hope passed over Gertie's face as she reached up to give my hand a squeeze before continuing to her car. As I watched her walk away, I said a silent prayer that my own intuition was dead wrong.

CHAPTER THREE

I'D JUST FINISHED BREAKFAST WHEN MY CELL PHONE SIGNALED I had a message. I picked it up and my pulse quickened when I saw it was from my friend Ally, who should be neck-deep in breakfast service at Francine's Café.

re: Ida Belle There's a mob outside the police station.

Hell! I grabbed the keys to my Jeep and hurried into the garage, pressing in Gertie's number as I jumped in the driver's seat.

"I'm picking you up in two minutes," I said as soon as Gertie answered. "I'll explain when I get there."

Before she could utter a single word, I disconnected the call and threw the Jeep in reverse. As I squealed away from the curb, my mind whirled with all the reasons a mob might be assembled. But unless it was a "Free Ida Belle" movement, I had serious doubts it was going to be good news.

Gertie was standing at the curb when I screeched to a halt. She attempted a quick leap inside the Jeep, but the weight of her enormous handbag set her off balance and she ended up sprawling across the passenger's seat and my lap. It took a bit of work to get her upright and her handbag straps unwound from the stick shift, but with minimal embarrassment and a brief apology, we were finally on our way.

I filled Gertie in on Ally's text as I drove. Based on her grim expression, I could tell she wasn't expecting anything good, either. But what we saw as I pulled onto Main Street was even worse than we expected.

Paulette stood in front of the police station, wailing like a wounded cat and screaming for justice. Sheriff Lee, who was probably old enough to be Paulette's great-great-great-great grandfather, was trying to reason with her, but a 200-year-old man didn't have a chance against a thirtysomething emotionally bent woman.

Hell, short of knocking her out, I wasn't sure what would improve the situation.

A crowd of people were assembled behind Paulette, all grumbling and shaking their fists at the sheriff. I parked in front of the café and as we approached the crowd, I could begin to make out some of the comments.

"This town used to be safe!"

"How many murderers can one town have?"

"What the hell are we paying you for?"

As we approached the crowd, one of the angry protestors caught sight of me and shook his fist. "Things like this never happened before Yankees came to town."

Five feet eleven, two hundred eighty pounds of flab, high blood pressure, incredibly low IQ.

"Given that the victim is also a Yankee," I said, "I fail to see your point."

His face turned a bit red but my logic didn't stop him from blustering on. "You know exactly what I mean."

I raised one eyebrow at him. "Are you saying he was killed because he's a Yankee? If that's the case, then I'm the one who should be worried, not you."

"No, damn it! That's not what I'm saying at all."

"Really?" I asked, intent on carrying the absurdity as far as he was willing to travel. "Because that would make sense given that the victim before him was living in California. That's kinda like Yankees, right?"

Several of the mob nodded in agreement and I held in a sigh. Humor had no place in Sinful.

"You're twisting my words!" he raged.

"Your words were already ridiculous," I said. "I didn't have to so much as bend one for everyone to get that."

"You meddling bitch." He started toward me.

I smiled. "You forgot 'Yankee.'"

Sheriff Lee, finally noticing the exchange, rushed forward at a good clip of negative two miles per hour. I have no idea what he thought he was going to do against the charging wall of ignorant flab coming at me, and I was almost sorry that he wouldn't arrive in time for me to see it, but the situation in front of me was about to require action.

Flabby Man took another step toward me and lifted his hand, palm open.

Oh, hell no! He did not think he was going to bitch-slap me like some girl.

"Stop!" Sheriff Lee yelled, but I barely heard him over the crowd. Flabby Man never slowed, so either his ears were insulated with a layer of blubber or he was ignoring the sheriff like most everyone else did.

He took that final step, his arm swinging downward at the same time. He couldn't have indicated his strike more if he'd sent me a text beforehand. In a single deft move, I stepped to the side, grabbed his thumb and twisted. He howled in pain and bent over to follow his thumb, and I kept pushing it lower. It didn't take long for gravity to take over and he went tumbling down onto the street.

"She assaulted him!" Another man in the crowd yelled.

I glanced over, taking only a second to dismiss him as a threat. He looked like Flabby Man's twin.

"Good," I heard a woman's voice chime in. "He's an asshole."

"You can't say 'asshole' in the middle of Main Street," another woman complained. "It's illegal."

"What are you going to do about it, asshole?"

Sheriff Lee, who'd finally managed to make it over to me, waved his hands in the air, trying to get the attention of the clearly escalating crowd. "Everyone calm down. There's no need for violence."

I looked over at Gertie and shook my head. She raised her eyebrows, clearly no more confident than I was that Sheriff Lee could get the crowd under control. The voices continued to escalate in pitch and level. More and more people began shouting and pointing fingers, and I could no longer tell who was angry at whom and for what.

And then all hell broke loose.

Such a simple thing—one shove—and the entire mob erupted. Men swung wildly at each other, mostly missing their intended target and hitting the women, who had handfuls of each other's hair and were bent over turning in a circle like performing some insane dance.

It was a bar fight without the bar.

Although it pained me, I knew retreat was the best option. I turned to grab Gertie and pull her out of the fray, but as I swung around, I caught a glimpse of her dropping to the ground and crawling through the crowd toward the sheriff's department.

What the hell was she doing?

I knew it was a suicide mission, but I couldn't abandon a man in the field, so I ducked down and pushed through the crowd, trying to follow Gertie, who scrambled on all fours through the mass of thrashing idiots. I was just about to step onto the sidewalk when someone grabbed hold of my ponytail and yanked me backward. I saw a flash of glittery hot pink and knew Paulette was the culprit.

It took me less than a second to assess my options, and none of them were good. If I didn't get my hair out of Paulette's grasp, those extensions were likely to rip right off, leaving me exposed in a way I couldn't afford. By the same token, I could hardly assault the widow in the middle of Main Street and in front of a bunch of screaming witnesses.

I grabbed the base of my ponytail as I heard the first rip of hair and at the same time, a spray of water hit my face. I looked up and saw Gertie standing on the sidewalk directing a water hose onto the fighting crowd. Paulette screamed like a banshee and showed no sign of letting up, so I did the only thing possible.

I clenched the ponytail as tightly as I could and swung around, flinging Paulette toward the sidewalk. She stumbled as she whirled around, and let go of my hair as she completely lost her balance and ran straight into Gertie, knocking her to the ground.

Carter chose that exact moment to open the door to the sheriff's department, and the spray of hose water caught him right in the face.

It was like a gunshot went off. All fighting ceased and the mob scattered in every direction, leaving only me, Gertie, and Sheriff Lee standing there, dripping and clearly guilty.

Carter wiped his hand across his eyes then shook the water off. He pointed at Sheriff Lee. "Go to the Williams house and sit on Paulette. I don't want her walking out her front door until I say so."

Sheriff Lee, looking happy to escape, hustled off down the street at a faster clip than I thought possible.

Carter turned to Gertie, who still clutched the dripping hose. "You, put down the weapon and go home." He pointed at me. "You, get inside."

I threw my hands up in the air. "I never even threw a punch. I'm the victim here."

Carter raised one eyebrow. "Somehow I find that impossible to believe. Inside. Now."

He stepped to the side and held open the door.

Gertie sprang up from the sidewalk. "She's telling the truth. You've got a lot of problems in this town, but Fortune is not one of them."

He pointed his finger at her. "Home. Now. Or I'll arrest both of you."

Gertie's mouth set in a grim line. She glanced over at me, and I gave her a small shake of my head. Whatever Carter had in mind for me, Gertie's continued protesting would likely only make it worse.

I could tell she wasn't pleased, but Gertie shut off the water and with a final glare at Carter, stalked off down the sidewalk, her shoes squishing as she went.

Ida Belle sat in a chair in front of the metal desk at the front of the sheriff's department, and looked up in surprise when I stepped inside. Deputy Breaux perched in the chair across from her, looking even more uncomfortable than he had at Ida Belle's house. The blinds on the front windows of the sheriff's department were drawn, so they couldn't have seen the fray, but I was certain they'd heard it.

Carter pointed to a room diagonal from where Ida Belle sat and I stepped inside and flopped into a chair in front of a makeshift desk. Carter closed the door behind him and it didn't take a second before he unloaded.

"What the hell were you thinking?"

My mouth dropped. "What was I thinking? Look, I know you find it impossible to believe that I'm not looking for trouble, but I assure you, I did not start that fight. I was only defending myself."

"Uh-huh." He didn't look remotely convinced. "Do you realize you have to defend yourself more than anyone I've ever met in my life? Professional football players defend themselves less than you do. Freedom fighters pale in comparison to the record you've established in just two weeks in Sinful."

"I see. So it's my fault this town is full of bigots and idiots."

He stared at me for several seconds, his expression a mixture of aggravation and exhaustion. Finally, he sighed and slumped into the chair behind the desk.

"You don't have to tell me about this town's prejudices. I'm not stupid nor am I deaf and blind. But you unnecessarily aggravate an already-volatile situation simply by your presence."

"So you're saying I should spend my entire summer in Sinful locked in my house so that I don't cause the kindergartners to get restless and create more work for you?"

"No, damn it." He ran a hand through his hair. "But can't you exercise a little more discretion? Did you really think it was a good idea to approach that mob when everyone knows you've taken up with Ida Belle and Gertie?"

"You forgot the part about my being a Yankee."

"I thought that part was a given."

I frowned. "In hindsight, I suppose it was a bad idea."

"It was a horrible idea. Look, I know you care about Ida Belle and you're worried about what's going to happen, but you're only going to make the situation worse if you incite an already high-strung crowd to another level of stupidity."

I knew he was right, but I wasn't quite ready to give up the charge. "Has it ever occurred to you that you incited that crowd by hauling Ida Belle down here for questioning? Couldn't you have been more discreet?"

"Ha. Yeah, because this town thrives on discretion. Short of interrogating her by text message or sending professional kidnappers to whisk her away to a private island, no way could I question her without everyone in town knowing within minutes. This isn't the big city, Fortune. Nothing goes unnoticed here."

"Except murderers."

His jaw twitched and a dark flush crept up his neck.

Okay, so it was a low blow, but I was pissed off.

"I know it may seem to a big-city girl," he said, "that we're nothing but a bunch of hicks who can't walk without tripping, but I assure you that no one is going to get away with murder on my watch. Regardless of your confidence in my ability, I promise you, I will do my job."

Okay, so that made me feel a little guilty.

"I'm not questioning your ability...exactly. But I don't understand why you hauled Ida Belle in here when you and I both know there's no way she murdered that man."

"My personal beliefs have no bearing on the job I have to do. The state prosecutor doesn't give a damn what I know. He only wants facts to make a case. It's my job to collect all those facts so that he can make an educated decision about pursuing prosecution, regardless of whom he chooses to indict."

"Even if those facts point to an innocent person?"

"This job didn't come with any guarantees that I'd love it. But I promised to uphold the law and that's what I have to do, with a belief that the system will work properly. I can't choose to do my job only when it makes me happy. Maybe one day, you'll understand that."

His words hit me like a bucket of cold water, completely knocking me off my high horse. How many times had I been schooled not to get personally involved when I was undercover? The reasons were numerous and varied, but all boiled down to the same thing—personal involvement equaled a conflicted assassin, and conflicted could equal hesitation, which could equal death.

In other words—mission failure.

In all my undercover assignments with the CIA, I'd never even been tempted to get personally involved. The people I'd associated with hadn't merited my interest, but I'd been incognito in Louisiana less than a day before I'd formed alliances with locals. Granted, I didn't have a target in Sinful, so it was a different sort of undercover than what I was used to, but you boiled it right down to basics, my life would be a lot easier if I'd kept the same standards about personal involvement.

For the first time in my life, I'd made real friends and now, everything was complicated. This was exactly what Carter dealt with every day—investigating people he knew, people he had relationships with and probably liked—every time a crime occurred. They couldn't all be domestic disputes and fishing violations. Sometimes, he'd draw the difficult case. The case that made him take a hard look at people he'd known his entire life and ask himself if all this time he'd been unaware of the monster that dwelled within them.

Immediately, I felt guilty for giving him such a hard time since I'd arrived. I'd thought him narrow-minded and rigid, but the reality was, he spent every single day managing a delicate balance between being a Sinful resident and having the rest of the residents under a microscope.

Lately, that microscope had been working overtime.

I was trying to formulate a response when Deputy Breaux knocked twice on the door then stuck his head inside.

"I'm sorry to bother you," he said, "but Ally called and there's a bit of trouble over at the café."

"What kind of trouble?" Carter asked.

"Paulette is there demanding Francine close for the day in her husband's memory. Francine not only refuses to close, she wants Paulette arrested for dripping on her new entry rug and ruining it. Sheriff Lee's not making headway with either of them."

No surprise there. A successful businesswoman like Francine wouldn't have a bit of use for a piece of fluff like Paulette.

Carter closed his eyes for a second, then rose from his chair and looked down at me. "You're free to go, but I want you to think about everything I said. You're already a handy scapegoat for people. Try not to make it any easier on them."

I gave him a nod as he walked out of the office, then jumped up from my chair and hurried out behind him, pausing by Ida Belle's chair.

"Let Ms. Morrow out," Carter instructed Deputy Breaux, "then lock the door behind her and don't open it for anyone but me or Sheriff Lee."

Ida Belle tugged on my yoga pants. "Find out what killed Ted," she whispered.

I glanced at the front door where Carter was still issuing instructions to a confused-looking Deputy Breaux. "How am I supposed to do that?"

"Check his office."

Carter's office was in the back corner of the building. I knew this because of the small matter of breaking and entering that Ida Belle, Gertie, and I had pulled off a week ago, but I couldn't see any way to get back there when I was supposed to be leaving the sheriff's department to go straight home and try to blend into the woodwork.

"Ma'am?" Deputy Breaux stood at the front door, his hand poised on the knob. Carter was nowhere in sight.

"Uh, I don't suppose I can use the ladies' room before I go?" I had zero idea where the restroom was, but I hoped it was somewhere at the back of the building and not upstairs.

Uncertainty washed over Deputy Breaux's expression. "I don't know...Deputy LeBlanc said I have to lock the door after you leave. I really need to lock the door."

"And I really need to go to the ladies' room. It's a girl thing."

"Oh...ummm." Deputy Breaux's face grew so red it looked as if it were glowing.

Got him.

"You can lock the door while I'm gone," I said, "then let me out when I'm done."

He hesitated a moment, clearly afraid he'd make the wrong call and incur Carter's wrath.

I moved in for the kill. "It's this medical thing, you see. The doctor says—"

"That's okay, ma'am." He held both his hands up to stop me from continuing, then immediately dropped one back down to grasp the doorknob. "Go ahead and I'll let you out when you're done."

"Thanks." I gave him my fake grateful smile. "If you could just tell me where it is..."

"Oh, right." He pointed at the hallway behind him. "Down this hall, then turn right on the back hallway. It's the second door on the left."

"Great." As I hurried away, I looked back at Ida Belle and gave her a wink.

CHAPTER FOUR

I HUSTLED PAST DEPUTY BREAUX AND TOWARD THE BACK hallway. I heard the dead bolt on the front door slide into place as I rounded the corner. I shook my head. Deputy Breaux was nothing if not dedicated to following orders.

I opened the bathroom door to check out the lock, then let out a sigh of relief when I saw the very old, very loose locking mechanism. I could jimmy that in half a second with my driver's license. I stepped inside the bathroom to turn on the water for the sink then locked the door and pulled it closed behind me before hurrying down the hall to the next door on the left—Carter's office.

The office door was locked but contained the same old, flimsy door lock that the bathroom had. I made quick work of it with my license, then slipped inside, locking the door behind me. I moved immediately to his desk and shuffled through the stack of paper in front of his computer. Bills, insurance policy, receipt for filing cabinet. Crap. I clicked the mouse and the screen popped up to the password entry box. Another dead end.

As I turned to look in the waste basket, a sheet of paper on the printer caught my eye. I pulled it off and scanned it, my pulse ticking up a notch with every word.

Arsenic!

No wonder they'd figured out cause of death so quickly. Arsenic poisoning wasn't exactly the easy-to-hide kind of death.

"Miss Morrow?" Deputy Breaux's voice sounded from the hall. "Are you all right?"

Crap!

My pulse shot up another notch as I slid the paper back on the printer and tried to come up with a plan. Maybe if I waited long enough he would go away.

A second later, he knocked on the bathroom door and called out again. "Miss Morrow?"

I looked around the office, hoping to create a miracle. The bathroom didn't have a window, so even though I could get out of Carter's office I had no way of getting back inside the bathroom. Not to mention it wouldn't take Carter two seconds to figure out what I'd done, especially when he found his office window unlocked.

I glanced up and that's when the miracle occurred. The office had one of those acoustic ceilings with those big white tiles. I pulled myself up onto the filing cabinet against the wall Carter's office shared with the bathroom and slid the tile over, hoping there was a crawl space in between.

I blew out a breath of relief when the tile opened up to a two-foot-high area that contained the air-conditioning ductwork. I rose up on my tiptoes and pushed back the corresponding tile on the bathroom side, then stuck my head over the wall.

"I'm fine," I said, praying it sounded like I was in the bathroom. "I'll just be another minute."

"Okay," he said and I felt some of my tension slip away.

And then, as Ida Belle would say, it all went to hell in a handbasket.

"Deputy Breaux!" Carter's voice boomed down the hallway.

"You're supposed to be up front with Ida Belle. You couldn't wait five minutes to pee?"

Holy crap!

My body froze in place, in direct opposition to my mind, which wouldn't stop whirling. This was so not good. The getting arrested and cover blown kind of not good.

"It's not me," Deputy Breaux said. "Ms. Morrow had to use the restroom. She's been in there a while and I came to check on her."

"And you believed that. I see." Carter knocked on the bathroom door. "Party's over."

I knew before I did it that it was a bad idea, but it was the only one I had.

Here goes nothing.

I pulled myself up into the crawl space, careful to keep my weight centered on the wall framing. I peered down into the bathroom and smiled when I saw the sink directly below me.

"Fortune?" Carter called.

"I'm almost done," I said. "Just washing up."

"Go home and shower. I don't have time to waste."

Balancing my midsection on the frame, I carefully spun myself around until I could lower my legs down the bathroom wall side. As soon as my toes touched the edge of the sink, I slid the rest of my body out of the ceiling and put both panels back in place.

Pleased with my resourcefulness, I brought my feet flat down to rest on the sides of the sink, and that's when things went horribly wrong. My right foot slid on the sink's edge as if it were ice. I waved my arms and crouched, trying to regain my balance, but it was too late. I pitched off the side of the sink headed straight for the toilet.

"I'm opening this door." Carter's voice boomed from the hallway.

I managed to restrain from yelling or cussing, which was a plus, but it was the only plus to be found. I dragged my hands down the wall as I fell, trying to stay upright. If I hit the toilet on my side, I gave the toilet a slim-to-none chance of remaining attached to the floor. My left leg hit the floor first and I reached for the back of the toilet to balance, but only succeeded in wrenching the lid from the toilet bowl. At the same time, my right foot came crashing down in the toilet and promptly lodged in the drain at the bottom.

Water splashed up toward my face and I held the lid up to block the spray. A split second later, I heard the lock on the bathroom door click and the door flew open.

If I wasn't certain I was about to be arrested, I would have laughed. The look on Carter's face was priceless—a mixture of confusion, incredulity, and when the exact location of my foot registered, a little bit of disgust.

"What in God's name are you doing? No, wait. I don't think I want to know."

It wouldn't have passed muster on a *CSI* episode, but I tossed out the first thing I could come up with. "I stepped on gum outside and was trying to clean it off my shoe."

He blinked. "And you thought the toilet was a good option?"

"I didn't think I could get my foot all the way up in the sink."

"Why didn't you take the shoe off—no, never mind. I don't even want to know. Just get your foot out of my toilet and go home."

"I can't. I lost my balance and now my foot's stuck."

Carter closed his eyes and rubbed his forehead with his hand. I wondered if he was counting to ten or weighing the potential cost of shooting me where I stood.

"That's why I'm holding the lid," I said, deciding I may as well invest everything in my ridiculous cover-up. "I was trying to fix it."

He opened his eyes. "You can't fix a stuck foot with the—you know what, it doesn't matter. Put the lid down."

I placed the lid on the toilet bowl and awaited further instruction.

"Untie your shoe," he said.

I blanched. "You want me to stick my hands in the toilet water?"

"Well, I'm sure as hell not going to do it. You already thought it was a good place for your foot. It's not a huge stretch."

I looked down into the toilet bowl and grimaced. The water looked clean enough, but something about deliberately shoving my hands in a toilet bowl didn't seem right at all.

"I don't have all day," Carter said. "Either you untie your shoe and pull your foot out or I leave you here and call a plumber."

I weighed my options. "A plumber sounds good."

"Sure. Of course, Sinful only has one plumber and he's offshore fishing until next week. It will be an inconvenience to the office staff having the only toilet in the building out of service, but we can always use the restroom at Francine's or the General Store. You, however, might find the circumstances harder to manage."

"Fine." I took a deep breath and shoved my hands in the toilet bowl, scrambling to undo the laces as quickly as possible. As soon as the laces were loosened, I yanked my hands out of the water and gave my leg a good jerk.

My foot slid out of the tennis shoe far easier than I'd expected and I tumbled backward into a storage cabinet, bringing the entire thing crashing down on top of me. I flailed around a bit in a stack of broken pressboard, toilet paper rolls, and cans of room deodorizer before Carter grabbed my shoulder and hauled me to my feet.

He pointed at the shoe, still lodged in the toilet, then at the door. I assumed at this point he was so angry he'd decided to stop speaking. I was probably better off.

I plucked my shoe out of the toilet and gave him an apologetic look before dashing out of the bathroom and down the hall past a stunned Deputy Breaux. In the front office, I waved my dripping wet shoe at Ida Belle before unlocking the front door. She raised one eyebrow before lifting a hand to wave.

Then I stepped out onto the sidewalk, placing my bare foot square into wet gum.

Karma is a real bitch.

———

AS I APPROACHED MY JEEP, I TOSSED THE WET SHOE INTO THE backseat and heard a muffled cry. I peered over the side and saw a still-damp Gertie huddled on the back floorboard.

"What in the world are you doing?" I asked.

"I wasn't going to just leave you here," she said. "Although if I'd known it was going to take this long, me and my bad hip would have reconsidered our options. Can we get out of here before someone sees me?"

"You don't have to ask me twice," I said as I hopped into the Jeep and started it up. "My house or yours?"

"Mine. I need to get out of these wet clothes before I become one big wrinkle."

"Got it," I said as I pulled off down Main Street.

"What's with the shoe?"

"I had a little bit of trouble with the sheriff's toilet." I told her the whole sordid mess as I drove.

Gertie's jaw dropped when I told her about the arsenic, but when I moved onto my creative escape from Carter's office, she started giggling. By the time we arrived at her house, she was collapsed in a lump of wailing hysteria.

I parked in her driveway and looked back at her. "Do I need to get you oxygen?"

She fanned her face, still gasping for air. "One minute... I can't believe... Oh my God..."

"That pretty much sums it up."

"You're such a dichotomy—easily the most resourceful person I've ever met but with the absolute worst luck. It's a wonder you've ever made it back from a mission."

I frowned, trying not to recall the reason I'd been shipped off to Sinful in the first place. "My training didn't cover Sinful, Louisiana."

Gertie nodded. "A perfectly valid argument. In a lot of ways, I found navigating Vietnam easier than living here."

Sinful, Louisiana, or this country's most ill-conducted conflict. Yep, I could see her point.

"All my bad luck aside, I did manage to find out what killed Ted. Now, I want nothing more than to go home, soak my tennis shoes in bleach, and stand in the shower until the hot water runs out."

Gertie pushed herself into a sitting position, then paused. "I think we have a problem."

"What now?"

"My legs are asleep." She stretched out her arms. "You're going to have to help me out."

Sighing, I grabbed her arms and pulled her up to the edge of the Jeep, then dangled her over the side. "If I pull you out, can you stand?"

"I think so, as long as I can lean on you. I'm getting dizzy though."

I slid my arms underneath her shoulders and pulled her over the side of the Jeep, expecting her to gain a little balance when her feet hit the ground. That didn't happen. Instead, her feet hit the lawn and her legs collapsed as if made of rubber.

She didn't weigh much to speak of, but the bulk was a problem. I tightened my grip and shuffled one foot back, trying to prevent her from crashing onto the lawn, but my shoed foot caught on something and sent us both sprawling backward. When we hit the ground, the sprinkler head my shoe had caught on snapped.

A second later, the sprinkler turned on and water gushed out of the pipe like Old Faithful, drenching both of us. I bolted up and dragged Gertie out of the gusher and onto her front porch where I collapsed in a heap, leaning against her door.

Gertie looked over at me, her silver hair plastered to her head, her makeup now resting on the collar of her dress, and started giggling again.

"What in the world are you laughing for?" I asked, certain she'd lost her mind.

"I was just thinking," she said in between chortling, "that we both wanted to go home and shower, but technically, we've been showering all day."

I squeezed a gallon of water from my ponytail and stared at my bare foot.

If this day got any more ridiculous, I was going to blow my cover and turn myself over to the terrorists. I couldn't help but think it would be easier.

CHAPTER FIVE

I MANAGED TO GET GERTIE INTO A KITCHEN CHAIR AND PLACED her cell phone in easy reach. If circulation didn't return to her legs in fifteen minutes or so, she was supposed to call 911. Apparently, the morning's activities hadn't spoiled her appetite, because she had me fix her a ham sandwich before leaving.

My stomach grumbled the whole drive home, and that ham sandwich seemed permanently affixed in my mind, which made sense. After all, I'd been up for hours, doing manual labor, and all I'd had to eat was a couple of eggs and muffins and that wasn't enough. The stress of the morning alone had probably worked those off as I swallowed.

When I got home, I headed straight to my bedroom and shed the wet clothes, tossing them across the shower rod to be dealt with later, then toweled off and pulled on shorts and T-shirt. The long, hot shower I'd envisioned before had taken a backseat to my rumbling stomach.

I did pause long enough to wash off the questionable foot with soap and water, but the rest of me was going to wait until after I ate. My stomach rumbled like a jet engine as I hurried back downstairs, and my head started to pound. I needed calories and I needed them fast.

I had just polished off the last bite of toast with homemade blackberry jam when I heard a knock at my back door. I'd been researching household poisons while I ate, so I closed the laptop before I jumped up to answer. I flung open the door, expecting to find my friend Ally standing there, and blinked in surprise when I saw Celia Arceneaux on my back porch.

"Can I come in?" Celia asked.

"Of course," I said and stepped back to allow her inside. "I just made a fresh pot of coffee. Would you like a cup?"

She shook her head. "I just need to say my piece."

"Okay." My curiosity piqued a bit because I had zero idea what "piece" Celia thought needed saying, especially to me.

"I heard about everything happening," Celia said, "including what that silly woman, Paulette, said when they were hauling Ted's body away."

"I wouldn't worry about it," I said. "I doubt the prosecutor puts much stock in the rantings of hysterical wives, even in Louisiana."

"I'm sure you're right, but with the poison being arsenic, it gives a whole different set of things to consider, and none of them good for Ida Belle."

I stared. "How do you know what killed him? I didn't think they'd released any information yet?"

"I have my sources, same as the Sinful Ladies. Let's just say I have a friend of a friend down at the coroner's office."

Well, it just figured. I'd spent my entire morning risking my cover, my physical health, my tennis shoes, and my mental stability, and all of my not-so-stealthy ability had been supplanted by another nosy old woman with the right connections.

"Okay, but even if we assume your source is right, why do you think that arsenic specifically implicates Ida Belle?"

"Everyone knows she's had a gopher problem for years. She

insists on growing that damned bamboo in her backyard, and gophers just love that stuff. She's spent a year or more fighting those critters."

I blinked, wondering if Celia had been dipping into some Sinful Ladies cough syrup. "What the heck does Ida Belle's gopher problem have to do with anything?"

Celia sighed. "I forget you're a Yankee. You probably live in one of those sterile high-rise buildings with fake plants and even faker neighbors. Arsenic is one of the ingredients in gopher poison, and I happen to know Ida Belle has a bag of it because I was at the General Store when she picked up the order."

My mind flashed back to the bag Carter had removed from Ida Belle's storage shed and I frowned. Maybe Celia was onto something.

"So anyway," Celia continued, "I want you to know that I don't believe for one minute that Ida Belle killed that fool Ted. Ida Belle is a lot of things, but mostly she's efficient. She'd never waste time and energy killing someone who doesn't matter one whit in the big scheme of things."

I stared at her for a moment, marveling over this apparently small-town, Southern method of determining innocence and guilt. Perhaps it was as simple as the good among them all considering "wasting time" a sin.

"I agree with you," I said.

"Good. Then you'll find the real killer."

"Me? I'm a librarian," I said, remembering my cover. I held up my hands. "That's not something I'm remotely trained for."

Celia narrowed her eyes at me. "But you caught my Pansy's killer."

"A more accurate description is I narrowly escaped being killed myself by Pansy's killer."

Celia frowned. "Well, if you want to get picky, I suppose that's true. But still, you managed to put together more than any of the rest of us would have ever figured out because we were too close to the people involved. Being new in town, you have the advantage of being able to see everyone as a suspect."

"Like the way everyone in town sees me?"

Celia gave me a rueful smile. "Something like that."

"Even if we assume what you say is true, I also have the disadvantage that the locals won't lay their secrets at my footstep. In fact, a lot of them won't even make eye contact."

Celia frowned. "True, and everyone knows you're friends with Ida Belle, so the guilty party certainly won't be sharing confidences with you any more than they would Gertie."

"Exactly."

Her eyes widened a bit and I saw her energy level spike. "But I can be your ears."

I was fairly sure I didn't want Celia serving as any of my body parts, but I'd never seen her this excited, so before I could stop myself I asked, "What do you mean?"

"Through the GWs. Granted, most of them are so silly I'm amazed they can walk without tripping, but I have a trusted few who have their wits about them and are in complete agreement with me on this situation."

Celia nodded, her expression growing more and more animated. "In fact, the more I think about it, the more I realize what a wonderful idea it is. Given my past with Ida Belle, I'm the perfect confidante for anyone who wants to see her go down."

I put my hands up to stop her before she went any further. "Hold up. I don't disagree with anything you've said. However, do you realize you're suggesting that you attempt to engage in personal conversation with a murderer?"

Celia froze and I saw the flicker of fear in her eyes.

"I'm not trying to be mean," I continued, "but Pansy's situation came as a total shock to you, and you had been around the killer every day of your life. You said before that I can see things you don't because I'm basically a stranger and that's true, but the opposite is true as well. Without even knowing it, you could put yourself or your friends in a lot of danger."

Celia's shoulders slumped. "You're right. I guess I didn't think things through."

"It's only been a week since everything in your life changed," I said quietly. "Give yourself a break."

She gave me a small smile. "I know it's not common knowledge and you probably don't even want it to be, but you're a nice person, Fortune."

"Yeah, I'd rather that didn't get out." Especially since I wasn't nearly as convinced of my "niceness" as Celia was.

"Regardless," Celia said, "I'm still going to beat you to Francine's on Sunday, even if I have to cheat." She made the sign of the cross and looked upward, probably asking for pre-forgiveness for whatever cheating she had planned.

I smiled, not even remotely worried about her plans. Unless the Catholics had acquired Usain Bolt or planned on shooting me, I wasn't worried. "I'm looking forward to it."

She gave me a nod. "I should get out of here before someone sees me. I have a reputation to protect."

"Of course," I said as I walked to the back door and pulled it open. "And no sleuthing, right?"

She sighed. "No sleuthing, but if I notice anything unusual, I'll let you know."

I raised one eyebrow. Like anything in Sinful was normal. "My version of unusual or yours?"

"Ha!" she laughed and slipped out the door without answering.

I pulled the door shut behind her and sank back down into my chair. Her idea wasn't an awful one. Ted had attended the Catholic church, so Celia would have access to any services, visitation with the widow, and all other Southern small-town traditional things. Gertie and I could hardly expect to be welcome at any of those, and based on the arsenic information Celia had provided, Ida Belle might not even be at liberty to go home.

I shook my head. No matter how bad things looked, my launching an investigation using Sinful residents as informants was too much of a risk. Civilians weren't trained to spot killers or protect themselves if they got backed into a corner. It was one thing for me to run around playing Bond girls with Ida Belle and Gertie. They had military training they'd managed to hide from the Sinful population for decades, so role-playing was second nature. But random residents would assume a huge risk playing detective.

I blew out a breath and slumped down lower in the chair. I was more than a little worried about the gopher poison. If Celia was right about Ida Belle being the only person in Sinful with gopher problems, on the surface it looked like an open-and-shut case. Even though I was certain Carter didn't think Ida Belle had murdered Ted, notoriously overworked and underpaid prosecutors didn't take the personal feelings of local law enforcement into consideration when deciding to pursue an indictment.

They only took into account what they could prove, and as things currently stood, all fingers pointed to Ida Belle.

I drummed my fingers on the table, the facts of the situation running through my mind. If Ida Belle's gopher problem was common knowledge, then everyone in Sinful probably knew about it. Which also meant that any number of them might know she had gopher poison.

It would be a simple matter to sneak into Ida Belle's shed and take a sample of the poison, and probably equally as simple to drive to New Orleans and pick up the same brand, assuming the killer knew what brand she used.

The bottom line was, there was a killer in Sinful. Again.

And this time, he'd framed one of the only people I had ever called a friend.

A thought hit me and I sucked in a breath so hard, my head spun. What if the fatal bottle of cough syrup had been the one I'd given Ida Belle at the rally? My fingerprints would be all over it. If

Carter decided to run those prints, I'd be in an even worse position than Ida Belle.

I jumped up from the table and grabbed my car keys. My shower would have to wait.

Gertie and I had an investigation to launch.

————

I WAS HALFWAY TO GERTIE'S HOUSE WHEN MY CELL PHONE rang. I didn't recognize the phone number and was surprised to find Ida Belle on the other end of the call.

"They're cutting me loose," she said. "Can you pick me up? I don't want Carter giving me a ride home. I'm more than a little miffed at him right now."

"Sure." I pulled a U-turn in the middle of the street and headed for the sheriff's department, my spirits picking up a bit. Maybe Ida Belle's gopher poison hadn't been a match for whatever killed Ted. Maybe this entire thing would only cost me a pair of tennis shoes and a bit of dignity.

Ida Belle must have been watching from the window because as soon as I turned onto Main Street, she hurried out of the sheriff's department and hopped into my Jeep before I'd even come to a complete stop. Figuring this was no time and place for chitchat, I pressed the accelerator and sped off. Ida Belle gave the building the finger as we pulled away.

"I was on my way to Gertie's when you called," I said.

"Good," Ida Belle said. "We need to talk."

I glanced over at her. Her jaw was set and I could practically feel the tension coming off of her. I hoped it was leftover anger at Carter and the wasted morning, but somehow, I doubted it.

She didn't utter a word the entire ride, walked straight into Gertie's house without even knocking and stalked down the hall to the kitchen, poured herself a cup of coffee, then sat at the kitchen table. Apparently hearing the commotion, Gertie came running downstairs dripping wet with soap all over her head and wearing a towel. Even more disturbing, she ran into the kitchen, her eyes clenched shut and waving a nine-millimeter.

Ida Belle didn't even blink. "Put that damned thing down before you shoot someone," she said.

"Ida Belle?" Gertie wiped one eye with her free hand. Unfortunately, that was also the hand holding the towel.

Ida Belle shook her head. "I'm going to need a drink if you plan on conducting this meeting naked."

I covered my eyes with my hands. "I'm going to need therapy."

"To hell with both of you," Gertie said and I heard her stomp off down the hall.

I waited until I heard the pound of footsteps above me before removing my hands from my face. Ida Belle sat there, completely unfazed sipping her coffee.

"If she doesn't want people seeing her naked," Ida Belle said, "she should lock her front door."

"That was my fault. I forgot to lock the door behind me when I left earlier."

Ida Belle raised one eyebrow. "Were Gertie's legs broken?"

"Well, actually..." I filled Ida Belle in on what had happened to me at the sheriff's department, then explained how Gertie had managed to temporarily paralyze herself.

During my recount, Ida Belle's expression went from incredulous to shocked to amused. When she started laughing, I thought she'd never stop. She guffawed, then chortled, then wheezed, then chortled more before finally collapsing on top of the breakfast table, gasping for air.

I was just considering CPR when Gertie came back into the kitchen, this time fully clothed and sans the nine-millimeter. She took one look at Ida Belle and shook her head. "I guess you told her about our morning?"

"Yeah. Like you, she seems to have gotten a much bigger kick out of it than I did."

Ida Belle wheezed again, her shoulders still shaking.

"Can she breathe?" Gertie asked.

"I'm not sure I care," I shot back.

Gertie poured us both a cup of coffee. By the time she'd taken a seat, Ida Belle was upright and semi-composed.

"You're awfully cheerful for someone who's been accused of murder," I said.

Ida Belle waved a hand in dismissal. "I didn't kill anyone and Carter knows it."

I shook my head. "No matter what Carter knows, he has to turn over all the evidence to the district attorney. They make the decision, and I've got to tell you, it doesn't look good."

The smile faded from Ida Belle's face. "What do you know?"

"During my adventures in bathroom destruction, I found out that Ted was poisoned with arsenic. According to Celia, who paid me a visit earlier to offer you her anonymous support and who had already gotten that bit of information from a friend at the coroner's office, everyone knows you had gopher problems. My guess is the gopher poison is what Carter removed from your shed."

"Shit," Ida Belle said.

Gertie gasped. "What do you think will happen?"

"If that cough syrup bottle contains trace evidence of the poison, then Carter will pull the prints and turn everything over to the DA."

Ida Belle's shoulders slumped. "I gave him a bottle of cough syrup after the rally."

"Shit," I said, repeating Ida Belle's earlier sentiment. "Both our prints are on there."

Ida Belle's eyes widened. "What happens if Carter runs your prints?"

I blew out a breath. "They should pop back as Sandy-Sue's, but my boss at the CIA will get an alert."

"And that will be bad?" Gertie asked.

"That will be very, very bad," I said, the possibilities of fallout too numerous and unpleasant to even consider at the moment.

We all sat in silence for a bit, each of us lost in our thoughts. Then my cell phone rang, its shrill tone ripping through the silence of the kitchen and startling all of us. I pulled it out of my pocket, my heart plummeting into my feet when I saw the display.

Harrison.

CHAPTER SIX

I ANSWERED HARRISON'S CALL, THEN MOVED THE PHONE A couple of inches from my ears to protect myself from the yelling I knew would come.

"What the hell is going on there?" Harrison's voice boomed out of the phone so loud that it echoed across the room.

Since everyone could hear him anyway, I pressed the speaker button and put the phone down on the kitchen table, motioning to Ida Belle and Gertie to be quiet. "Could you be more specific?" I asked.

"Damn it, Redding, don't play dumb with me. Deputy LeBlanc just ran your prints so you best tell me why because when Morrow comes down here ready to shoot someone if they don't have answers, I want to give the man what he wants."

I looked over at Ida Belle and Gertie, who both sat frozen, staring at the phone. "There was a bit of a problem here today," I said finally.

"What kind of problem requires the deputy to run your prints?"

"The murder kind of problem?" I cringed, waiting for the bomb to drop.

"Jesus H. Christ! You've got one of the most dangerous men in the world looking under every leaf, rock, and grain of sand on the planet for you, and you still can't manage to keep a low profile. What kind of threat does it take to make you invisible?"

"The wrath of God?" I replied, hoping a bit of levity would improve the situation.

"Ahmad's wrath is far worse," Harrison said. "And when Morrow finds out, he may fly down there and kill you himself. The man's hair started thinning since you've been gone, and I swear I've aged ten years trying to keep him from knowing more than he already does."

"I appreciate everything you've done——"

"I can't cover this one up," he interrupted. "If Morrow finds out you're down there essentially implicating his niece in a murder and that I hid it from him, he'll fire me on the spot."

I knew he was right, so I didn't bother to argue. "But my cover held, right?"

"It's holding...for now. But don't be surprised if Morrow yanks you. This whole thing has been a mistake from the beginning. In fact, I'm going to start looking for a relocation site myself."

"No! It's critical that I don't leave Sinful—not now."

"Why the hell not? It's a spot of swamp that you didn't even know existed two weeks ago. Give me one good reason why you can't leave."

I looked across the table at Ida Belle and Gertie...my friends. And although it was infinitely depressing, the only real friends I'd ever had. I couldn't abandon them, even if it meant pissing off Morrow and losing my job.

"I can't leave," I said, "because the wrong person is going to be fingered for the murder."

"It's not your problem."

"Yes, it is."

"How in the world could it be?"

"Never leave a man behind," I said quietly.

For several seconds, the only sound in the kitchen was the ticking of the clock, then I heard Harrison sigh. "It's one of the old women, right?"

"Who's he calling old?" Gertie grumbled.

Ida Belle elbowed her in the ribs and put one finger across her lips.

"Yeah," I said.

"How do you know she didn't do it?"

"Because the target wasn't a threat. Remember, despite appearances, these women are not regular civilians. They operate by the same code we do."

"Shit," Harrison said, sounding tired and defeated. "And this Deputy LeBlanc is going to be a problem?"

"Not by choice. I'm certain he knows Ida Belle didn't kill the man, but he has to turn over the evidence to the DA, and it looks bad because of some convoluted mess concerning gophers that you don't even need to know."

"So his hands are tied."

"Yes. But mine aren't."

"You're not trained as an investigator," Harrison argued.

"I know that, but I'm the only thing she's got."

"Fine. I won't try to find you another cover...yet, but I can't make any guarantees about Morrow. If he says I have to pull you out, then I don't have a choice."

"I understand. And Harrison?"

"Yeah?"

"I owe you."

"Got that right," he said and disconnected the call.

I slumped back in my chair. "That went well."

"Do you think your boss will pull you out?" Gertie asked.

"If he thought it would eliminate his stress level, yeah. But he'd still have to find another place for me, and that won't be easy. Since the real Sandy-Sue inherited everything Marge had, the estate is covering all costs of my being here. It allows me to be completely off grid. No expense reports for Morrow to file for living expenses."

"So no paper trail for the traitor in the CIA to track you with," Ida Belle said.

"Exactly," I said.

"So worst case," Ida Belle said, "we've got some time to clear this all up and convince him to let you stay once everything is back to normal."

I nodded, but I had little faith that things in Sinful would ever be normal. I would be happy if people just stopped turning up murdered. The general weirdness was something I could live with.

"Let's get back to Ted," I said. Now that I'd made up my mind to get in the middle of another murder investigation, I wanted to get it over with as soon as possible. "The poison and your proximity to Ted last night at the end of the rally easily give you opportunity, but what they don't have is motive."

"What about the election?" Gertie asked. "Would that be enough reason to kill someone?"

"In DC maybe," Ida Belle said.

"Logically," I agreed, "you wouldn't think so. It's not like Ida Belle wins by default because her opponent is dead. Someone else will step up to run and the whole thing will start over again. Even if Ted had won, it wouldn't be a threat to Ida Belle's livelihood or quality of living, so if the prosecutor tried to make a case for an election murder, it would be a huge stretch."

Gertie looked happy with my assessment. "So if Ida Belle has no motive, what do we do now?"

"We figure out who wanted Ted dead," I said. "A poisoning isn't an opportunistic sort of murder. Someone had to acquire the poison and make sure it got into something Ted was likely to drink but Paulette wasn't."

"What if someone put the poison in a cough syrup bottle not even caring who they killed?" Gertie asked. "What if Ted just happened to be the unlucky one who drank it?"

I blew out a breath. "Then that would mean someone has a serious beef with the Sinful Ladies if they killed someone just to make the group look bad, or someone is batshit crazy and just wanted to kill a human being, period. If it's the latter, we won't know until someone else turns up dead."

Gertie's eyes widened. "Maybe we better stick to the Ted angle for now."

I nodded. "So if our bottle was used to poison him, the easiest way to narrow things down might be opportunity. We need to figure out how the poison got in the bottle. If we eliminate all the Sinful Ladies who prepared the syrup, and Ida Belle and I, who else had access?"

Ida Belle frowned. "I gave him the bottle before the speeches started—telling him he'd need it after I whooped him and all that."

"What did he do with it?" I asked.

"He put it in his blazer pocket," Ida Belle said.

I glanced at Gertie, who shook her head. "He wasn't wearing a blazer when the speeches started," I said.

Ida Belle's eyes widened. "That's right. It was so darn hot...I guess he took it off."

"Which means it was somewhere backstage where anyone could have accessed the bottle," I said and sighed. "We're right back to a suspect list that encompasses the entire town."

"So opportunity is a dead end," Ida Belle agreed. "I guess the only thing left is motive."

I nodded. "Then, hopefully, the murderer should be obvious."

"The most logical suspect is always the spouse," Gertie said.

"True," I agreed. "So what do we really know about Ted and Paulette? Was he a cheater? An abuser? Was she running around with a local and wanted him out of the way?"

Gertie shook her head. "I haven't heard anything along those lines, but I don't know either of them very well. Paulette stayed in New Orleans for spa visits and shopping most of the time. She never formed friendships with any of the Sinful women. I think she considered us and the town beneath her."

"Okay," I said, "what about Ted? You said he was always running around town giving away stuff. Was there anyone he formed a bond with?"

Ida Belle shrugged. "I never paid attention. He was an annoying man, always smiling too big and complimenting too much."

"And he was a front hugger," Gertie piped in.

"What's a front hugger?" I asked.

"You know," Ida Belle said, "those guys who insist on hugging you straight-on full frontal, regardless of how well they know you, and when a side hug would be more appropriate."

"I think they just want to feel your boobs," Gertie said.

I grimaced, not completely convinced that Ted was copping a chest feel of ancient boobs, but happy I hadn't been subjected to one of those full-frontal hugs. I had issues with my personal space.

"My guess is," Ida Belle said, "that most of the women in Sinful went out of their way to avoid him. I don't think we'll find much information through my usual channels."

"So maybe we need to ask a guy about Ted," I said. "What about Walter?"

Gertie perked up. "That's a good idea. Most of the men drop by the General Store every couple of weeks to shoot the breeze with Walter. If Ted was up to anything sketchy, Walter may know about it."

"Do you think he'd tell us if he does?" I asked.

Gertie raised one eyebrow.

"Oh, right!" I said, remembering that Walter had been in love with Ida Belle since the crib. "So first up is talking to Walter, but I don't think we should have that sort of conversation over the phone."

"No," Ida Belle agreed. "He may not be able to speak freely while he's at the store, and I don't want to wait until tonight."

"Well, then we've got a problem," Gertie said, "because I don't think any of us need to make a trip down Main Street again today. Carter may throw us all in jail if he thinks it will buy him a moment of peace."

I nodded. "He basically implied I should go home, close myself in my house, shut the blinds, and not even look out a window."

"That was rather rude," Gertie said, "even for Carter. Well, if he doesn't want anyone to see you, we'll take my boat. We can dock behind the General Store and go through the back door to the storeroom. That way we avoid being seen by the Main Street traffic."

"I thought you wrecked your boat in my azalea bushes," I said.

"That was *my* boat," Ida Belle said. "Gertie wrecked her own boat a couple of months ago."

"That's an awful lot of boat wrecks," I said.

Gertie threw her hands in the air. "How was I supposed to know a house would be there?"

I looked over at Ida Belle, not even wanting to guess how Gertie had managed to wreck her boat into a house.

Ida Belle mouthed the word "later" and I frowned, uneasy at the prospect of boating with Gertie again. "Maybe Ida Belle should drive this time."

Gertie shook her head. "Given the circumstances, I don't think Ida Belle should leave her house. In fact, we should probably call Marie to come over here and sit with her just in case she needs an alibi."

I sighed. "You're probably right. So I assume your boat has been repaired since the highly suspect boat-house accident."

"Uh, pretty much," Gertie said.

I narrowed my eyes at her. "What does 'pretty much' mean?"

"It was only a small hole. It will be fine."

I looked over at Ida Belle, who shrugged, clearly not up to speed on Gertie's boat repair status.

"Oh for goodness' sakes," Gertie said, "stop being such a chicken. It's just a five-minute boat ride and we've got a limited amount of time to work with."

I felt my back tighten and I fought the urge to stand and fight. Gertie had hit on my biggest weakness, and I'd bet anything she knew it. Nothing lit a fire under me as much as an accusation of being a coward. And it didn't help that Gertie was right about the ticking clock. The sooner we got all this settled, the more likely that Ida Belle would be in the clear and Morrow would leave me in Sinful.

"Fine, then let's get going," I said, leaving off the "before I wise up and change my mind" part.

Gertie jumped up from her chair. "Great! We can drop Ida Belle off at her house on the way to the boat dock. I just need to put on tennis shoes."

She hurried out of the kitchen and I looked over at Ida Belle. "Please tell me that boat is structurally sound."

Ida Belle shook her head. "I lent her my welder, but I have no idea if she did the patch correctly."

"Great."

"Hey, look at the bright side—at least you know how to swim."

CHAPTER SEVEN

THE BOAT DOCK WAS A PATCH OF DIRT LITTERED WITH RANDOM weeds that led to a makeshift slope of gravel used as a launch. A handful of trailered boats sat on each side of the launch path, all of them looking worse for the wear. No wonder Ted had gotten cheers when he'd promised to pave this place.

"That one's mine," Gertie said, pointing to an old green flat-bottom boat with yellow daisy slipcovers over the seats.

I held in a smile as I backed my Jeep up to the boat. In a sea of camouflage, who would have guessed?

Gertie jumped out and directed me right under the hitch, then lowered the trailer and latched it to the Jeep. I swung the Jeep around and backed the boat down the makeshift launch, Gertie unhooked it, and we were ready to roll. Or drift. Whatever.

"Hurry up," Gertie called from the boat as I parked the Jeep and headed to the launch. "I don't think it's a good idea to sit still for all that long."

I gave the boat a once-over before pushing it back and hopping inside, unable to squelch the feeling that this was not going to turn out well. I took a seat on the front bench and gave Gertie a thumbs-up.

"This isn't a race," I reminded her, "so there's no reason to go fast."

"Unless someone starts shooting at us."

"Is that really a possibility?"

Gertie shrugged. "Usually."

I wasn't about to ask. "Fine then. We'll go at a moderate pace unless someone starts shooting. Agreed?"

"Sounds like a plan." She pulled on a pair of aviator sunglasses and twisted the throttle on the outboard motor.

The boat leaped out of the water and I clutched the sides to keep from pitching off into the bottom. So much for moderate. Gertie set off down the bayou at a pace twice the speed I would have recommended, especially for someone with questionable vision who refused to wear glasses.

I turned to face the front and said a silent prayer as the boat swept just inches from a pier, casting a huge wave over a couple fishing. I called out an apology, but we were probably gone too fast for them to hear it. The bank blurred by so quickly, I couldn't tell where we were, but I thought I saw us speed past my house before making a hard turn that almost pitched me out of the boat.

I was just about to yell at Gertie to slow down when she cut the speed completely and I splayed across the bow of the boat, barely avoiding rolling off into the bayou. I rose up just in time to see Walter's dock inches from my face and grabbed the edge before we crashed into it.

"Maybe I should drive on the way back," I said as I jumped onto the pier and tied off the boat.

"You don't even know how to drive a boat," Gertie said.

"And yet, I'm certain I could do a better job than you."

"Everyone's a critic lately," Gertie grumbled as she climbed out of the boat. "Let's get inside before everyone sees us."

After that morning's mob run-in, she didn't have to tell me twice. I double-timed it to the back of the General Store and slipped through the back door and into the storeroom, Gertie hot on my heels. I cracked open the door to the front of the store and peeked inside, but the store appeared empty, except for Walter, who sat on his usual stool behind the cash register.

"Pssssstttttt," I whispered.

Walter lowered his newspaper and looked over at the door, his eyes widening when he saw my head poking out.

"I need to talk to you," I said.

He tossed his newspaper on the counter and hurried into the storeroom faster than I'd ever seen him move.

"Is Ida Belle all right?" he asked as soon as he closed the door behind him.

"She's fine," I assured him. "Carter questioned her and she's been released. She's at home now under the general orders not to leave town."

"Why not? What the hell is going on? I've left Carter three messages already today and apparently my nephew has conveniently forgotten I'm family."

"I don't think he's forgotten," I said, my heart going out to the obviously distraught store owner. "He's just doing his job. I imagine he's not any happier about it than we are."

Walter sighed. "I know you're right, but he's still going to hear about it when I get a hold of him. So what's going on? Do you know anything?"

I nodded and brought him up to date on everything except my CIA business. Ida Belle and Gertie were the only people in Sinful who knew my true identity, and even they didn't know my full name or job title. I figured they'd guessed the latter, but some things were better left unsaid.

When I was done, Walter rubbed his temples and took a deep breath. "It's worse than I thought. No wonder Carter won't return my calls. I have money. I can get Ida Belle the best attorney in the whole state."

The heart that I tried to pretend I didn't have clenched just a bit at Walter's devotion to his unrequited love. I swear if I were thirty years older, weren't a CIA assassin with a price on my head, and wanted to disappear forever in this ridiculous bayou town, I'd totally make a move on Walter.

"I don't think we're at that point yet," I said, "and God willing, we're not going to get there."

Walter shook his head. "Unless you've got a miracle up your sleeve, I don't see how we're going to avoid it."

"Gertie, Ida Belle, and I are going to do our own investigation and catch the real killer."

Walter stared at us for several seconds, his expression a mix of disbelief and fear. "I believe you're actually serious."

Gertie threw her hands in the air. "Of course we're serious, you old goat. Do you think I'm going to stand by and watch my oldest and dearest friend get railroaded for something she didn't do?"

Walter stiffened, his face turning light red. "No, what I think you're going to do is fall headfirst into something you're not the least bit qualified to do and end up sitting in the cell next to Ida Belle."

"Fine then." Gertie crossed her arms across her chest. "Now we all know our roles according to Jeff Foxworthy—you're the good friend that we'll call for bail. I'm the *great* friend that will be sitting in jail with her."

"Hmmm," I said. "A bit reckless, but I respect this Foxworthy's code. Is he a Sinful resident?"

Gertie sighed. "Later. Right now, we need to get on with business. That is if Mr. High-and-Mighty here will lower his standards to helping us. Unless, of course, you're afraid talking will get you arrested."

Walter shook his head. "Fine, you old fool. What do you want to know?"

"A reason someone might want to kill Ted," I said.

Walter's eye widened. "Straight to the point. But I'm afraid my answer is going to disappoint you. I have no idea why someone would want him dead."

"Not even a little reason?" I asked, unable to believe that Ted's used-car-salesman personality hadn't rubbed someone the wrong way.

"I think the women considered him a bit of a letch," Walter said, "so they mostly avoided him. The men mostly thought he was full of hot air and he could drive you to drink when he got on a roll and wouldn't stop talking, but that's not something you kill a man for."

"What about an affair?" I asked. "You said he was a letch. Maybe there's a woman in Sinful who didn't want to avoid him. Someone with a jealous husband."

Walter frowned. "I guess anything's possible, but I'd have no idea who it could be. I've never seen him talking to anyone in particular and certainly not carrying on in a way that I would suspect an affair."

Gertie sighed. "This is a pointless line of questioning. Walter would have to see Ted in bed with another woman to know he was having an affair. Men have blinders on when it comes to that sort of thing."

"Really?" I asked. My experience with men had mostly been limited to other CIA operatives. Being observant tended to keep you alive, so I was unaware of this pedestrian male blind spot.

"Maybe," Walter said, looking a bit indignant, "it's that women are underhanded and sneaky and men don't want to believe the worst about them."

Gertie waved a hand in dismissal. "Keep telling yourself that. Angelina Jolie could be a known archcriminal and men would still line up to have sex with her."

"Hmmm," Walter said, apparently lacking a good argument.

"Sex with Angelina Jolie aside," I said, "can you think of anything at all that Ted might have done to make someone angry enough to kill him?"

"I wish I could," Walter said, "but I haven't seen or heard anything that would make me think someone was gunning for him. If one of the men around here was out for Ted, either he was damned quiet about it or it's so recent the rumor mill hasn't gotten it around."

"Have you had any interaction with him recently?" I asked.

"Sure. He's been to see Scooter the last two weeks for repairs. That man really shouldn't own anything with a motor." Walter looked a little sheepish. "Well, I guess he doesn't anymore. That was awfully rude of me."

"You forgot," I said. "What kind of repairs?"

"Brake problems on his truck—nothing out of the ordinary. His boat motor was a different story. Damn thing melted—bad wiring, probably. Scooter said it wasn't worth repairing, so he had to buy a new one."

"And he seemed normal when he was here for those repairs?" I asked.

Walter nodded. "He was talking a blue streak about some show on cable. I pretty much tune him out once he gets going, but he seemed same as always to me."

"Maybe we're thinking about this the wrong way," Gertie said. "We're assuming someone was trying to kill Ted because of something he did, but maybe Paulette was the one having an affair."

I frowned. "You think a jealous lover killed Ted so he could have Paulette to himself?"

Walter grimaced. "If that's the case, he'll get off on an insanity plea. No one in their right mind would want that woman."

"I agree," Gertie said, "but most men aren't as discerning as you are, Walter."

"You did say Paulette spent most of her time in New Orleans," I said.

Gertie brightened. "That's right. Claimed she was at spas, but that would give her all the opportunity in the world to cat around."

I nodded. "And Ted or anyone else in Sinful wouldn't have been the wiser."

"Great," Gertie said. "So all we need to do is verify what Paulette does when she's in New Orleans."

"How do you propose we do that?" I asked. "She's not likely to take a spa trip given that her husband was just murdered."

Gertie scrunched her brow in concentration. "We need receipts. Then we could figure out where she was and maybe figure out a way to question staff."

I shook my head. "No way," I said, knowing already where she was going. "We're not breaking into Ted's house. Might as well wave a banner that says 'Arrest me. I did it.'"

Walter nodded. "Carter would put you under the jail."

"Well then, I'm out of ideas," Gertie said. "You got any better idea?"

"Just because I don't have a better idea," I said, "doesn't mean this is a good one."

"But it's the only one."

I stared out the storeroom window at the bayou, frantically seeking any alternative to Gertie's suicidal suggestion.

"You're thinking about doing it," Walter said. "I can't believe it. You're as crazy as the other two."

I smiled. If he only knew. "Since Paulette is Catholic, won't she go to church for something? If the house is empty..."

"Okay," Walter said, "this is where I take my leave so if Carter ever asks me, I don't know a damned thing. Call me if you need anything...of the legal variety."

Gertie waited for Walter to leave the storeroom before replying. "They sometimes do a prayer vigil right after the death. I figure Ted will be sent back east for burial, so there's a good chance Father Michael will do some sort of service tomorrow."

I nodded. "We'll break into the house then."

"And we have the added advantage of a good portion of Sinful being at the service. Most of those hypocrites don't step into church unless it's a wedding or a funeral, but it's less chance of being seen by one of the neighbors."

"Then it's a plan. Let's get the heck out of here before someone sees us and we cause trouble for Walter."

Gertie nodded and we headed out the back door and down to the dock. I untied the boat as Gertie fired up the motor, already dreaming of the hot shower I still hadn't managed. I push the boat away from the dock and jumped in it.

"Slower this time," I admonished Gertie, who rolled her eyes then twisted the throttle so hard the boat practically leaped out of the water.

Even worse, she was headed directly at another boat that was moving down the bayou.

"Look out!" I yelled.

Gertie yanked the motor to the side and the boat swerved, missing the other boat by an inch but throwing a wave of water over it. I looked over in time to see the shocked driver hold one arm up to protect his face from the sheet of water, then he dropped his arm and his gaze locked directly on me.

Crap. It was bitch-slap guy from this morning's mob.

I looked back at Gertie, who had slowed down to wipe the water from her eyes. "Remember when I said you needed to drive slower?"

"Yeah?"

"Forget everything I said."

She squinted at me, looking completely confused. "What—"

Bitch-slap guy's eyes widened. "Yankee, murdering bitch!"

Gertie looked back. "Oh no!" She twisted the throttle on the motor again.

The boat jumped forward once more and I braced my feet against the bottom of the hull to maintain my balance. A second later, Bitch-slap cranked the motor on his boat and came after us.

Gertie glanced back. "Looks like we got ourselves a boat chase!"

Oh goody.

I grimaced as the boat slammed down over the ripples the wind made on the surface of the bayou. The ride to the General Store hadn't seemed near as rough. I glanced back at Bitch-slap and felt my pulse tick up a notch when I saw he was gaining on us.

"Can you go faster?" I asked.

"Are you kidding me? I'm already going so fast I'm getting younger. Besides, my motor is maxed out."

I scanned the bank as it rushed by, trying to gauge how close we were to the dock. I thought we were close, but I wasn't sure. And at the rate he was gaining on us, we weren't going to make it to the boat launch, much less out of the water, before he caught up with us.

When I heard the first ping, I thought we'd hit something on the bayou, like a soda can, but then something tore through my sleeve and grazed the side of my arm. I peered around Gertie for a better look at Bitch-slap just in time to see him lower a pistol directly at my head.

I dove for the bottom of the boat. "He's shooting at us!"

Another ping echoed beside me.

"It's just a pellet gun," Gertie said. "It stings but it can't kill you. Just don't give him an eye to aim at."

"I don't want to give him anything to aim at. If he gets any closer, those pellets are going to do more than sting."

I scanned the bottom of the boat, looking for something I could use as a weapon. The anchor looked promising, but the rope attached to it looked too weak to allow me to catapult it. Instead, I grabbed an oar.

"When I yell," I said to Gertie, "I want you to cut the engine and swerve to the left about a foot."

"Okay," Gertie said.

No pause. No questions. Not even so much as the lift of an eyebrow. I wasn't sure whether to be overwhelmed by her confidence in me or frightened.

I pushed myself up into a crouching position behind the middle bench and peered around Gertie. Bitch-slap was only about ten feet behind her. When he reached five feet, it was time to launch.

Nine. Eight. Seven. Six. Five...

"Now!" I screamed as loud as I could.

Gertie cut the engine completely and the boat slammed down onto the bayou as if someone had hit the brakes. As a startled Bitch-slap blew by us, I jumped up and whacked him with the oar, sending him careening backward.

He yelled as he fell, clutching the motor handle with a death grip to keep from launching into the bayou, and pulled the entire thing around as he fell back on the bench. The boat shot off to the right and ran straight up the bank and onto the road that ran parallel to the bayou.

Where it promptly crashed into the side of Carter's truck.

"Let's get out of here," I said, dropping down to the bottom of the boat again.

And that's when I realized the bottom of the boat was filling with water.

"I think maybe my repair failed," Gertie said. "I probably should have put that patch on with something stronger than duct tape."

I peered over the side of the boat in time to see Carter jump out of his truck and start yelling at Bitch-slap.

"The dock's just over there," Gertie said. "We'll have to swim for it." She bailed over the side of the boat and started swimming for the shore.

Seeing no better alternative, I popped up from the bottom of the boat and dove in beside her. I swam underwater as long as I could to avoid identification by the good deputy, hoping I swam in the direction of the bank. When I finally had to pop up for air, I was pleasantly surprised to see the boat launch less than twenty yards away.

I looked around for Gertie and was surprised to see her only a couple of feet behind me, executing a perfect crawl. I launched into my own Michael Phelps routine and practically ran up the launch as soon as my feet hit solid ground. I didn't even look back as I dashed for my Jeep.

I threw it in reverse and peeled backward toward the boat launch, making it to the edge of the bayou just as Gertie crawled up the ramp. She clutched at the bumper of the Jeep to pull herself upright, then dashed to passenger's seat and fell inside.

As I took off, I glanced across the bayou and saw Carter standing at the edge of the opposite bank, shaking his head at me. I pressed my foot down on the accelerator, determined to go straight home and lock myself in my house, just as Carter had suggested I do earlier. At least for the rest of the night.

As I pulled onto the street, I looked over at Gertie, who sighed.

"Just like I told you," she said. "You never know when someone may start shooting."

CHAPTER EIGHT

I DROPPED GERTIE OFF AT HER HOUSE AND MADE HER PROMISE to go inside and stay there until tomorrow morning. I didn't even want her walking out the front door to check the mail. I was beginning to wonder if Carter wasn't onto something with that whole hibernation theory of his.

The trip to see Walter hadn't provided any information to speak of. Even worse, it had sparked more ridiculous ideas with Gertie, and then I'd gone right along and agreed with them. I shook my head as I pulled into my garage. I'd been running from fire to fire since I'd arrived in Sinful, and most days it felt like I was trying to put them out with a teaspoon of water.

As soon as this crisis with Ida Belle was over, I would seriously rethink how I handled the rest of my stay in Sinful.

I stood under the shower spray until I used every ounce of hot water in the house, and scrubbed my entire body with exfoliating gel and a loofah. I'd thought that kind of thing too girly, but my dip in Sinful Bayou had changed my mind. Losing a layer of skin may be the only thing that made me feel like the crud was off of me.

Unfortunately, even a thousand gallons of hot water and a

pound of sandpaper gel hadn't eliminated the sewer smell of bayou mud, so I threw on shorts and a T-shirt and ran downstairs to stick my nose in a can of coffee grounds.

The grounds did the trick *and* made me want a cup of coffee, so I brewed up a pot and deliberated between a handful of Gertie's chocolate chunk cookies or a slice of Ally's latest creation, a chocolate pecan pie. I finally decided that since the day had been doubly hard, I was twice as deserving of dessert and served up both before pouring myself a cup of coffee and placing my sugary buffet on the kitchen table.

I'd taken one heavenly bite out of the first cookie when my doorbell rang. I looked over at my pistol on the kitchen counter and seriously considered threatening whoever was at the door so that they'd leave and never come back.

The second buzz was more insistent and I rose from the chair with a sigh, but refused to put down the cookie. I shoved the pistol in a kitchen drawer before stalking to the living room. I threw open the front door, then froze when I saw Carter standing there.

"Please tell me you have more of those cookies," he said.

"Maybe?" I said. He didn't look angry or aggrieved so I wasn't sure of his angle.

"I don't suppose I could have one?"

I stepped back and waved him inside, then followed him back to the kitchen. Might as well find out what he was up to.

"Coffee?" I asked.

"That would be great," he said and slid into a chair at the kitchen table. "I hope you don't mind. It's been a long day."

"Ha. Yeah, that's sorta an understatement." I placed the coffee and a plate of cookies on the table in front of him and slid back into my seat.

"I should probably go ahead and get this out of the way," he said. "I'm not here to arrest you."

I swallowed a huge bite of pie. "About time, especially as I haven't done anything."

He raised his eyebrows. "Well, if I wanted to be a pain, I suppose I could haul you in for assaulting Shorty Johnson with an oar."

"Since he was shooting at us, I would just claim self-defense and make you look like a woman-hater."

Carter dropped his cookie and stared. "Shooting at you?"

"It was a pellet pistol. But those things sting and it ruined a perfectly good T-shirt of mine. Besides, people shooting anything at me tends to piss me off."

He laughed. "I'll bet. Since Shorty neglected to inform me of the shooting part of the event, I guess I'll let you off."

"So let me get this straight—you knew I assaulted Shorty with an oar but didn't know it was because he was shooting at us. Yet the first thing you said when you walked into my house was that you weren't going to arrest me. Why the heck not?"

He shrugged. "Knowing Shorty, I guess I figured he'd done something to deserve it, which turned out to be accurate. Besides, he trashed the side of my truck and since he doesn't have any insurance on that boat and is probably broke, I'm either going to have to pay for it myself or file on my own insurance and watch my rates go up."

"Sounds very reasonable...and very boring." I took a sip of coffee. "If you didn't come to arrest me, are you planning on telling me why you are here?"

He smiled. "Maybe I'm just here for the cookies."

"Oh, that's a story I could definitely buy except that you didn't know I had cookies until I answered the door."

"I'm a pretty good detective. Are you sure I didn't know?"

"Unless you broke into my house, I'm sure."

He laughed. "No, I'll leave all the breaking and entering to you and the Trouble Twosome."

"I'm sure I have no idea what you're talking about."

"I'm sure." He took a drink of coffee and stared out the window for several seconds. Finally, he turned his gaze back to me. "Look, the reason I came is to ask you for a favor."

"Really? Of all the things I imagined, that one was nowhere on my list. What in the world can I do for Sinful's finest?"

"You can keep an eye on Ida Belle for me—make sure she's never alone and do your best to keep her from interacting with the general population."

I frowned. "You want to tell me why you're asking me to babysit a woman old enough to be my grandmother?"

"As you witnessed this morning, emotions are running high, and a lot of people aren't making good decisions. Ida Belle is an easy scapegoat for fools and Sinful has more than its share of those."

He glanced out the window again and blew out a breath, then looked back at me.

"This isn't easy for me to admit, but I'm worried about the way things are going in this town. I know I gave you a hard time this morning, but I don't think you have anything to do with this mess, or any of the others. You just seem to have the incredibly bad luck of stepping in the middle of it."

I heard the part about my bad luck and Carter not thinking I had anything to do with Sinful's troubles, and normally, I would have taken a second or two to gloat. But instead, my entire focus was on his first sentence and the tone of his voice when he'd delivered it. It was surprising enough for Carter to admit he was worried, but it wasn't just worry I heard in his voice. It was also fear.

"It's just weird timing," I said. "All of it hitting at once. I know it's a lot on you, but it's not like any of the murders are related."

"I know, but they're all a big glaring neon sign that this town has changed and not for the better."

"Oh." I sat my coffee mug down and leaned back in my chair. "I guess I hadn't thought about it like that."

He sighed. "Yeah. When my time was up with the Marine Corps, I thought I'd come back home and try to forget those eight years in Iraq."

A wave of sympathy washed over me and I wished I could commiserate with Carter as the real me. Sandy-Sue Morrow, librarian extraordinaire, wouldn't have a clue what Carter had probably seen and done overseas, but Fortune Redding knew all too well what went down during war.

"I don't blame you," I said quietly.

"I was eighteen when I left Sinful for boot camp, and convinced this was the most boring town on the face of the earth. When I came back, I hoped like hell I'd been right."

"But it's not."

"It seemed that way at first—a honeymoon phase, I suppose— but now..." He shook his head. "Sinful's changed."

"I'm sure that's true, but you've changed, too."

He looked at me, a flicker of surprise passing over his face.

"You came back home," I continued, "hoping to find the same town you left as a boy, but you returned a man, with a whole different set of experiences shaping your view of the world. Even if Sinful hadn't changed, I bet you'd still see it differently."

He gave me a small smile. "You know, sometimes you can be pretty smart."

"Only sometimes?"

"You *did* have your foot stuck in my toilet this morning."

I laughed. "Well, if you're going to get picky..."

"Attention to detail is sorta part of my job." He glanced down at his watch. "And I need to get back to it. Will you please consider what I asked?"

I nodded. "I'll do my best to keep Ida Belle contained in her house and in front of witnesses who would look good at a trial, but I can't make any promises. She's sorta wily."

"Ha," he said as he rose from the table. "That she is."

I followed him to the front door, where he stopped and

turned around, standing only inches from me. "You said that my asking you for a favor was nowhere on the list of things you'd imagined I came here for. What else was on that list?"

It was just like the bad romance novel Gertie had made me read the week before as part of my induction into normal society. The smoldering eyes, the sexy smile...all so cliché. And damn it if it didn't work.

My pulse quickened and I felt a tingle in my belly.

My God, I'm officially a sixteen-year-old girl.

He brushed a strand of bangs away from my cheek with his finger and my body went into overdrive. Every inch of skin tingled from the brush of that one finger. Then he leaned forward and I knew he was going to kiss me.

My mind warred between shoving him out the door and locking it behind him and throwing him on the floor and molesting him on my living room rug. It was a rush of overwhelming emotion that made my head spin. Never had I had such an adrenaline reaction to a man before. Not even one I was about to kill.

I'd just decided to stand my ground and see what happened when my doorbell rang. The loud, annoying buzz broke the moment completely and sent us both backward in an attempt to put space between us.

"Thanks for the cookies," he said as he opened the door and stepped past my friend Ally. "Evening, Ally."

"Bye, Carter," Ally said then gave me a questioning look. "I suppose it's a good sign that you're not in handcuffs?"

A mental picture of me naked and in handcuffs ran through my mind and I felt a blush creep up my neck. Instantly, I shut the completely inappropriate vision down and waved Ally inside.

She followed me back to the kitchen and took a seat at the table, studying me while I poured her a cup of coffee. "I didn't interrupt anything, did I?" she asked.

"No, he was here on police business and was about to leave anyway."

She took a sip of coffee and narrowed her eyes at me. "Then why are you blushing?"

"I'm not blushing. It's June in Louisiana. I'm hot."

"Now you're lying." Her eyes widened. "Oh my God. He totally made a move on you!"

"No, he didn't." Although I was pretty sure he was going to make a move, he hadn't actually gotten to. So technically, I wasn't lying.

"Oh." Ally's expression fell a little. "Did you want him to?"

"No...I don't...I can't..." Crap. I had no idea how to finish those sentences.

She grinned. "You *did* want him to. Isn't that a real ripper? Of all the men in the world you could find attractive, you pick Carter, the one man who's always trying to stick you in a corner and make you behave."

I shook my head. This conversation was out of control and going places I wasn't ready to go. "I don't find Deputy LeBlanc anything but annoying."

"Now you're lying again. Come on, Fortune. Every woman with a pulse thinks Carter's hot. Unless you're dead or blind, you can't help but notice."

"I never said he wasn't hot. He's just not my type."

"Do tell? Tough, sexy, incredibly good-looking men with a solid job history and a strong moral code aren't your type? I'm afraid to ask what is."

I sighed. "You're not going to let this go, are you?"

"Hell no. Of all the things that have happened to you since you've arrived in Sinful—finding human bones, being accused of murder, almost being murdered yourself—this is the first time I've actually seen you uncomfortable. No way am I dropping this, so you may as well spill."

I studied her for a moment, her expectant, gleeful expression staring impatiently back at me, and I couldn't help but smile. This was what it felt like to have real friends. People who would back you up when you needed them but also had no compunction about picking apart your most intimate thoughts. In some ways, this was just as foreign to me as my erratic feelings about the enigmatic Carter LeBlanc.

"I can't really tell you anything," I said finally, "because I don't have any answers."

"Oh." Ally frowned, apparently sensing that I was telling the truth. "You really don't know if you like him?"

I shrugged. "I like him well enough when he's not giving me shit, and I don't really blame him for the times when he does give me shit because I've usually asked for it."

"And?"

"And yes, he's not hard on the eyes."

"But?"

I threw my arms in the air. "But why does that have to mean anything? *You* like Carter *and* you think he's hot, so why aren't you trying to date him?"

She frowned. "Hmmm. That's a valid question. I grew up with him, mostly with him looking out for me since I was younger and tended to get picked on. So I think I see him more as a big brother than a potential mate, but it doesn't prevent me from seeing him that way with someone else." She gave me a hopeful look.

"Well, I'm going to have to disappoint you. I'm only here for the summer. The last thing I need to do is get involved with someone."

Ally's shoulders slumped a bit. "I keep forgetting you don't really live here. Or maybe I just don't want to remember. I guess I was hoping..."

"I can't stay, Ally. My life is somewhere else." *As* someone else.

"And you love it?"

I paused for a moment, considering her question. Did I love my life in DC? Or was it simply all I'd ever known?

"It's what I know," I said finally. "It's who I am."

"You're young, Fortune. You still have time to be anyone you want to be. I'm not trying to push you into something you don't want to do, but you should think about it. Since you've been here, you've had a chance to see an entirely different life from your own. And maybe Sinful isn't your place, either. But that doesn't mean your old life is."

I stared out the window at the bayou. The setting sun cast an orange glow over the surface of the outgoing tide. It looked so deceptively peaceful, especially compared to the hustle of DC.

But it was all a lie.

Sinful had more than its share of dark secrets, and it seemed they'd all chosen now to bubble up to the surface. I only hoped those buried secrets didn't end up exposing my own.

CHAPTER NINE

"WHERE'S THE POPCORN?" GERTIE CALLED FROM THE LIVING room.

"You're not eating that crap on my new rug!" Ida Belle yelled back from the kitchen.

I stood in the pantry clutching the bag of popcorn, not certain whether to head for the microwave or my Jeep. The two of them had been impossible since I'd walked through the door, and I was ready to shoot them both. The fact that we were a mere ten minutes into my senior babysitting adventures was a really, really bad sign.

"How are we supposed to watch a movie without popcorn?" Gertie yelled.

"If you're going to eat popcorn, you have to stand in the hallway," Ida Belle shouted back.

I stalked to the microwave, determined to restore peace if it was the last thing I ever did. "Wouldn't it just be easier to move the rug? Because I have every intention of eating and drinking and I'm not going to stand in the hallway to do it. Nor am I going to sit at the kitchen table with you two squabbling as my only source of entertainment. Because I have to tell you, you're not all that entertaining."

Ida Belle stared at me. "Who pissed in your cornflakes?"

"You did. And her. The two of you are like battery acid tonight. One more word and I'm going home. Carter can get someone else to babysit. If I wanted children, I'd give birth."

"Touché. I suppose we're both a little on edge."

"Well get off the edge. Roll up the damned rug, pop this popcorn, grab us a couple of beers, and let's get this show on the road. I am so tired of conflict, I'm ready to join a Zen cult."

"I don't think they'd approve of your chosen profession," Ida Belle said. "Fine, we'll roll up the damned rug and cart all manner of food and drink into the living room. What are we watching anyway?"

"I don't know. Gertie picked."

Ida Belle grabbed the bag of popcorn and shoved it in the microwave. "Probably another one of those horrible chick flicks."

"For your information," Gertie said as she strolled into the kitchen, "I rented *The Expendables* 1 and 2."

I held in a grin. "A bunch of old mercenaries getting involved in things they have no business doing. How appropriate."

"You are really catching up on modern film," Gertie said approvingly.

"The other night, I watched a Rambo series marathon."

The microwave dinged and Gertie rushed over to remove the popcorn. She ripped into the bag, then dropped the entire thing into the bowl and ran to stick her fingers under cold water. Ida Belle shook her head, pulled the bag from the ends, and dumped the popcorn into the bowl.

"She's never going to learn," Ida Belle said as she walked past me and into the living room.

I grinned and grabbed three beers from the refrigerator before traipsing behind her. The opening credits had barely finished when the doorbell sounded. We all froze, then looked at one another, probably all afraid that whoever was outside brought more bad news.

Finally, Ida Belle got up and opened the door. "Damn it, Marie," she said as she waved the other woman inside. "Why didn't you call? We all thought you were Carter coming to arrest me."

"Oh, I'm so sorry," Marie said, clearly dismayed that she'd given us a scare. "But I needed to tell you something and that woman got me so flustered with her talk—tell her right away, don't use a phone because they might be listening—I thought I'd have a heart attack on the way over here."

"What in the world are you talking about?" Ida Belle asked. "What woman? And sit down before you pass out."

Marie dropped onto the couch, clutching her purse. "Babs Gaspard. That friend of Celia's."

"What in the world did Babs say that's got you so upset?"

"It wasn't what she said. It was all that spy stuff. Do you really think someone is always listening to our phone conversations, because I got into a fight with my cousin the other day and said some things about her I'd rather not be repeated, even though they were true."

"Your cousin Shirley?" Gertie asked.

Marie nodded.

"That makes sense," Gertie said. "Most everything said about Shirley is true."

Ida Belle waved a hand at Gertie. "Forget about Shirley. And forget what that silly woman said. No one is listening to your phone conversations."

"Are you sure?" Marie asked and looked over at me.

"I'm fairly certain," I said. "It's not as easy as one might think to get an order for a wiretap or to intercept a cellular signal."

Marie's eyes widened.

"At least, that's what I've read," I said, trying to cover my faux pas.

"Oh right," Marie said, her expression clearing in understanding. "I bet you read a lot of different things while you're working in the library."

"You know it," I said. "So what did Babs say that you needed to tell us?"

"She said there's a man at Ted's house. No one's ever seen him before. He's young, probably Paulette's age, and showed up this evening."

"Ted's family?" I asked.

Marie shook her head. "Babs didn't know. She just said Celia told her to get the information to me and to tell me to take it straight to Ida Belle."

"Why in the world would Celia Arceneaux think I'd want to know about some strange man visiting Paulette?"

I sighed. "Because that's Celia's way of helping."

Marie looked even more confused.

"Celia paid me a visit this afternoon," I explained, "expressing her support of Ida Belle's innocence—to remain anonymous, of course—and asked me to find the real murderer. I thought I'd convinced her that it would be dangerous for civilians to attempt to corner a killer, but apparently, stubbornness runs in the water supply around here."

"Oh, I see," Marie said, "and Celia didn't want to talk to me directly, so she sent Babs instead. Like a secret messenger."

"Some secret," Ida Belle said. "Babs's mouth flaps like sheets in a hurricane."

Gertie sighed. "Impolite, but true."

"So what else did Babs say?" I asked.

"That's it," Marie said.

"What do you mean, that's it?" I asked. "That's barely more than nothing at all. You know, if people are going to insist on playing Nancy Drew they should really make sure they have something worth sharing before they go all covert operation."

"Maybe it's not Ted's family," Gertie said. "Maybe it's Paulette's boyfriend."

Marie's eyes widened. "Paulette has a boyfriend?"

"We don't know," I said. "It's just a theory that if Paulette spent her time in New Orleans fooling around with another man, that he might have gotten jealous and killed Ted."

"Oh, that's a good theory," Marie said. "Except that it's Paulette. Would a man really kill someone over Paulette?"

"Therein lies the rub," I said. "And even if Paulette was having a torrid affair, I hardly think that man would show up at her front door the same day her husband was murdered. No one could be that stupid."

"Well..." Ida Belle said. "But I happen to agree with you on this point. So I guess we need to find out who this man is."

"Oh, Babs said Celia was going to handle that," Marie said. "She's going to bring Paulette a casserole tomorrow. She'll pass the information on to Babs as soon as she's done, then Babs will tell me, then I'll call you first to let you know I'm coming, then come over here to tell you what she says." Marie sighed. "Jeez, I'm tired just thinking about all of it."

"Me too," I said.

Marie jumped up from the couch. "Well, I guess I'll let you ladies get back to whatever it is you were doing."

"Watching a movie and eating," Ida Belle said. "Why don't you join us?"

"I can't. I left a casserole baking and it was done about five minutes ago." With that, she dashed out the door, slamming it behind her.

I shook my head. "Marie is far too nervous to make a good operative."

"And she'll burn her house down," Gertie said.

"What do you make of this guy at Paulette's?" Ida Belle asked.

"Nothing yet," I replied. "Too many possibilities. I guess we'll have to wait until Celia finds out more."

"I guess so." Ida Belle flopped back on the couch. "Fire up the movie, Gertie."

I settled back in the recliner and tried to focus on the movie. It was a decent flick, but my mind kept wandering back to Paulette and her New Orleans trips, the strange man who had arrived in town the day of the murder, and the gopher poison that the whole town knew about.

I was completely lost in my thoughts when glass broke on the window behind the couch and something came flying into the living room, crashing into a lamp on the far side of the room. Ida Belle and Gertie hit the floor and I flipped backward over the recliner. I peered around it and saw something large and covered with paper surrounded by vase shards.

Tires squealed outside and I jumped up to get a look at the vehicle, but all I could manage in the dim streetlights was a dark-colored truck.

"Don't touch it!" Gertie yelled at Ida Belle. "It could be a bomb."

I turned around to see Ida Belle leaning over the lump, about to pick it up.

"Then touching it isn't going to make a difference, is it?" Ida Belle said.

I hurried over as Ida Belle picked up the object.

"It's just a rock covered with paper," Ida Belle said as she removed the rubber bands to peel the paper away from the rock.

Yankee-loving murderer.

"Now, there's a sophisticated message," Ida Belle said. "If only we could narrow down the pool of suspects to less than the entire Sinful population."

"We can," I said pointing to the back of the paper. "The idiot wrote that message on his utility bill."

Ida Belle flipped the bill over. "Looks like Shorty didn't learn his lesson with that boat mishap."

"I'm calling Carter," Gertie said.

I looked over at Ida Belle, expecting her to protest, but she just nodded. Apparently, she saw the wisdom in being the victim.

———

IT ONLY TOOK CARTER FIVE MINUTES TO SHOW UP AT IDA Belle's house. It took five seconds for him to sigh in disgust at the message on the utility bill.

"I don't know whether to be happy he's made my job so easy," Carter said, "or pissed off that someone that stupid not only roams the earth, but lives in my hometown."

"I'm voting for pissed off," I said and tapped the bill. "Notice those big red words 'Cancellation notice' written on here. If he's not paying his water bill, I seriously doubt he has the cash for your truck or Ida Belle's window."

Carter perked up. "That makes things easier on me. I figured locking him up would mean no pay and that means no money for my truck, but if he's not paying his bills anyway, there's no loss. Sorry about the window, Ida Belle."

"No worries," Ida Belle said. "I wanted to get some of those new high-efficiency windows anyway. But I'm pressing charges. That vase was expensive."

"I'm pressing charges too," I said.

"For what?" Carter said. "You assaulted him this afternoon."

"For shooting at me—did you forget that part? And at this point, I can make a good case for stalking."

Carter gave me an aggrieved look. "You really want me to press charges for stalking? This town isn't as big as a postage stamp. When it comes down to it, we're probably all stalking one another as soon as we walk out our front doors."

"I know that, but you can use it to threaten him to stay away from us."

He smiled, understanding my angle. "That I can do. Normally, I'd want the three of you at the sheriff's department tomorrow to give statements, but given that our toilet is broken," he said as he looked at me, "I can't have civilians in the building."

"Can we do them here?" I said, feeling slightly guilty.

"I'll bake muffins," Gertie said and clapped her hands. "It will be a party."

Carter stared at Gertie for a moment, apparently not on the party train with her. "I have to go pick up Shorty. I'll see you here tomorrow morning at ten. If something changes, I'll call to reschedule."

Carter left and I locked the door behind him. "Do you have something to cover that hole?" I asked.

"There's trash bags and duct tape in the kitchen," Ida Belle said. "I'll cover it with a tarp on the outside tomorrow. Eddie is the only window guy in Sinful, and it will take forever for him to get to the work. Guess I'll look like a vagrant until then."

"Is he busy with hurricane repairs?" I asked.

"Hell no," Ida Belle said. "He's busy being drunk. I have to wait until he runs out of money for booze before he'll take the job. He just finished installing new windows in the school cafeteria so it could be fall before he needs to work again."

I shook my head. "If Walter can order the windows, I'll install them myself."

Ida Belle and Gertie stared. "You can install windows?" Ida Belle asked.

I shrugged. "Understanding building structure was part of the job...you know, for access purposes. And sometimes we had to build our own shelter. They were makeshift mostly, but I know how to work with wood. Should be a lot easier here without sand blowing in my face and the fear..."

"Fear of what?" Ida Belle asked.

I laughed. "I was going to say without the fear of someone shooting at me, but apparently that doesn't apply."

Gertie shook her head. "It's like I always say, you never know—"

"When someone might start shooting," I interrupted.

Famous last words.

CHAPTER TEN

I SPENT THE NIGHT ON IDA BELLE'S COUCH, WHICH WAS A BIT risky given the local natives' choice of rock throwing, but if it happened again, I wanted to be close enough to the door to catch them and hand out my own form of judge and jury. Carter's method was the legal one, but it didn't tend to work on crazy. In my experience, the only thing that worked on crazy was crazier, and I could definitely top anything Sinful could deal out.

But apparently, all the crazy was in for the night, and instead, all I got for my efforts was a crick in my neck that took a good hour to work its way out. Gertie was up at the crack of dawn, baking muffins, but they smelled so good I couldn't complain about her banging pots at 6:00 a.m. She also might have mollified me with a taste...or maybe two. Okay, it was three muffins, but who's counting?

Carter showed up at ten on the dot, took our statements, and had us sign. Some of the Sinful ladies arrived just after Carter left to work on a quilt, so I headed for home, figuring I was off the babysitting hook for several hours.

I took a hot shower, working out the last remnants of my neck kinks, then headed downstairs where I grabbed a bottle of water from the refrigerator, then stood in the middle of the kitchen processing the uneasy feeling of not knowing what to do.

It was one of the only times since I'd arrived in Sinful that I didn't have a single thing to work on. I should probably start the inventory for the estate, but I really didn't feel like it. And part of me kept hoping that Ahmad would be captured, the price on my head would be lifted, and I'd get to leave Sinful before summer was over and the inventory was due. Then the real Sandy-Sue could handle her inheritance the way she saw fit.

I drummed my fingers on the kitchen counter, staring out the kitchen window, and finally decided to focus on Ida Belle's home repairs. I needed to measure before getting with Walter to order replacement windows, but in order to do any of the work, I needed tools. I'd seen some tools in Marge's storage shed, but I hadn't paid much attention to what she owned, so I headed outside to check it out.

The summer sun beat down on me and the humidity had me covered with a layer of sweat before I'd even made it off the back porch. At this rate, I'd need another shower by the time I went back inside.

The shed sat behind the house to the right, midway between the house and the bayou. It was shaded by a giant oak tree and had a row of hedges running beside it. I was halfway there when I saw a shadow pass across the window of the shed—the inside of the shed.

I immediately reached for my piece, then cursed when I remembered that it was on the kitchen counter and not strapped to my hip as it always would have been before I came to Sinful. I hurried back inside, grabbed the nine, and then exited the house by the front door, planning to sneak down the row of hedges and catch whoever was in my shed before they caught sight of me and had a chance to run.

I crept down the back side of the hedge, hoping the neighbor I shared the hedge with didn't look outside and see me creeping across his lawn with a handgun. When I reached the shed, I found a good spot to push through the shrubs, then dropped on my hands and knees and crawled through to the back of the shed.

The back of the shed didn't have a window, so I stood back up and placed my ear to the wall. Everything was silent for a bit, then I heard something rattle, as if someone had bumped against something inside the shed. I slipped around the corner of the shed and crouched down as I eased past the window. When I reached the end of the shed, I lifted my right arm up, pistol in ready position, then jumped around the corner and threw open the door.

Before I had a chance to focus, much less aim, something hit me square in the face, screeching like a banshee and clawing the top of my head. I scrambled backward, accidentally firing off one round before I could reposition my finger. The creature on my head launched off and scurried into the bushes.

I repositioned my trigger finger and whirled around, preparing to go to war in the shrubbery, when I heard laughter behind me. I glanced over to see Ally standing there, bent over and laughing so hard she was crying. Her boat was pulled up the bank in my backyard.

"Some wild animal attacked me," I said, feeling a bit outraged at her obvious glee. "And you think that's funny?"

She gasped a couple of times, then straightened up and drew in a deep breath. "That wasn't a wild animal."

"I can feel the cuts on my scalp. That's wild enough and it's not going to set up house in my shed."

Ally walked past me and leaned over, peering into the bushes. "Here, kitty kitty."

The bushes rustled a bit and a small black cat peered out. It took one hesitant step out of the bushes, then strolled right past Ally and wound around my legs, purring.

Ally grinned. "I think you've got a new friend."

"Oh no. I don't know a thing about taking care of a cat, and besides, my head is throbbing from those claws. It would be like living with live razor blades."

"Come on, Fortune. The razor blades might make a good backup security system. Besides, cats can see ghosts, so if you're haunted, Kitty will be able to tell you."

"I don't want to know if I'm haunted, and I have all the backup security I need in a second magazine." I pointed to my gun.

"Uh-huh. Would that be the gun you just shot out your own window with?"

Ally pointed to the second story of my house where I could see the small pane of glass missing from one of the guest room windows.

"Great. I guess I'll be replacing two sets of windows."

Ally frowned. "What are you talking about?"

"I'll tell you all about it, but let's get inside out of this heat." I pointed at the cat. "You need to go home."

The cat looked up at me and meowed.

"I think he likes you," Ally insisted.

"I don't care, and how do you know it's a he?"

She shrugged. "Because he caused a rash of shit and thinks rubbing on your legs and looking pitiful will fix it."

I laughed. "Let's get inside before we melt." I pointed at the cat. "You stay here."

The cat sat down and started cleaning his paw.

"He probably wants to get my blood off his nails," I said, then we headed inside. "Beer, water, or soda?" I asked as I poked my head in the refrigerator.

"It's after noon, so beer me."

I grabbed two beers and took a seat at the kitchen table. "Is that noon thing another one of Sinful's odd laws?"

"No, that's a personal one. I figure drinking before lunch is crass."

"Why aren't you at the café?"

"It's my day off. Between all the excitement yesterday and staying late to help Francine bake pies, I slept like a brick. I didn't even wake up until nine, which is unheard of for me."

"Yeah, I completely forgot to ask you yesterday what happened with Paulette at the café. I was at the sheriff's department when Carter went over there to break up a fight between Paulette and Francine...something about a new rug."

Ally nodded. "I thought Francine was going to shit kittens. I don't think I've ever seen her that mad in my life. Not even when old Mr. Bullard smacked her on the butt and called her a prize heifer."

"I'm surprised old Mr. Bullard is still alive."

"He's not, actually, but Francine didn't have anything to do with that. At least that's what she claims. He had a heart attack in the café, so who knows. Anyway, Paulette stormed in there, looking like a wet hooker, and started yelling at Francine that she was a horrible person for keeping the café open."

I shook my head. "The woman has some balls."

"Francine didn't even miss a beat. She kept pouring coffee and told Paulette that people didn't stop getting hungry just because someone died and to stop dripping on her rug or she'd be buying a new one."

"Wow. That's blunt, even for Francine."

"Paulette once called Francine tacky white trash, and Ted used to hit on her."

"Never mind. Francine was more than polite."

Ally nodded. "I thought so too. If it had been me, I would have accidentally spilled that pot of coffee on her."

"Sneaky, and effective," I said approvingly.

"So Paulette started wailing like a banshee that Francine couldn't make her get out and that she was the victim. Then Francine told her that the only victims were the rug and everyone who was listening to her bitch."

I laughed.

"So Paulette starts to lunge forward, and I'm thinking 'This is about to get good' because Francine is the only girl in a family of eight siblings and can fight better than most men."

Francine's stock went up a hundred points in my mental tally.

"Then Carter walks in," Ally continued, "and grabs Paulette before she can make a move. He lifted her right off the rug and carried her outside to her car, then waited until she drove off before going back to the sheriff's department."

I shook my head. "Why does he have to be so efficient? It takes all the excitement out of everything."

Ally laughed. "I know. Some of the customers were disappointed he showed up so quickly. They figure someone called and ratted, but no one would fess up to it."

"That Paulette is some piece of work. I heard some guy showed up at her house yesterday and seems to be staying there."

"Really? Who is he?"

"No one seems to know, but I'm sure it will come out sooner or later."

"You don't think she's already getting some on the side, do you?"

"Technically, it wouldn't be 'on the side' since Ted's dead, but no. Even after everything I've heard about Paulette, I still can't believe she'd be foolish enough to parade a boyfriend through Sinful the day after her husband's murder."

Ally slumped back in her chair. "Probably not, but it would have been interesting, right? Especially with Ted being murdered and all. Do you think Paulette did it?"

"I don't know. The spouse is always the usual suspect, but you still have to prove it. Without evidence that Paulette had access to the murder weapon and a motive for doing it, it would all amount to nothing."

Ally frowned. "I heard about the arsenic, and everyone knows that Ida Belle had gophers, so I assume that's why Carter questioned her. But no one with two brain cells thinks Ida Belle killed Ted, so that means someone else did."

"Yeah, but who?"

"I have no idea. I hope Carter is smarter than we are."

"Me too." But I was afraid he was running into the same lack of information that Gertie and I had.

"Anyway," Ally continued. "Paulette's apparently wasting no time getting Ted in the ground."

"What do you mean?"

"The coroner released the body this morning. I guess they have all the evidence they need. Father Michael was in the café yesterday evening making notes. I asked if he was working on a sermon, and he said that he was preparing for a candlelight vigil tonight and the funeral tomorrow."

I sat up straight. "Wow. That *is* fast." Which meant I only had this afternoon to plan my trip through Ted's house with Gertie. I hadn't expected to have my hand forced so quickly.

"What time is the vigil?"

"In the summer, they usually start late because they're held at dusk. There's no point in everyone holding a candle if daylight is streaming through every window of the church." She stared at me. "You're not thinking of going, are you?"

"Heck no! I just wondered, is all. I've never known anyone who had a vigil."

"The GWs will probably start making phone calls about it this afternoon. Sinful being so small, people don't need much in the way of notice, and most people will just show up for the funeral tomorrow."

Suddenly, it dawned on me that Ted was going to be buried in Sinful. "I don't get it—why bury Ted here when they're from up north?"

Ally frowned. "I hadn't really thought about it, but that is weird. Maybe he had a falling-out with his family or something and didn't want to be buried back home."

"Or maybe he has no family left."

For the first time in my life I thought about what would happen if I died. I had a will. Everyone in the CIA was required to keep an updated copy on file with human resources. Morrow was my executor, so I assumed he'd pick some plot and schedule the standard service. People I worked with would come...unless they were on a mission. In that case, my funeral would probably be attended by the priest, Hadley, Morrow, and the guy with the shovel.

How depressing.

"Fortune?" Ally's voice broke into my thoughts. "I lost you there for a moment."

"Oh, yeah. Just thinking. So much has happened since I arrived that it's sometimes a lot to take in."

She nodded. "I've lived here practically my entire life but I've had trouble keeping up these past few weeks."

"Carter thinks the town has changed."

Ally tilted her head to the side, her brow wrinkled. "He said that?"

Instantly, I felt guilty. "I shouldn't have repeated that. Please don't say anything to anyone about it."

"No, of course not. But I find it interesting."

"Why is that?"

"I feel the same way. I mean, I know the whole 'you can never go home again' thing because you change while you're gone and then nothing is the same as it was before, but this is something different."

"It's like everything bad is bubbling to the surface at once."

"Yes! That's it exactly. And it's stuff that I never imagined would go on in Sinful." She shook her head. "I guess that's my own naïveté or maybe just wishful thinking. I suppose evil is everywhere."

"Sometimes it's just plain ole greed." I straightened up. "Ted was always giving stuff away, right? Maybe Paulette killed him for the money."

Ally shrugged. "It's as good a reason as any." She rose from the table. "I better get going. I just wanted to check in on you. Everyone's talking about your run-in with Shorty yesterday, but I'm not foolish enough to think he got the better of you. I should really get on my laundry. Aunt Celia will expect me to attend the service with her tonight, and I don't have a single pair of clean underwear to my name."

"Go commando."

Ally's eyes widened. "It's illegal to go into a church in Sinful without underwear."

I sighed. "Of course it is."

———

"You're sure the house is empty?" Gertie peered out Marie's front window.

"You've asked the same question ten times now," Marie complained. "You watched the same thing I did. Paulette and that man Celia said is her cousin came out and drove away. If anyone else is in that house, I'm not aware that they were inside to begin with."

"I just want to make sure," Gertie said. "You don't have to get pissy about it."

"The only way we're going to be sure," I said, "is when we go in there and it's empty. How long do these candlelight vigil things last?"

"It depends on how far off on a bunny trail Father Michael gets," Marie said, "but usually about an hour."

Marie's cell phone rang and we all jumped. "It's Ida Belle," Marie said. "Again."

"Give me that," I said and answered. "You have to stop calling.

We're about to go in and we need this line clear. As soon as we know anything, we'll call."

I disconnected before Ida Belle could protest and handed the phone back to Marie.

Gertie shook her head. "Asking that woman to take a sideline seat is like asking Johnny Depp to stop being hot."

"It's for her own good," I reminded Gertie. "The last place Ida Belle needs to be seen is across the street from Ted's house. Why do you think I parked my Jeep around the corner?"

"I know, but try telling her that," Gertie said.

"We need to get this show on the road." I gave Gertie a hard look. "Be careful to put everything back exactly as you found it. We don't want to give Paulette or her cousin any reason to suspect we were there."

"Remember," Marie said, "Babs said that Celia unlocked the patio door when she called on Paulette earlier. Unless she double-checked before leaving the house, you should be able to stroll right in. Babs said there's no security system."

I nodded. "I have my phone on vibrate. Do not leave this window. Don't even blink. If you see anyone approach the house, send me a text."

"Got it," Marie said.

I pulled out two sets of plastic gloves and passed one to Gertie. "Let's do this."

CHAPTER ELEVEN

GERTIE AND I HEADED OUT THE BACK DOOR AND SKIRTED around the block, coming at Ted's house from the back side. Marie had already identified the neighboring homes as Catholics, so unless they were being heathens, they should all be at the vigil.

"I wish it was completely dark," I said.

"I don't know," Gertie said. "My night vision isn't what it used to be."

"All of your vision isn't what it used to be. You just refuse to admit it."

"My vision is perfectly fine. I don't know why you and Ida Belle always have to harp—"

I heard a grunt and looked back to see Gertie and her perfectly fine vision slumped over the air-conditioning unit she'd just walked straight into. I shook my head. "Awful how those AC units just jump right out in front of you."

"You distracted me by talking."

"Then by all means, I'll shut up before you walk right through a window and give us away." I had my back to her, but I would have bet anything she gave me the bird.

When we reached the back of Ted's house, we inched around

the side to the front fence gate. I pulled the lever down and breathed a sigh of relief when it opened. A six-foot fence was no big obstacle for me, but Gertie and fences had a somewhat check-ered past.

When the patio door slid open without a hitch, I wasn't sure whether to be relieved again or worried. Investigating with Gertie and Ida Belle didn't usually go this well. I was waiting for the other shoe to drop.

"Where do we start?" Gertie asked.

"Upstairs. Half of Sinful has traipsed through the downstairs today. Nothing incriminating would be on display. If that guy staying here is really her cousin then he'll be in a guest room. See if you can find something on him. I'll take the master bedroom."

Gertie nodded and we crept upstairs. The first two rooms we came to were completely empty, which seemed odd given that they'd been living in Sinful for two years, but maybe they were the kind of people who weren't attached to things. The next was a bathroom, then after that a guest room with a duffel bag in the middle of the bed. I waved Gertie in and continued down the hall to the last door, which must be the master bedroom.

I blanched when I looked inside. It was like a gold-and-red lamé fabric assault. A bed with giant posts stood in the center of the back wall, giant bolts of fabric draped from column to column. The same fabric hung over every window, covered every pillow and seat cushion, and was even draped over the dresser, the nightstands, and a makeup table.

I couldn't imagine how anyone managed to sleep in this horror story. You'd need sunglasses for the glare alone.

I moved immediately to the nightstand on the right side of the bed, but all I found was lotion, gel packs for eyes, and sleeping pills. I checked the name on the bottle—Paulette Williams. Nothing of interest there.

I moved to the other side and found it even less revealing. A car magazine was the sole occupant. I frowned and moved to the dresser. The first drawer was clearly Paulette's and I said a prayer of thanks that I was wearing gloves. Her underwear was even more garish than her bedroom decor, but despite what I'd seen in movies, nothing was hidden in the back of the panty drawer. None of the other drawers coughed up a clue either.

I checked the drawer on the makeup table, but only found one of everything from Walmart, then moved into the master bathroom, which was equally sterile. I muddled through the walk-in closet of boring tan slacks and polo shirts with equally opposite spandex and glitter, but came up empty. If Ted and Paulette had any secret vices, they weren't hiding them in their bedroom.

I stepped out in the hall as Gertie walked out of the guest bathroom. "Anything?" I asked.

She shook her head. "The cousin must have his wallet on him, and the duffel bag didn't have a luggage tag or anything."

"Probably carry-on," I said.

"Did you find anything in the master?"

"Aside from the most offensive decorating in the world, not a single thing seems out of the ordinary."

"Well, shit."

I nodded. "The other bedrooms were empty, so I guess we move downstairs."

I could tell by Gertie's expression that she was disappointed, and so was I. This entire escapade had been risky and was headed straight toward being a total bust. I had just reached the top of the stairs when I felt my phone vibrating in my pocket.

Alarmed, I yanked it out, hoping the message was from anyone but Marie.

Two people just went through fence gate. Too dark to see who.

"Marie saw two people go through the fence gate," I said.

Gertie's eyes widened. "Paulette and her cousin would use the front door."

"I know. And it's a little late for lawn work."

"You locked the patio door behind us, right?"

As I nodded, I heard glass breaking downstairs. "I don't think it mattered," I whispered. "We have to hide."

"Where?"

A damned good question. The two empty bedrooms didn't provide anything in the way of cover and the other two bedrooms and baths were being used. Unless the others were breaking in to steal televisions, no doubt they'd be upstairs to search the bedrooms.

"This way," I said and hurried into one of the empty rooms. Maybe we'd luck out and find an exterior window with a nearby tree. We dashed into the bedroom, closing the door behind us. I made a quick check of the windows, but unless we wanted to make a twenty-foot drop straight onto a concrete patio, they weren't a viable option. I could have made the drop, but no way would Gertie and her ancient bones be able to come out of it walking.

I heard footsteps on the stairs and grabbed Gertie's arm and pulled her toward the closet. I was surprised to find it much larger than I'd expected, until Gertie turned on her cell phone flashlight and pointed to the back wall. In the dim light, I saw a doorknob, so I eased it open and found a narrow staircase.

Gertie peered around me and pointed up, indicating it was the staircase to the attic. I didn't like the idea of moving us another floor higher from the ground, but we couldn't exactly be picky. With any luck, the other guys would get whatever they were after and exit without checking the closet. And hopefully, leaving Gertie and me enough time to get out before Paulette and her cousin returned home.

As we crept up the narrow staircase, I said a silent prayer that nothing creaked. Old houses made noise, but people who broke into old houses tended to investigate noise, regardless. We made it up the stairs without incident and I pulled a penlight out of my pocket as we stepped into the attic so that we could get our bearings. The last thing we needed was to trip over something.

The attic was practically barren except for a makeshift desk in front of a dormer window. Unable to control my curiosity, I inched over to the desk to see if it contained anything of interest, Gertie close behind. When we reached the desk, I froze at the sound of two men speaking. I whirled around, looking behind us, but no one was standing there, nor did it sound like anyone was accessing the stairs. Gertie tugged on my sleeve and pointed to a grille near the floor and I nodded. The voices were coming up through the ventilation system from the second floor.

I motioned to the floor and eased myself down until I knelt in front of the vent. Maybe if we could overhear their conversation, we'd know who was in the house and why. Gertie inched down beside me until we both crouched there, silent and waiting for the voices to start up again.

"Those pictures have got to be here somewhere," a man said.

We heard the sound of drawers banging and glass breaking, then another man said, "What if he has them on one of those smarty phones or something?"

"He showed us prints, remember? And even if they're on one of them phones, the phone should be here unless they're planning on burying him with it."

"I hope they don't do that. I really hate digging up graves."

I looked over at Gertie, whose eyes widened. What the hell kind of people made digging up graves a regular habit?

"If we don't find those pictures," the first man said, "the only graves we're going to be digging is our own."

"Maybe the bitch has them. Maybe she's going to start cashing in."

"I can handle the bitch."

"How's that?"

"Same way someone handled Ted, which is what we should have done a long time ago. Check in the bathroom. I'm going to take a look in those empty rooms, then we'll blow this joint."

My cell phone buzzed again and I felt my heart drop when I read the text.

Paulette and cousin pulling into drive.

Crappity, crap, crap, crap!

I showed Gertie the text and the color rushed out of her face. I was just thinking things couldn't get much worse when the universe proved me infinitely wrong.

"That bitch is pulling up out front!" the second man yelled.

I heard scuffling in the room below us and jumped up, scanning the room for a potential hiding place.

"There's a staircase in this closet," the first man yelled. "Get in here!"

No time left and no hiding place in sight, I jumped on top of the makeshift desk and opened the dormer window. The slope of the roof wasn't as drastic as it extended away from the window, so I figured even Gertie would be able to manage it. How we were going to get down was a whole other story and one I didn't even want to think about.

I waved at the window and gave Gertie huge props for climbing up on the desk and out the window without even a moment's hesitation. As I stepped outside to follow her, a small wooden box on the corner of the desk caught my eye. I grabbed the box before stepping onto the roof, then closed the window behind me.

Gertie had scrambled up the roof to the right, and was crouching below some low-hanging tree branches. The branches perked me up a bit. If they were sturdy enough, we'd just found our way down. I shoved the box into my sports bra. It was the most restricting garment I had on besides my jeans and I didn't figure I'd be using my breasts to shinny down the tree.

"What about those men?" Gertie whispered.

"What about them? I assume they're hiding in the attic."

"What if they kill Paulette and her cousin?"

Shit. I'd been so busy trying to escape that I hadn't even

thought about what might happen to Paulette and her cousin with those guys cornered in the attic. I reached up and pulled on the largest branch above us and decided it was strong enough to hold us.

"Start down," I said. "And get back to Marie's. I'll take care of the rest."

"But—"

"Go!" I hissed.

She grabbed hold of the branch and stepped off the side of the roof and into the tree. Now, as long as she didn't fall on the way down, we were good. I waited until she was halfway down, then pulled out my cell phone and called Marie.

"We're outside of the house and on our way back," I said as soon as she answered. "The bad guys are in the attic. Call Carter and say you saw two people go through Paulette's back fence a couple of minutes ago and then she drove up."

"What—"

"I'll explain later. Just do it." I slipped the phone back in my pocket and hoped Marie followed instructions. Now I just had to get Gertie and me out of the tree and back across the road before Carter got there, and hope that the bad guys hadn't gotten impatient and put a cap in Paulette and her cousin.

I shinnied down the tree with the skill of a panda, passing Gertie on my way. The limbs had been trimmed at the bottom to allow for walking space, so the lowest branch was still a good ten-foot drop. I jumped off of it and rolled as I hit the ground, then turned around to help Gertie.

Apparently, Gertie had forgotten her age or she'd decided to channel me because instead of hanging from the lower branch and dropping, as I thought she'd do, she barreled off the branch like I did, except she forgot the rolling part. Instead, she crashed right into me and we both went tumbling onto the lawn.

I saw Gertie's eyes widen as her feet hit the ground and her hands flew up to cover her mouth. I bolted up and grabbed her by the shoulders, hauling her to her feet.

"My foot," she whispered.

I realized she was only standing on one foot and began to panic. The only exit from the backyard was through the gate and if Marie had followed instructions, Carter would be pulling up there any minute. I reached under her arms and lifted her off the ground on the bad foot side, then hurried across the back lawn, half walking, half dragging Gertie.

When I got to the gate, I peered outside just as Carter's truck pulled up to the curb. Panicked, I scooped Gertie up and over my shoulder and went running for the back fence. When I got there, I shoved her up at the top and left her dangling half over and I jumped up and over.

"This may hurt," I whispered as I pulled her over the wooden boards and grabbed hold of her before she crashed into the turf again. Her feet had no sooner hit the ground than I hefted her over my shoulder again and skirted two houses down before running down the side of a house and checking the street.

Carter wasn't in his truck and I couldn't see him anywhere outside. I'd picked a good spot to cut through because the streetlights were too far apart and left a dark strip that ran directly across the road. I scanned the block one more time, then hauled it across the street as far as I could manage, only slowing when I rounded the backside of the houses on Marie's block. My shoulders and legs were burning with the strain, so I put Gertie down and went back to the underarm method of walking/dragging until I got her into Marie's house. Gertie managed to put some weight on her foot, so the going was a little easier.

Marie stifled a scream when we rushed in her back door, then almost passed out from relief when she realized it was us.

"What happened?" she asked as she saw Gertie limp to the kitchen table and slump into a chair.

"She fell," I said, not about to go into the whole roof debacle right now. "Carter is sure to come over here. We need to hide."

Marie shook her head. "It won't do any good. He came down the block from the opposite direction of his house. He would have seen your Jeep parked around the corner."

I looked down at my shirt, covered with grass stains from Gertie's knees. "If he sees me like this, he'll know something was up."

"I'll go grab you one of my shirts," Marie said and took off down the hall but before she even got to the stairwell, her doorbell rang.

"Mrs. Chicoron. It's Deputy LeBlanc."

CHAPTER TWELVE

Marie ran back into the kitchen and before I could even make a suggestion, she yanked an apron out of a drawer, held it to my waist, and told me to tie it. I was just securing the strings at my back when she put a carton of eggs and a bowl on the counter, and poured flour in the bowl.

Certain she'd lost her mind, I reached out to grab her arm and that's when she hit me with a shot of water from the salad sprayer, then tossed a handful of flour on me. I coughed as the flour went up my nose and wiped my face with my hand, completely stunned and uncertain what action to take next.

"I'm teaching you to bake," Marie said. "You're not very good." She pointed at Gertie. "Stay there where he can't see that limp or your pants legs."

Then she ran out of the kitchen like a bat out of hell.

I looked over at Gertie, a little shell-shocked.

Bones, Marie's ancient bloodhound, lifted his head from his bed in the corner and stared at us both for a couple of seconds before lowering his head and snoring again.

"She's good," Gertie said. "How about you bring me a glass of milk and some cookies...make things look more authentic."

I heard Marie open the front door and grabbed the milk and cookies for Gertie and myself. No sense in Gertie getting all the benefit of the cover-up. It wasn't like she'd carried me for a block.

I shoved the milk and cookies in front of Gertie and hurried back behind the kitchen counter and grabbed a cookbook from a shelf just as Carter and Marie stepped into the kitchen.

He gave Gertie a suspicious nod, then took one look at me and raised his eyebrows. "Should I even ask?"

"I'm teaching her to bake," Marie said, "or trying to anyway. It might be more expedient for the rest of us to continue to provide her with baked goods."

Carter didn't look even remotely convinced.

I shrugged. "What can I say? I have a skill for eating, but not necessarily for baking. I never knew it was this involved...or this messy."

"So I'm supposed to believe you have been in here all evening baking?"

"No," I said. "We'd just gotten started a little before you knocked on the door. Earlier, I was busy eating. You know, getting a taste for my future creations."

"Uh-huh. How come you parked your Jeep around the corner?"

"There wasn't any parking in front of Marie's house when we got here," Gertie chimed in. "Probably half of Sinful was delivering casseroles to Paulette."

"I see, and why isn't Ida Belle here in the middle of this cooking lesson?"

"We didn't figure it was a good idea," I said. "You know, with Paulette living across the street and all. And besides, she's quilting with some of the Sinful Ladies Society."

Carter shook his head, but he must have decided that we weren't up to anything for a change or if we were, he'd never get it out of us, because he changed the subject and got down to the police business at hand.

"What exactly did you see, Marie?" he asked.

"Oh, well, I was straightening the living room—we'd been sitting in there before watching television—and I saw someone across the street. I thought it was odd because everyone had left for the vigil earlier, so I stepped up to the window to get a closer look."

"And you saw someone enter Paulette's back gate?"

"Two people, but their backs were to me. I didn't see what they looked like at all."

"What did you do then?" he asked.

"I yelled for Fortune and Gertie to come look but the people were already in the backyard. We waited a minute but they never came back out. Fortune said I should call you and as I was doing so, Paulette and her cousin pulled up. They went inside. We watched for a couple of minutes, then went back to the kitchen."

Carter narrowed his eyes at her. "Just like that. You came back here as if nothing was going on?"

Marie shrugged. "All Ted has back there is an old grill. And it had gotten completely dark by then. For all I knew, they could have left already. I wouldn't have been able to see them."

Marie sucked in a breath. "Paulette and her cousin are okay, right? Those people didn't go inside, did they?"

"As a matter of fact, they did. A back window was broken out and apparently, the men went up to the attic to hide when Paulette and her cousin Tony arrived home. Paulette went straight to her bedroom and Tony to the guest bathroom. The men tried to sneak out of the attic but Tony walked out of the bathroom before they made it downstairs. One of the men clubbed him with a crowbar and they both fled out of the back of the house."

Marie's hands flew over her mouth.

"Oh, my God," Gertie said. "Is Tony all right?"

Carter nodded. "The guy wasn't a good shot. Tony will have a hell of a bruise on his shoulder, but I don't think anything's broken."

I shook my head. "What kind of people commit a robbery while the widow is at a vigil?"

At that moment, the box in my bra dug into my rib cage and I said a silent prayer that God wouldn't send lightning right through Marie's house and onto my head for my hypocrisy.

"I don't know," Carter said. "I have Paulette checking to figure out if anything is missing. They may not have had time to get anything. It's a good thing you saw them, Marie."

Marie shook her head. "Some days, I don't know what this town is coming to."

Her thoughts so closely mirrored Carter's that I watched his face closely for a reaction. But apparently, when Carter was working, his innermost thoughts were locked tightly away, because his expression never changed.

"I'm sure opportunists exist in every town. Sinful has always had its share. I can't say that I've seen any this crass, but then the whole world seems to be slipping in standards. Why should Sinful be any different?"

Marie sighed. "I suppose you're right."

"Thanks for the information," Carter said. "I better get back across the street before Paulette unloads on Deputy Breaux. It's bound to happen before the night is over."

He gave us a nod, then left the kitchen. Marie hurried behind him and we heard the front door close and lock before she ran back into the kitchen and collapsed into a chair across from Gertie.

"Oh my God," she exclaimed. "I don't know how you two do this sort of thing all the time. I feel like I'm going to have a heart attack."

"We don't do it all the time," Gertie said. "It just seems that lately, the call for stealth has been a bit higher than usual."

"You were really, really good," I told Marie. "Like professional good. I would never have come up with that cover so quickly."

Marie smiled. "That's because you really don't know a thing

about baking. I just grasped at the one thing I turn to every time I'm in trouble. This time, it happened to *save* my butt instead of make it wider."

"Hey, I don't really have to cook something, do I?"

"No!" Both Gertie and Marie held their hands up.

"Well, don't everyone give me their opinion at once. Jeez."

Marie jumped up from her chair and hurried into the kitchen, apparently worried I might challenge her directive. "Take off that apron, wipe off your face, and grab yourself some cookies. I'll put everything back in order."

She didn't have to tell me twice. I grabbed a handful of cookies from the counter and a soda from the refrigerator, and headed to the table.

"So what kind of pictures do you think those men were looking for?" Gertie asked.

"How do you know they were looking for pictures?" Marie asked.

"We heard them talking through the vents." I reached into my sports bra and pulled out the box. "I don't know what pictures they were looking for but I'm hoping they're in here."

Gertie's eyes widened. "Where did you get that?"

"I stole it from that desk before we went out onto the roof."

Marie sucked in a breath. "You went out—no, never mind. I don't want to know."

I pulled at the lid, but it was locked. "Do you have an ice pick?"

Marie shook her head. "I know it might be hard to believe but we've had refrigerators with ice makers for a lot of years."

"Marie doesn't fish," Gertie said. "If we were at mine or Ida Belle's we'd have an ice pick."

"Anything small and thin," I said.

Marie frowned for a minute, then brightened. "How about a knitting needle?"

"Perfect."

She hurried to the living room and returned shortly with a long, thin needle. I inserted it in the lock and wiggled it around until I heard a click. Marie leaned over me and Gertie scooted around the table to get a closer look as I lifted the lid. Inside was a stack of photographs.

I lifted the stack and looked at the first one. "I don't get it. It's a man and a woman, kissing in a bar."

Marie's hand flew up to cover her mouth and Gertie's eyes widened. "Not just any man," Gertie said. "That's our banker and that woman is his wife's sister."

I flipped the photo over and moved to the next one.

"That's one of the St. Claire brothers," Marie said, pointing to the man smoking.

"He's smoking a joint," I said.

"Seriously?" Marie leaned over to get a better look at the photo. "I've never seen one in person. His mother would have a fit."

"He's a grown man," I pointed out. "His mother would get over it."

Gertie shook her head. "His younger brother died of a drug overdose. Nona St. Claire hasn't been the same since. If she knew another of her boys was using..."

A bad feeling came over me and I flipped to the next picture. It was a picture of a beefy man entering a shack on the bayou. "Is there anything wrong with this situation?" I asked.

Gertie whistled. "Only if you take into account that man's wife reported him missing at sea seven years ago and just had him declared legally dead."

"Wishful thinking?" I asked.

"Insurance policy."

I set the pictures down on the table. "I think I know what's going on here."

"What?" Gertie asked. "Because I'm completely lost."

"I think our friend Ted was blackmailing people."

"Oh my God," Marie said and slumped into the chair next to me.

Gertie whistled. "And then he was using the money to buy stuff and give it to people, making him look like a good guy. What a tool."

I nodded. "And what do you want to bet that some of the people he gave gifts to were the same people he was extorting money from?"

"No wonder the men seemed to tolerate him but not really like him." Gertie shook her head. "That takes some kind of balls."

"Not to mention running for mayor," Marie pointed out. "What the heck was he thinking? People will kill over..."

"Exactly," I said.

"But which one?" Gertie said. "There must be twenty photos here, and he may have more hidden somewhere else."

Marie frowned. "I didn't like Ted. He always gave you that look—you know, like he was mentally undressing you—but I never figured him to be this stupid or to take such a risk. Do you think he needed money that badly?"

"Maybe," I said, "or maybe he was just doing what came naturally."

"What do you mean?" Gertie asked.

"What do any of you really know about Ted's life before he moved to Sinful?"

"Not much," Gertie said. "And only what he's said about it."

I nodded. "So what if Ted didn't inherit anything? What if he came here to hide from his past?"

"Hide in Sinful?" Marie asked. "It doesn't seem a likely place."

"Oh," Gertie said, giving me an amused look, "I think Sinful is the perfect place to hide. Who would ever look here?"

"I see what you're saying," Marie said. "But we don't know for sure that's what happened."

"I think it's as good a guess as any," I said. "Did either one of you know about the things going on in these photos?"

They both shook their heads.

"But yet, a man who'd only lived here for two years managed to get the dirt on everyone in town. How likely is that unless he's done it before—often and well?"

"Not very," Gertie said. "So what the hell do we do about it?"

"I think you should turn the photos over to Carter," Marie said. "One person already died over them. I'm as worried about Ida Belle as you two, but I don't want any more of the people I care about at risk. Tonight almost gave me a heart attack, and that was before I knew you went traipsing across the roof."

I held in a sigh. Marie was one of the nicest people I'd ever met, and I hated disappointing her, but I was about to anyway. "I can't turn the photos over to Carter without explaining how I got them. Somehow, I don't think he'd take kindly to Gertie and me breaking and entering, especially as someone else did the same thing and assaulted one of the occupants."

"Oh!" Marie's face fell. "I hadn't even thought about that."

I ran through a number of possibilities for getting the photos to Carter, but none of them offered a chain of evidence without exposing myself. And without a chain of evidence, a judge would never allow the photos during trial.

It was the ultimate catch-22. I'd found evidence to prove why others would want Ted dead, and it was highly unlikely Carter would ever have found the evidence because he had no reason to execute a search warrant on Ted's house. But I couldn't use the evidence.

At least not through legal channels.

"I know that look," Gertie said. "You've got an idea."

"Two, actually."

"Well, out with them. I'm not getting any younger."

"First, we need to do some digging into Ted and Paulette's past. Then we need to follow up on the people in these photos."

"Follow up?" Marie asked. "You mean spy on them?"

I nodded. "Exactly."

CHAPTER THIRTEEN

Ida Belle cleared out the Sinful Ladies and we reconvened at her house. Since Carter's truck was still parked outside Paulette's house, Marie stayed put to keep an eye on things and because I was afraid to involve her any more than she already was. It was also easier for me to talk when it was only Ida Belle and Gertie. Then I didn't have to worry about maintaining cover.

Ida Belle was pacing like a caged animal by the time we got to her house. She opened the front door and started waving us into the house before I'd even put my Jeep in park. By the time we got inside, I thought she'd pop a cork.

"What happened?" Ida Belle asked as soon as she shut the front door. "Jesus, you left me hanging for hours."

Gertie rolled her eyes. "It wasn't hours and we were a little busy."

"This isn't a good time for that patience speech of yours," Ida Belle warned.

I held my hands up to stop the barrage before it got started. "No need for violence." I brought Ida Belle up to speed on everything that had happened and showed her the photos.

She grabbed the stack and flipped through them, exclaiming with every new reveal. "Wow. Ted really had the goods on people. I suspected a lot of these, but didn't have proof."

"You didn't go looking for proof, either," I pointed out.

"True."

"I don't understand," Gertie said. "If Ted had so much money, why risk doing something like this? Even if he knew how to do it well, this is Louisiana, not Boston or wherever he's supposed to be from. People will shoot you here."

"People will shoot you in Boston, too," I said, "but you make a valid point. If he didn't need the money, then it must be for fun. But that makes him crazy."

Ida Belle shook her head. "I don't disagree with the crazy part, but I'm starting to wonder if the inheritance story wasn't a lie."

"Why is that?" I asked.

"One of the Sinful Ladies is a receptionist over at the bank. She said she overheard the loan guy talking about having to do a foreclosure on Ted and Paulette's house. She's not the sharpest tool in the shed, so I figured she'd heard wrong or gotten her facts mixed up, but after seeing those photos, I have to wonder."

"If Ted was broke," I said, "that effectively eliminates Paulette as a suspect. She has absolutely nothing to gain, especially if Ted's blackmailing schemes were paying for all those spa visits."

"Darn," Gertie said. "After seeing how she decorated her house, I really wanted her behind bars. That shouldn't be legal."

"So what do we do now?" Ida Belle asked.

"First thing," I said, "is going over these photos and making a list of everyone in them. Then I want you two to figure out if we can eliminate any of them from the suspect list."

Ida Belle nodded. "You mean, like they were out of town the night of the rally...things like that."

"Exactly."

Ida Belle pointed toward the back of the house. "Head to the kitchen. I'll go grab my laptop."

Ida Belle hurried off upstairs for her laptop and I trailed after Gertie to the kitchen, where she started a pot of coffee. Ida Belle hustled back into the kitchen a minute later and slid into the chair next to me.

"You two talk," I instructed as I pulled the laptop over in front of me and opened it. "I'll take notes."

Gertie slid into a chair next to Ida Belle and they started flipping through the photos, talking so fast I had to stop them occasionally to catch up and ask for clarification on some of the Creole and Cajun names that I had no idea how to spell. Finally, they delivered on the last photo and I looked at the list.

"Eighteen people," I said. "Now, let's see if we can narrow it down any."

They spread the photos out in front of them and started up again.

"These six were offshore."

"These two were working evenings on the road crew outside of New Orleans."

"He was at his aunt's funeral in Baton Rouge."

"He moved to Alaska to work the pipeline, and this one moved to Texas."

I verified names and tapped in the information as fast as my fingers would work. When they paused for a couple of seconds, I checked the list.

"That gets us down to seven," I said. "Anyone else you can take off the list?"

Gertie shoved three photos over in front of Ida Belle. "Weren't these three in jail in New Orleans?"

Ida Belle brightened. "That's right!"

I paused. "All three...at the same time?"

"They were off on a gambling trip the weekend before the rally. They got a little drunk and tried to hold up the casino with water pistols. The casino management pressed charges."

"I wonder why," I mumbled and made a note next to the three men.

Too stupid to actually commit a real crime.

"Okay, so that leaves us with four. Toby Anderson, Lyle Cox, Blaine Evans, and Shelly Fisher. A boat thief, a drug dealer, a poacher, and an adulterer. Any of those that you think absolutely, positively couldn't kill someone?"

Ida Belle and Gertie looked at each other, then back at me, and both shrugged.

"So you're cynics like me," I said, "and think all it takes for someone to be a killer is the proper motivation?"

"I guess so," Gertie said. "Jeez, we're a depressing bunch."

"I prefer realistic," Ida Belle corrected. "The bottom line is Fortune's right. Any of the people on that list could have been desperate enough to murder Ted if it meant keeping their secret and stopping the financial hemorrhaging."

"What's their financial status?" I asked.

"All of them have limited means," Ida Belle said, "and all but Lyle have spouses who would leave if they had any idea of these things. The spouses being the ones with actual steady employment."

"So four it is," I said, already pleased at how many we'd eliminated from the list. "Four is manageable." I looked at Gertie. "I don't suppose you recognized the voices of the guys in the house as any of the men on this list?"

"No, it was too muffled and to be honest, I was a little stressed."

"No matter," I said. "Any of these people except Shelly could have been the ones in the house. The opportunists in the group would have thought the vigil was the perfect time to gather up anything incriminating to prevent it coming to light."

"What now?" Ida Belle asked.

"Step B of my plan," I said.

Gertie clapped her hands. "Fortune thinks we should look into Ted and Paulette's past."

"I'm as nosy as the next person," Ida Belle said, "but why focus on their life before Sinful?"

I pointed at the photos. "Do you really think this is the first time Ted has done something like this?"

Ida Belle frowned. "Maybe not. It all seems rather..."

"Calculated?" I supplied. "Professional?"

"That's it," Ida Belle said. "It seems professional."

"If Ted pulled this sort of thing before, maybe he's got a record for it."

"Or maybe someone he was extorting money from before followed him down here," Gertie said.

"That's a possibility I don't want to think about right now," I said. "At least not until we've eliminated everyone local."

"Researching Ted and Paulette is a good idea," Ida Belle said, "but we don't have much to go on. They didn't talk much about their past."

"Which is interesting," I said, "considering how much of a blowhole Ted was."

"True," Ida Belle said.

I frowned. "Come to think of it, I didn't see any pictures in their house. Did you?" I asked Gertie.

Gertie scrunched her brow for a minute then shook her head. "Not that I can recall. We didn't spend any time downstairs though, except to move through it. But even then, I recall some crystal vases with gold gild—tacky as hell, but that appears to be Paulette's decorating motif—but not a single picture frame."

"You said Ted inherited money, right?" I asked Ida Belle.

"That's what I heard."

I went back to trusty Google. "Let's do some digging on Ted. I figure Paulette was only in it for the paycheck, so we won't find much of relevance on her."

Ida Belle moved her chair over closer to me so that she could see the screen while Gertie poured us all a cup of coffee. I typed in a search of Ted's name. Nothing. Tried a variation. Nothing again. So I started typing in every possible combination I could come up with for Ted and Paulette, but as far as Google was concerned, they were nonexistent.

Ida Belle shook her head. "Not a single thing out of all of that."

"Is that normal?" Gertie asked, then slurped her coffee.

"It's not completely unheard of," I said. "Not everyone is into social media, but if there was really a big company sale and inheritance, you'd think there would be mention of his name somewhere."

"What about The Sorcerer?" Gertie asked. "Surely he can find something on Ted."

I perked up. Ida Belle's online gaming friend had proven to be something of a wizard when it came to information-gathering. In fact, he made the CIA look rather amateurish.

Ida Belle shook her head. "He's gone dark. Got picked up last week by a couple of guys in a black Cadillac."

I stared. "He was kidnapped?"

Ida Belle snorted. "Only if the federal government can be accused of kidnapping. My guess is your people have him."

"Crap." If the CIA figured out even half of what the ten-year-old hacker was capable of, he'd never see daylight again.

"What about picture matching?" Gertie asked. "You know, like they do on that show *Catfish*?"

"They match pictures of fish?" I asked.

"No, it's—never mind. You can upload a picture to Google and see if it matches anyone else on the Internet."

"Oh!" I perked up. "That's cool. Does anyone have a picture of Ted?"

Ida Belle and Gertie looked at each other and both shook their heads.

"Sorry," Gertie said, "but why would anyone want one?"

"We never figured we'd need it," Ida Belle agreed. "He didn't even use his own photo for his election flyers. He had that strange cartoon drawing instead."

"Can you think of anyone else who would have one that we could ask and not look suspicious?"

Ida Belle shook her head. "I can't imagine anyone in my crew having something like that, and Walter's not really the picture-taking type. I wouldn't feel safe asking outside of that group of people."

Gertie nodded. "Me either."

I slumped back in my chair, frustrated that such a good idea would come to nothing.

"I know how we could get one, though," Gertie said.

I shook my head. "Oh no. I'm not breaking into Ted's house again, and besides, I just said earlier that I didn't see any photos."

"I'm not suggesting we break into Ted's house..." Gertie said.

"Then what?"

Gertie glanced at Ida Belle, her face reddening a little. "Well, I mean, it's not like Ted's completely gone yet."

I jumped up from my chair, instantly cluing in on her train of thought. "Are you insane? You're suggesting we break into the church and take a picture of the body?"

Ida Belle brightened. "That's a great idea."

"Absolutely not." I crossed my arms and gave both of them my stern look. "We are not breaking into a church that sits, I might add, across the street from the sheriff's department, all to molest a dead body by taking pictures."

"Oh, for Christ's sake," Gertie said. "Who said anything about molesting? We'll just open the casket, take a quick picture, and leave. It's not like you're going to startle him with the flash or anything."

I threw my hands in the air. "You think it's a bad idea to ask people you've known all your life if they have a photo of Ted, but you think breaking into a church and defiling a casket is a good idea? On what planet does that compute?"

Gertie raised her hand. "Oh, oh, I know this one. Earth." She smiled, obviously pleased with herself.

"Now we're defiling a casket?" Ida Belle asked. "Make up your mind what our offense will be."

"Your biggest offense will be committing the dumbest crime ever. How will it look if we're caught inside the church?"

Ida Belle smiled. "And that's why we'll make sure we don't get caught. Look, I appreciate your concern and your outrage, but don't you think Ted himself would prefer that the real killer go to prison instead of me taking the rap for killing him?"

Double crap.

I flopped back down in my chair. Yeah, from what little I knew of the man, the real Ted would probably be handing us flashlights and crowbars and asking what the hell was taking so long.

"Gertie's injured," I said, throwing in the last vestige of an argument I had.

"Actually," Gertie said, "my foot feels fine now. It may be a bit stiff tomorrow, but I'll put some cream on it and I'll be good to go."

"Fine," I said, knowing they were going to do it with or without me, and that with me, the odds of a successful getaway usually increased dramatically. "But we have to plan this carefully, you have to do everything exactly like I say, and we have to wait until after every light in Carter's house is out and we're certain he's asleep."

Ida Belle gave me a single nod and sat back down. "Midnight tonight then."

I sighed. I hadn't even recovered from my rooftop adventures and now we were planning on breaking into a church to get a photo of a body that one of us was likely going to be accused of murdering. I was going straight to hell for this one. I was sure of it.

"Hey, have either of you heard what the rush is to get Ted buried?" I asked.

Gertie nodded. "Rumor has it that Paulette is moving back east where her family is. That cousin Tony came down to help her settle things up and pack. At least, that's what Marie heard from Celia's crew."

I frowned. "So if she's going back east, why bury Ted here? Why not take the body back east where *his* family is?"

"According to Sinful Lady intelligence," Ida Belle said, "Ted was estranged from his family and hasn't been in touch with them since they moved to Sinful. Paulette says he was always clear with her that he never wanted to be around them again, even as a corpse."

"That seems a little extreme," Gertie said.

Thinking of my own nonexistent relationship that I'd had with my impossible-to-please and now-deceased father, I shook my head. "Not necessarily."

Gertie gave me a strange look but before she could question me, Ida Belle said, "So the funeral is tomorrow at the Catholic church. Burial to follow at Sinful Cemetery. And my guess is Paulette will hightail it out of Sinful as soon as she can pack up that tacky decor of hers."

Ida Belle nodded. "She never made a secret of how much she hated it here."

Heaven only knew how much I hated the idea of breaking into a church to take a picture of a corpse, but the tone of Ida Belle's voice removed any remaining doubt that I was doing the right thing. In the short time I'd known Ida Belle, I'd heard her angry, frustrated, happy, annoyed, and sad, but I'd never heard the sliver of defeat that I did now.

I sighed. This was officially the longest day ever.

CHAPTER FOURTEEN

"Stop pushing me," I hissed. "If I trip over something, I'll wake up everyone in the neighborhood."

"You're the one who nixed flashlights," Gertie whispered.

"Yeah, because a bunch of flashlights bobbing along behind the Catholic church wouldn't look remotely suspicious. It's like you're trying to get caught." I inched my foot forward, claiming another twelve inches in a most exasperating crawl to the back side of the church.

"Stop talking," Ida Belle said. "Ever since Old Lady Fontenot got that hearing implant, she has ears like a bat."

I shook my head and slid my foot forward another step, gently feeling the air with my hands. I'd already heard enough about Old Lady Fontenot and her implant on our trek through the swamp from the clearing where Ida Belle had me stash my Jeep. I didn't think for a moment that this Fontenot lady would be able to hear us talking, even though she lived across the street directly behind the church. But if I fell over a trash can, she'd probably dial 911 before I could pick myself up off the ground.

It felt like I'd shuffled across the entire state, but finally, my foot connected with something solid. I reached down and felt the cold, hard concrete that made up the back steps.

"We're at the steps," I said. "Give me a minute to check the lock."

I crept up the steps, then felt around until my hand closed over the doorknob. Ida Belle had assured me the locking mechanism was the old variety and the church had never installed a dead bolt, but I wasn't betting on it until I saw for myself. Using my fingers as my eyes, I gently felt the surface of the keyhole, then jiggled the knob and pressed against the door.

When I felt movement in both, I felt my spirits tick up a notch. I pulled Ida Belle's ice pick from my back pocket and went to work on the flimsy lock. It didn't take but a couple of seconds before I heard it click.

"I'm going to open the door," I whispered, giving them warning. We were fairly sure that no type of alarm was attached to the back door, but on the off chance that something sounded, we would all be ready to run in different directions. As well as anyone could run in the pitch black, anyway.

I grasped the knob and turned, then gently pushed the door open. Other than a tiny squeak, not a single sound came forth.

"Inside," I hissed and hurried inside, pushing the door all the way open as I went. Ida Belle and Gertie crept up the steps and huddled in the hallway as I used antibacterial gel to wipe any fingerprints off the doorknob. I handed Ida Belle and Gertie plastic gloves, donned a pair myself, then shut and locked the door behind us.

"The worship space is straight down at the end of the hallway," Ida Belle said.

I took out my penlight and shone it on the old carpet that lined the hallway. It was just enough light to keep us from falling over one of the many decorator's tables that littered the hallway, but as long as I kept it directed downward, it shouldn't catch the attention of anyone who glanced at one of the windows of the classrooms that lined each side of the hall.

When we reached the end of the hallway, I pushed open one of the double doors and stepped into the worship space. A dim glow was emitted by a light directly over the altar, giving us some welcome light. The doors opened at the front of the worship space, along the side of the steps to the altar and risers that led to the choir loft. I eased around the main platform and saw Ted's casket, standing centered directly in front of the altar.

We all crept over and stood in front of it.

"How hard will it be to open, you think?" Gertie looked at me.

"How the heck should I know?" I replied. "My job is to put people in them. Not get them out."

"It shouldn't be sealed yet," Ida Belle said. "I think you just lift the top piece."

Gertie and I stared at her.

"I got my times messed up and got to a funeral early one time," Ida Belle explained. "I saw them setting up. And since a woman Gertie's size and twice her age propped the thing open, I'm guessing it's not that heavy."

"Okay," I said. "Then open it."

"I'm not going to open it," Ida Belle said.

"Me either," Gertie said. "That's just creepy."

I threw my hands in the air. "This was your idea."

"I never said I was going to do all the work," she shot back.

"Since you haven't done any of the work, I'm thinking now is a good time to start. Now open that damned casket or I'm leaving the two of you here and going straight home for a hot shower and bed."

"Fine," Ida Belle said and pushed up the top piece of the casket.

We all leaned forward to get a better look and sure enough, there was Ted. He didn't look as vibrant as he had when giving that whopper of a political speech, but that sorta stood to reason.

"He doesn't look so good," Gertie said, echoing my thoughts.

"He's dead," Ida Belle said. "He didn't look good alive. Did you think he would improve?"

"Just move," I said and pulled my cell phone from my pocket, ready to get this over with.

"Wait!" Ida Belle said. "Did you hear that?"

I froze. "Hear what?"

"Someone is walking outside."

"You're sure?"

Ida Belle put a finger to her lips. I slowed my breathing and strained to hear someone in the silence. I was just about to decide she was imagining things or had heard some animal rummaging around when I heard the sound of glass breaking in one of the classrooms down the hallway.

The hallway was off-limits for escape and Ida Belle had already said the front door had an alarm on it. No matter really, as we probably wouldn't have time to get out the front of the church before whoever broke that window showed up. I gestured to the choir loft and we hurried up the steps on the side of the altar to the back row of the loft, which was just out of reach of the overhead light.

We crouched down behind the bench back from the row in front of us and peered over to see what was going on. A minute later, two large men wearing ski masks walked into the worship space and over to Ted's coffin.

"That's definitely him" the first man said.

"What the hell?" the second man said. "They don't close the top at night or something?"

"What difference does it make? He's dead."

"I guess." The man reached into his pocket and pulled out a camera.

What the hell? What were the odds that two separate groups of people would break into the church to take a picture of a corpse? And what the heck did *those* guys need one for?

I nudged Ida Belle and raised my eyebrows, but she shook her head. Apparently, she had no idea who the guys were or what they were doing. Just what we needed—another mystery.

The guy with the camera stepped up to the casket and leaned over to get a shot of Ted. As he leaned over, the unmistakable sound of expelled gas echoed through the worship area.

"Jesus, I know you have no respect for the man" the first man said, "but this is a church. Can't you hold that until we get outside?"

"What?" the second man said, straightening back up. "That wasn't me. I thought it was you."

"You think I'd rip one in a church? For Christ's sake, my aunt's a nun."

"Well, I'm telling you it wasn't me."

"Forget about it. Just take the picture and let's get the hell out of here."

As the man with the camera leaned over again, the sound of expelled gas repeated, this time louder.

"Motherfucker!" The second man jumped back from the coffin. "It was him!"

"Bullshit! A corpse can't rip one. Stop screwing around."

The first man snatched the camera from the second man but as he lifted it up to take the picture, Ted's hand flew up in the air and seemed to point directly at them.

"Jesus, Mary, and Joseph!" the second guy shouted and shoved the first man out of the way as he bolted for the front doors.

The first man hit the coffin with a thud and I sucked in my breath as I watched it teeter on the stand. Finally, the man stabilized and ran after his buddy, who threw open the front doors of the worship space.

A second later, alarms went off all over the church.

CHAPTER FIFTEEN

I JUMPED UP FROM THE CHOIR LOFT AND VAULTED OVER THE railing, pausing only long enough to snap a picture of Ted before heading for the back door. I heard Ida Belle and Gertie bumping along behind me as I ran down the hallway, the alarm making my pulse race and my ears ring.

"Wait!" Ida Belle yelled halfway down the hall. "We can't go out the back door like this. Old Lady Fontenot will be out there with a camera and a spotlight. I guarantee it."

"You got any better ideas?" I asked.

"We had a backup plan," Ida Belle explained and motioned to Gertie. "Hurry up!"

Gertie pulled three Mardi Gras masks out of her purse and tossed us each one.

"This is your backup plan?" I asked.

"You got anything better?" Ida Belle shot back.

I pulled the mask on and took off for the back door, too pissed off that I didn't have a backup plan and not about to admit it. I only hoped Old Lady Fontenot was slow with her camera aim. I paused long enough to unlock the back door and wave Gertie and Ida Belle out before sprinting down the steps behind them. No use taking the time to lock the door behind us. That cat was sorta out of the bag.

No sooner had we reached the edge of the alley than a spotlight hit me right in the face. I ducked out of the beam of light and a flash went off, catching me right in the eyes again.

"I got you dirtbags!"

Partially blinded by the spotlight and the flash, I stumbled across the alley, blinking to clear my vision, and snatched the camera right out of the woman's hand. Clearly, she wasn't expecting a direct attack because she never moved an inch from that spot, either before or after I grabbed the camera from her. She was still standing there, staring after us as we rounded the corner of the alley and ran into the swamp.

As soon as I hit the tree line, I pulled off the mask and flung it into the brush, but the path through the swamp wasn't nearly as easy to traverse in the pitch dark and at a run as it had been walking with a penlight. The branches ripped at my arms, and I knew that despite wearing a long-sleeved shirt, I'd have the scratches to show for it in the morning.

I was pretty sure we were almost at the clearing where we'd left my Jeep when Gertie, who was running in front, tripped and fell flat on the path. Ida Belle, who was running with an odd stride and apparently unable to control her forward momentum, kept running right over her and out into the clearing. I skimmed to the side of Gertie's prone figure and hesitated for a moment, deliberating between checking her pulse or just hauling her up.

Figuring I was going to have to haul her up either way, I skipped the pulse part and pulled her up by her shoulders. She wobbled and slumped, only half-conscious as I dragged her into the clearing and tossed her over the side of my Jeep and into the backseat. Ida Belle was already in the passenger's seat, so I jumped in and we hauled butt out of the clearing and straight toward Ida Belle's house.

"She got a picture of us," Ida Belle said, sounding somewhat frazzled.

"Not exactly," I said and tossed the camera in her lap.

She looked down at it and started laughing. "You stole her camera?"

"Took it right out of her hands. Those masks weren't going to fool anyone."

"No, but I'm not sure taking her camera will solve the problem either. She knows Gertie and I well enough to know our clothes."

"Does your fireplace work?"

"Sure."

"Then we'll burn them as soon as we get to your house."

"What about yours?" she asked.

"Everyone in the world owns jeans and a black T-shirt. You and Gertie are the only people in existence who would insist on wearing slacks and printed blouses to commit a crime."

Ida Belle crossed her arms across her chest. "It was a *church*. It would have been disrespectful to wear jeans or sweats."

I shook my head. As long as I lived, I was certain I would never understand Southern manners.

Ida Belle was silent for a moment, then finally said, "I don't blame those guys for freaking out. What the heck is up with Ted's body?"

"It's decomposing," I said. "Either the embalming job wasn't very good or Paulette opted to save some money and skip it altogether, which may also explain why she's rushing the funeral."

"Which goes back to the theory of Ted being broke."

"It might."

I turned off my headlights before turning the corner to Ida Belle's house, then rolled to a stop in her driveway. With any luck, none of her neighbors were on nosy patrol. Gertie had roused herself a bit and Ida Belle and I hefted her out of the Jeep and towed her inside.

Ida Belle ran upstairs to get a change of clothes for her and Gertie, and I fired up the fireplace. She came back downstairs a couple of minutes later, wearing a long nightshirt and carrying a nightshirt for Gertie and the slacks and blouse she'd worn for our nightly escapade.

Ida Belle tossed her clothes on the fire and I poked them around a bit as Ida Belle helped a still-groggy Gertie change into the nightshirt. A minute later, Ida Belle eased Gertie into the recliner and tossed her clothes on the fire. The two of us stood there watching until the last of the cloth melted away.

Ida Belle sighed. "I really liked that blouse."

"What the hell were those guys doing in the church?" I asked.

"It looks like they were doing the same thing we were," Ida Belle said.

"But why? Why would anyone else want a picture of Ted's corpse?"

"I have no earthly idea. I've been racking my brain all the way home, but I can't come up with anything that makes sense."

"Did you recognize their voices?"

Ida Belle frowned. "No. They didn't sound Southern at all."

I nodded. "I think they were Yankees."

"I agree, but why would Yankees come all the way down here to get a picture of Ted's corpse?"

"I don't know, but I'd bet everything it's important that we find out."

"Maybe Ted's infighting with his family was something epic," Ida Belle said. "Maybe some of them came down here to be sure he was dead."

I shook my head. "That would be the family feud to end all feuds."

Gertie groaned and we looked over to see her holding her head with both hands. "I feel like I got run over by a truck. What happened?"

"You got run over by a truck," I said.

Ida Belle elbowed me and walked over to Gertie, checking out the purple circle already forming around Gertie's eye. "That's probably going to turn black," Ida Belle said.

I nodded. "These scratches on my arms aren't going to look so hot either."

"Let me see," Ida Belle said.

I rolled up my sleeves and Ida Belle leaned over to inspect my arms. "None of them were deep enough to break the skin, but they're going to welt up some. Why didn't you run with your arms tucked in front of you?"

I stared. "Why in the world would you do that?"

"To keep from getting scratched, of course. Do you see any scratches on Gertie and me?"

"No, but the balance that arms to the side provides might have prevented Gertie from face-planting."

Ida Belle shrugged. "It's a trade-off."

I was just formulating my next argument in this most absurd conversation when I heard a vehicle pull to a stop in front of Ida Belle's house. We both ran to the window and I felt my pulse spike as I saw Carter exit his truck, the frown on his face perfectly clear.

"Don't panic," Ida Belle said, although it was clear she was on the verge of panicking herself. "We'll just play it cool like we're having a pajama party."

"Seriously?" I said. "How the hell are we going to explain Gertie's eye? Or the fact that she's only half-conscious and can't stand without assistance?"

"I canth stan..." Gertie pushed herself up two inches, then fell back into the chair.

As the doorbell rang, Ida Belle ran for the hall closet and threw boxing gloves at me. "Put those on. You were showing us some moves you learned at a self-defense class."

I didn't believe for a moment that Carter would buy it, but

with no proof to the contrary, I supposed he wouldn't have a choice.

"Coming!" Ida Belle yelled as the doorbell rang again. She pulled a glove on her left hand and tossed the other on the couch, using her free right hand to unlock the door. I rolled down my sleeves, pulled on the gloves and stood in the middle of the living room, feeling incredibly stupid.

Ida Belle threw open the door. "What the hell, Carter? It's the middle of the night."

I barely held back a grin. Offense as defense was one of my preferred methods as well.

Carter looked at Ida Belle, then past her to me and Gertie. "Can I ask what you're doing?"

"Firth rule of fight club," Gertie said and held up her hand. It immediately dropped back into her lap.

"Fortune was teaching us some self-defense moves from a class she takes back home," Ida Belle explained. "I accidentally clocked Gertie, but she'll be fine."

"Uh-huh." His brow creased and I could tell he didn't even know where to start. Two old ladies in nightshirts, one wearing boxing gloves and the other sporting what would become a banner black eye, were probably not anywhere in the sheriff's department training manual. He glanced over at the fireplace and frowned.

"It's hot as hell," he said. "Why do you have a fire going?"

"We were going to roast marshmallows when we're done," Ida Belle said. "Don't you know anything about pajama parties?"

He looked me up and down.

"I don't wear pajamas," I said.

He sighed. "Yeah, I know. I don't suppose you three know anything about the break-in at the Catholic church tonight?"

Ida Belle and I feigned surprise.

"Heathen," Gertie mumbled.

"Why would someone break into the church?" Ida Belle asked. "Everyone knows they don't keep money there."

"Someone opened Ted's coffin."

"Creepy," Gertie said.

"I have to agree with Gertie," I said, getting into the mix. "Was he buried with expensive jewelry?"

"No," Carter said, "and corpse-robbing does not happen in Sinful, so don't even go there."

"Some weird cult thing?" I suggested.

Carter's face turned red. "There are no cults in Sinful, either."

I shrugged. "Well, all of this is interesting and all, but why are you asking us about it?"

"Because Ms. Fontenot said she saw three people running out of the back of the church wearing Mardi Gras masks."

"What's a Mardi Gras mask?" I asked.

"Later," Ida Belle said and waved her hand at me.

"Ms. Fontenot is positive one of those three was Ida Belle. Said she recognized your 'hideous' purple blouse with red stripes."

"Like she's a fashion plate," Ida Belle said. "Old Lady Fontenot might be able to hear like a bat but she's also blind as one."

"She says she took a picture, but the tall, lanky one grabbed her camera and ran off with it." Carter looked me up and down. "I don't suppose you know anything about that?"

I widened my eyes and forced myself not to glance at the camera, which was peeking out from under a decorative pillow on the end of the couch. "Why would I?"

Carter threw his hands in the air. "You know what, never mind. I don't even think I want to know the answer to this. I just want that man in the ground, that woman out of town, and someone sitting in my jail on murder charges."

"As long as it's not me," Ida Belle said, "I'm right there with you."

"Fine. Great. Then go back to...whatever." He whirled around and stalked out of the house.

Ida Belle looked back at me and raised her eyebrows, then closed and locked the door behind him. "He's awful testy."

"Yeah," I said and frowned. The man who'd left wasn't the Carter I'd come to know. That man was frustrated and on edge. He looked ready to chuck the whole thing, and I wondered how close he was to doing just that. I hadn't helped matters with that cult comment, and I felt a bit guilty, but it had served the purpose of getting his attention off of us.

Ida Belle pulled the glove off her left hand and tossed it on the couch with the other one. "Get those things off and let's run that photo through Google before something else goes wrong."

Gertie was still woozy, so we helped her into the kitchen. Ida Belle microwaved some of the coffee from earlier and pushed it in front of her. The strong aroma worked like smelling salts, perking Gertie right back up to almost normal...while she was sitting, anyway. The jury was still out on whether she could stand, and I definitely wouldn't have bet money on walking.

I pulled out my cell phone and accessed the pictures, then groaned when I got to the one of Ted. That creepy, floating hand of his was blocking half of his face. I showed the phone to Ida Belle who cussed.

"Now what?" I asked. "We certainly can't risk going into the church again, and even if you had someone willing to do it, someone snapping a picture during the funeral might stand out a bit."

Ida Belle jumped up from her chair. "Yes, they *would* stand out." She ran into the living room and I looked over at Gertie, who shrugged.

A couple of seconds later, she was back with Old Lady Fontenot's camera. "She's Catholic," Ida Belle said as she shoved the camera at me and sat back down, "and just enough of a weirdo that she might have taken a picture at the vigil."

"Seriously?" I picked up the camera and accessed the photos.

"Oh yeah," Gertie said.

The first one up was the three of us running out of the church. I took one look and was thankful that I'd stolen the camera. Even with the masks, anyone in Sinful would have pegged Ida Belle and Gertie, which means I'd have been pegged as well.

But the next picture...the next picture was golden.

"Unbelievable," I said as I stared at the perfectly clear photo of a very deceased Ted. "You're right. She's weird, but I'm glad. I don't suppose you have a USB that fits this camera?"

Ida Belle took the camera from me and studied it for a moment. "I think the cord for my camera will fit this. Hold on."

She jumped up and rummaged through a kitchen drawer and finally pulled out a cord. "Try this one," she said and tossed it to me.

I let out a breath of relief when the plug slid easily into the camera. After all of this, if we'd had to wait until the next day to make a trip to New Orleans for a camera cord, I might have dived straight into a bottle of Sinful Ladies cough syrup and never come up for air.

I downloaded the pic to Ida Belle's laptop, then uploaded it into the Google picture search thingie and set it to work. A couple of seconds later, the screen filled with links, but not a single one of them referenced the name Ted Williams. I clicked on the first link, expecting to find it had all been a mistake, and gasped.

The picture was definitely a match but the name attached to the mug shot wasn't Ted Williams. It was Gino Rossetti.

"You got a hit?" Ida Belle asked.

I scanned the article attached to the picture. "I got a hit all right, and I think I know why Ted was in Sinful." I turned the laptop around and pointed to the headline.

Maselli Underboss Pinched for Extortion of New Jersey Mayor.

CHAPTER SIXTEEN

IDA BELLE WHISTLED. "NEW JERSEY MAFIA. HOLY CRAP!"

"Let me see," Gertie said and pulled the laptop over, her eyes widening as she read the headline. "I can't believe it."

"So the Yankees in the church were people Ted...or, er, Gino, knew from his secret past?" Ida Belle asked.

"That would be my guess," I said.

"But why?" Gertie asked.

"Maybe a rival mob and they wanted proof he was dead. Maybe friends of the mayor. When Paulette said Ted was estranged from his family, she was certainly underselling it."

"Do a search on his real name and two years ago," Ida Belle said. "That's when he came to Sinful."

I pulled the laptop back in front of me and typed in the search info. Seconds later, the page populated with articles again.

FEDS SWEEP MASELLI FAMILY WAREHOUSES.
Maselli Mob Bosses Indicted for Drug Smuggling and Murder.
Gino Rossetti Disappears.

. . .

I CLICKED ON THE ONE ABOUT GINO'S DISAPPEARANCE AND started reading.

MASELLI FAMILY UNDERBOSS GINO ROSSETTI DIDN'T SHOW UP IN court today to answer charges concerning the alleged extortion of Mayor Rawlings. But according to those who knew him, that's not unusual. Apparently, Mr. Rossetti isn't keeping any of his scheduled appointments. His personal physician, tailor, barber, and even his priest claim they haven't seen him or his wife, Paulette, in weeks and the speculation has already started.

"THEN IT GOES ON TO TALK ABOUT THE CHARGES," I SAID, "AND Ted's history with the Maselli family."

Ida Belle shook her head. "It's absolutely mind-blowing. But what I still don't get is why Sinful?"

"Maybe he really did meet that guy...Parker...and remembered the town. Maybe he stuck a pin in a map and came here. Unless Paulette decides to tell, I don't think we'll ever know."

"Carter's going to shit," Gertie said.

I sucked in a breath and looked at Ida Belle, whose eyes widened.

"We have to tell him," I said.

"But how?" Ida Belle asked. "Even if we come up with some outlandish reason that we found out who Ted really was, we still can't give him the blackmail photos without giving you and Gertie away."

I slumped back in my chair, trying to think of any way to get the information to Carter without incriminating ourselves, but I kept coming up empty. And guilty. What we knew could be the key information needed to solve this case. Ted would be in the ground. Paulette would leave town, and the murderer would be behind bars. Everything Carter said he wanted. Everything that would clear Ida Belle's name. And the only thing standing in his way to happiness and Ida Belle's path to freedom was me and my lies.

"This is the biggest mess ever," I said finally.

Ida Belle nodded. "I hate to agree with you, but we really stepped in it this time."

Gertie's face fell as her still-addled brain caught up with Ida Belle and I. "We were only trying to help, and we've made it even harder for Carter to do his job."

"Not really," I said. "Think about it—Carter had no reason to search Ted's house and unless he did, he would never have found those photos. And if we hadn't taken them those other guys might have found them just like I did. Then we wouldn't have the proof either."

Gertie brightened a little. "So really, we saved the evidence."

"You could look at it that way."

Ida Belle sighed. "The evidence that doesn't do me any good."

The disappointment and defeat of the two strongest women I'd ever met overwhelmed me and I felt my heart beat a little bit harder. These were good women, and more importantly, they were my friends. I had to make this right.

I sat up straight in my chair and looked at both of them. "The evidence does us plenty of good."

"I don't see how," Ida Belle said.

"Because. We can use it to catch the murderer. Wasn't that the plan all along?" I pulled up my list of the photo suspects and pointed to the screen. "One of these four people is probably the killer. We need to figure out which one."

"How?" Gertie asked. "It's not like any of them are going to admit it if we ask them."

I drummed my fingers on the kitchen table. "If only we could be at the funeral services tomorrow."

"Good Lord, why?" Gertie asked.

"To people-watch," Ida Belle said.

I nodded. "It would be interesting to see how these four people react at the services."

"Wouldn't it be smarter for them to just stay home?" Gertie asked.

"No," I said. "They would think that would look suspicious. Everyone being blackmailed knows these pictures exist and that if they came out, Carter would take a hard look at them for Ted's murder."

Ida Belle nodded. "The blackmail victims, likely including the killer, have to attend the funeral and pretend to mourn along with everyone else. That's why it would be beneficial if we could be there watching—looking for that person whose actions seem strained or stilted."

Gertie sighed. "I see the value, but none of us can walk into that service without causing a huge problem."

Ida Belle stared at her for a moment. "No, but we could watch at the cemetery."

"I don't see how," Gertie said. "Some people are bent if you so much as walk to your mailbox. How are you going to show up in the cemetery when you're the main suspect?"

Ida Belle grinned. "From a distance."

"Oh," Gertie said, then her eyes widened and she sat up straight in her chair. "Oh, that's a great idea!"

"Will someone please fill me in?" I asked.

"Sinful Cemetery is at the far end of town with the swamp creating the back border. There's only one road in and out but the bayou runs behind the tree line where the swamp begins."

A picture began to form in my mind. "So you want to sneak up the bayou and watch the funeral from the tree line using binoculars?"

"Yes," Ida Belle said, "except there *is* the issue of slope."

Gertie frowned. "I didn't think about that, but the ground does slope off from the cemetery toward the tree line. I don't know that we'd have a clear view."

"Then we'll have to climb trees," Ida Belle said.

"Oh no," I said, a million different endings for that scenario playing out in my head, and none of them good. "It's risky enough to attempt to watch the funeral, and will only make things worse for Ida Belle if she's caught, but to do it dangling from trees is simply asking for trouble."

I looked at Gertie. "Don't you remember what happened the last time you were in a tree—you know, at Ted's house? Or the stakeout when we were trying to find Pansy's killer?"

Gertie blushed a bit but waved a hand in dismissal. "That could have happened to anyone. But I agree with you that it wouldn't be good for Ida Belle to get caught. So it looks like the two of us will have to handle it."

"No way." I shook my head. I'd have better odds walking down the center aisle of the Catholic church during the middle of the service than I had trying to get Gertie into a tree without breaking a hip or me.

"I agree it's not optimal," Ida Belle said quietly, "but it's the only thing we've got."

I blew out a breath, knowing that despite all the things that were wrong with the idea and the million more that could go wrong with the execution, come tomorrow, Gertie and I would be dangling from trees, watching a funeral through binoculars. Even though it was a lousy one, it was the only option we had at the moment.

"I'll do it," I said. Sure, climbing trees with Gertie was risky and the even larger worry was that if we got caught, it might be the straw that broke the camel's back for Carter. If he poked lightly into my background, my cover would remain intact, but it wouldn't hold water under harsh scrutiny.

Regardless, it was a risk I had to take.

It was the last risk we had available.

———

IT WAS CLOSE TO 3:00 A.M. BEFORE I DRAGGED MYSELF HOME. I was exhausted, achy, itchy, and for the first time in my life, I actually felt whiny. I grumbled and complained all the way upstairs, and not even the steaming hot shower could improve my mood. The revelation about Ted's real identity had been a shocker I was completely unprepared for, and now, a jumble of thoughts ran through my mind. It was as if someone had loaded all the pieces to the puzzle into a cannon and then shot them out.

Now, I had a million torn pieces to pick through—trying to decide which ones were important and which ones were merely interesting. Unfortunately, the day had left me with no brainpower and limited physical reach. It was beyond time to hit the bed. If there was a God, he'd let me sleep in tomorrow. After all, dealing with Gertie and trees was going to require both mental and physical strength.

I managed to pull on a tank top and underwear and shorts, thinking I'd take a couple of minutes to make some quick notes on my laptop before things slipped away, but instead, I collapsed in the bed. The cool sheets felt so good against my tired body that I practically wept. I couldn't remember the last time I'd been this exhausted.

Despite my whirling mind, it took only seconds for me to doze off, but I didn't stay that way for long. I couldn't have been sleeping more than ten minutes when I bolted straight up in bed and then froze as I heard the sound of glass shards clinking together in the bedroom across the hall.

The window!

With everything that was going on, I'd completely forgotten that I'd shot a hole in the guest bedroom window. I hadn't even remembered to clean the glass off the floor, which had turned out to be a good oversight since that broken glass had alerted me that someone was in that room.

I lifted my nine-millimeter from the nightstand and slipped out of the bed, silently placing my bare feet on the cool wood floors. I eased across the bedroom, careful to slide my feet rather than lift, hoping to avoid any creaking. Moonlight streaming in my bedroom window illuminated my bedroom and carried into the hallway, making passage easier.

When I reached the doorway, I peered around the corner into the hall. It was empty so I slipped out of my bedroom and across the hall, then flattened myself against the wall right next to the guest bedroom doorway. I held my breath and listened, waiting for any indication that the intruder was still in the room.

Finally, I heard the brush of something against the fabric of the bedspread. As if someone had walked too close to the bed and I heard the sound of their pants rubbing against the bedspread. I gripped my pistol, counted to three, then burst around the corner, gun leveled at what should be center mass for most people.

A second later, something hit me square in the face, and I squeezed off a round as I stumbled backward into the hall.

CHAPTER SEVENTEEN

As soon as the claws dug into my scalp, I knew my friend the cat was the culprit. I flipped on the bedroom light and saw the offending tree limb perched right outside the pane of glass that was missing from the window.

The first pane of glass, that is.

Thanks to my furry intruder, a second pane of glass was going to need replacing as well. I looked down at my legs where the cat was weaving in and out of them, rubbing against my bare skin and purring so loudly I could hear him.

"Dude, I can't keep cactus alive. You don't want to live here."

The cat let out a loud meow and sat, gazing up at me with huge emerald-green eyes. I felt myself soften and the cat flopped onto the floor and rolled, rubbing his head on my feet.

Crap.

I'd just acquired a cat.

"I assume you're hungry, but I don't have any cat food. I do have some leftover baked chicken. Would that be good?"

The cat sat up and meowed and I narrowed my eyes at him. If I didn't know any better, I would swear he understood what I'd just said. My eyes widened and he strolled off and headed downstairs. I shook my head and followed him into the kitchen where I started chopping up a hunk of chicken breast. The cat sat patiently next to me, gazing up at me with those big green eyes.

I'd just placed the plate of chicken on the floor when my doorbell rang. I strode to the front door, ready to tell whoever was standing there that unless my house was on fire, I didn't care. No matter what they had to say. I didn't care one bit.

I flung the door open and saw an exhausted Carter standing on my porch. Immediately, my heartbeat quickened. What if the house or church intruders had returned and something had happened to Ida Belle? What if that lump on Gertie's head had been a concussion?

"Is something wrong?" I asked.

"You tell me," Carter said, sounding as exhausted as he looked. "Your neighbor reported gunfire here."

"Oh crap! I didn't even think about someone calling the police."

He raised one eyebrow. "I take it there's a lot of middle-of-the-night gunfire where you're from?"

Considering I "lived" most of the time in the Middle East, it was a loaded question, but as long as I concentrated on my apartment in DC, I could answer without lying. "No, of course not."

"So do you want to tell me why you were firing a weapon inside your house in the middle of the night? Giving gun-shooting lessons now, maybe?"

I rolled my eyes and motioned him inside. "This way."

I strode off to the kitchen assuming he'd either follow me or leave. Either way, I could get this over with and go back to bed.

"There." I pointed to the cat, who'd just finished up the chicken and was now cleaning his face. I couldn't help myself from smiling. He was awfully cute.

Carter looked at the cat. "You were shooting at the cat? If you'd just stop feeding him, he'd go away."

"I wasn't shooting at the cat. Well, not exactly. I heard something moving in the guest room across the hall and thought someone was breaking in. When I went into the bedroom, the cat jumped on my head and startled me, and I accidentally shot out a window pane."

Carter sighed. "With all the strange things going on in this town right now, why in the world would you leave a window open, especially on the back side of your house?"

"Oh, I didn't leave it open. He came through another pane I accidentally shot out this morning when I thought the cat was breaking into my shed. I guess my neighbor wasn't at home to hear that one and report me."

Carter ran one hand through his hair and shook his head. "I don't even know where to start, except to say, you need to get some Mace or a baseball bat, or just use that boxing that knocked Gertie out if you come across an intruder. But you are someone who should never, ever own a firearm."

"In this town, you think I'm the person most likely to have an accident with a firearm? Really?"

"Well, this makes three accidental shootings since I've known you—all with your house as the victim. In that same span of time, *two* accidental misfires is the most I've logged on anyone else. So yes, you are the top of the list of most likely."

"Hmmm." That was rather distressing. I knew I'd lost some of my edge since I'd been living in Sinful, but I didn't think I'd topped the locals for stupid behavior with firearms. Hell, I hadn't even thought it possible to top the locals after seeing some of Gertie's mishaps.

"Look," Carter said. "I'm not even going to ask you where you got the gun because quite frankly, I don't want to have to arrest the person who gave it to you. So just give it back and we can both pretend we never had this conversation."

I shrugged. "Okay." I had no intention of telling Carter that Marge had a veritable arsenal behind a secret panel in the master bedroom closet. "Sorry you had to get back out of bed over this."

"Ha. You're assuming I've been to bed."

He turned around and strode out of my house without another word. I locked the door behind him, then peeked through the mini-blinds and watched him drive off. As much as I tried to tread lightly around the good deputy, I felt sorry for him. He might possibly have had an even worse day than I did.

And you feel guilty for withholding information that could help his investigation.

I sighed and mentally gave my conscience the bird. Why couldn't I have been born a sociopath? I was quite convinced my father had been one, and it had seemed such an advantage. Never caring about another person's feelings made it super easy to do what was only convenient for oneself.

Before I came to Sinful, I'd thought I was just like my dad, except for the successful career part, and I'd ceased thinking I'd ever measure up to my golden father's standards years ago. But since I'd been in Sinful and met Ida Belle, Gertie, Walter, Ally, and even Carter, I was starting to realize that I wasn't anything at all like my father.

I'd just been pretending to be.

The cat meowed and rubbed my legs. I reached down to pick him up. "Since you've decided you own me, I guess I should think of something to call you."

He purred and stretched his head out to bump my hand, clearly informing me I was supposed to be petting him. I smiled and scratched him behind his ears.

"How about Merlin?"

He looked up at me with a satisfied expression and meowed again.

"Merlin it is then." I started up the stairs. "Maybe you'll work some magic and bring me a solution to this situation with Ida Belle. Think you can do that?"

He looked up at me again, and I swear, he winked.

Or maybe I was sleep-deprived.

———

DESPITE THE FACT THAT I DIDN'T GET TO SLEEP UNTIL AROUND 4:00 a.m., I only managed to sleep until seven. Having a rigid mind and a habitual temperament was a real bitch sometimes. I tried to force myself back to sleep, but I lasted another ten minutes that were filled with frantic, horrible dreams before giving up and climbing out of bed. I stretched my arms above my head, then reached down for the floor, trying to limber up all the muscles that had gotten a workout the day before.

I noticed that neither our late night nor my stretching routine seemed to affect Merlin's ability to sleep. He lay curled up in the middle of the spare pillow, his whiskers occasionally twitching. If only I could achieve that level of relaxation.

I headed downstairs to the kitchen and reached for the coffeepot, then decided instead to head into town and have breakfast at Francine's. Given my friendship with Ida Belle and general Yankee status, I might catch some flak, but I was going to have to go into town anyway to buy cat food for Merlin. And if I was going to be harassed, I might as well get a good meal out of it. One that I didn't have to cook or clean up afterward.

I hurried back upstairs, tossed on yoga pants, T-shirt, and tennis shoes, and brushed my hair before pulling it back into its standard ponytail. Merlin opened one eye, yawned, and rolled over. I didn't know much about cats, but it didn't appear as if he were going to make a good sentry at all.

It hadn't gotten ridiculously hot yet, so I opted for a jog instead of driving. Cat food couldn't possibly weigh that much and if I ended up buying more, I could always have Walter hold the stuff for pickup later. Besides, Sinful had been hell on my waistband. Even my yoga pants were protesting a bit and they were elastic waist. If I wanted to keep eating all the baked goodies that came my way, I was going to have to step up the exercise portion of things.

My house wasn't much of a jog from town, but I stretched it out by circling around a couple of blocks before heading straight up Main Street. The General Store wouldn't open for a bit, so I headed to Francine's, where the smell of cinnamon buns overwhelmed me as soon as I stepped inside.

My friend Ally waved her order pad at me and pointed to an empty table in the corner. The café was usually busy this time of the morning, and today was no exception. That two-seater in the back was the only opening at the moment, but that was perfect for me.

I noticed an uncomfortable lull in conversation as I walked through the café, and forced myself not to sigh. I slid into the chair, my back against the wall so that I could see all entry points into the building. It was a habit I hadn't been able to break, even though I was technically a civilian in Sinful. So far, I'd managed to restrain myself from rearranging the living room furniture at my house, but every time I sat in that recliner with my laptop, that window behind me felt like a semiautomatic weapon aimed directly at my back.

Ally slid a cup of coffee in front of me. "Did you hear about the break-in at the church last night?"

"Yeah. Carter showed up at Ida Belle's to see if we did it."

Ally's eyes widened. "What is wrong with him? Ida Belle and Gertie have done some strange things in the past, I'll give him that, but this is just too weird."

"Hmmm," I said and directed my attention to the coffee. I hated lying to Ally, but it was far easier on her if she was left out of the loop, especially as she didn't know my real identity. I'd gotten comfortable around her so quickly that I sometimes caught myself about to slip into conversation about the real me.

"I can't talk now," she said, "and I've got the funeral after work, but I'll try to come over this evening and we can exchange gossip. Do you want breakfast?"

"Absolutely. I'll have the special, eggs over easy."

She made a note on her pad and gave me a smile. "Got it."

As she walked to the kitchen to put the order in, I sipped my coffee and pretended to gaze out the plate-glass windows of the café. What I was really doing was watching the other patrons. It was a difficult skill to learn, but one that was infinitely handy. Most everyone had gone back to their conversations, but it was easy to tell which of the customers had turned their talk toward me. They cast furtive glances in my direction, then immediately jerked their heads around when I locked my eyes on theirs.

Amateurs.

My senses were so well developed that on a mission, I could lock in on a bird staring at me from outside a window. Civilians sneaking glances in an open room were child's play. I recognized some of them from my visits to the café and the General Store, but didn't know any of them by name. None of them looked like members of the mob who had incited the riot in front of the sheriff's department.

It only took a couple of minutes for Ally to return with my plate of eggs, bacon, and biscuits and I dug in. I couldn't recall the last time I'd sat down to a meal of real food, but I was fairly sure I'd consumed my weight in desserts and coffee the day before. It was no wonder I was craving protein and exercise. My body probably thought I'd abandoned it.

"I like a woman with an appetite."

The voice sounded above me and I barely kept myself from jumping as I looked up at the man I'd met at the rally...Bobby, I think he'd said. I'd been concentrating so hard on Ida Belle's current dilemma and focusing on my breakfast that I hadn't even seen him approach.

"You think most women don't eat?" I asked, then popped the last bite of biscuit in my mouth.

He laughed. "Not in front of men."

I swallowed and took a sip of coffee. "Then they're stupid."

I knew this was his attempt at flirting with me, and he wasn't a bad-looking guy, but something about his cocky stance grated on me. I knew this guy. I worked with a bunch of this guy, which is exactly why I didn't date other agents.

"Sandy-Sue, right?"

I blanched a bit at the real name of the woman I was pretending to be. "Everyone calls me Fortune."

"Why is that?"

"Because Sandy-Sue sucks?"

He grinned down at me. "You are a real piece of work, aren't you? I can see why ole Carter is having a hard time keeping you under wraps. You got a problem with authority?"

His question hit a little too close to the mark for my taste, and if my boss, Morrow, was there, he'd have yelled "yes" so loud it would have burst people's eardrums.

"Only when they're wrong," I finally replied. It was as close to honest as I was going to get.

"No wonder Carter thinks you're trouble. According to the local buzz, he's setting a record lately for pissing people off."

I bristled at his insinuation. Carter wasn't the strictest law enforcement officer I'd ever come across—thank God, or I'd have been sitting in a jail cell practically since the day I arrived in town —but he wasn't deliberately antagonistic. Sometimes, it might feel like he was giving me grief, but the reality was, I'd always been the one crossing the line.

"I think it's called 'doing his job,'" I said.

"Yeah, well," Bobby shuffled a bit, apparently catching my tone, "the way he's going about it seems to be making a lot of people unhappy."

"I don't think keeping people happy is in his job description, but catching criminals and keeping this town safe is. If people take issue with his methods, then I suggest they live in a country where the police are part of the problem, and then start flapping their jaws about how he ought to do his job."

"I appreciate the vote of confidence." Carter's voice sounded behind Bobby. "But it's not necessary."

CHAPTER EIGHTEEN

Bobby whirled around and gave Carter a sheepish grin. "It wasn't me talking that way. I'm sure you're doing a fine job."

"Uh-huh," Carter looked over at me. "That seat taken?"

"Just waiting on you," I said.

Bobby raised his eyebrows and looked from me to Carter as Carter walked past him and took the seat across from me. Carter never even glanced at him.

Ally stepped up to the table and gave Carter a smile. "Can I get you some breakfast?" she asked.

"The special looks good."

"Got it," she said and gave me a wink before hurrying off.

"Well, I'll guess I'll see you around," Bobby mumbled.

I watched him walk out of the café and felt a guilty sense of accomplishment. "He didn't even stay to eat breakfast. I must have hacked him off good."

"He was expecting you to invite him to sit down," Carter said.

"That wasn't going to happen."

"But yet, you invited me."

I shrugged. "He pissed me off."

Carter grinned. "You're great for a guy's ego."

"Ego inflating isn't part of my job description. Besides, I was just stating facts. Your job sucks and unless someone's done it before, they have no right to an opinion on how it should be done."

"If only everyone in Sinful shared your opinion. I'm afraid most of them have gone the complete opposite direction. Deputy Breaux is fielding at least fifty calls a day from people screaming that I need to arrest someone."

"And do they have someone in mind?"

"Some want Ida Belle behind bars. Others vote for the usual drunken douche bags who cause trouble and one thinks I should arrest Pastor Don."

"The preacher?"

"She didn't like his sermon on obesity."

I laughed as Pastor Don's stock inched up in my mind. "He's got some serious backbone to preach on obesity in a town that structures its entire religious schedule around banana pudding."

Carter nodded. "He said the Bible isn't multiple choice."

Talk of the pastor brought my mind back around to church and the night before, and I sobered. "Did you ever figure out what happened at the church?"

"No. And I shouldn't be discussing it with one of the suspects, but since Old Lady Fontenot is a horrible witness and some of the evidence doesn't match her report, I'm not going to pursue her claims."

"What evidence?"

He raised one eyebrow. "Normally, this is where I'd tell you that it's none of your business, but I imagine everyone in Sinful already knows that the front doors of the church were open and set off the alarm. That's what I responded to."

"But if the intruder ran out the front doors..."

"How could Old Lady Fontenot see them run out the back? Exactly. And the odds of two different groups of people breaking into the church at the same time have to be astronomical."

I nodded. Astronomical and also exactly what happened, which made me wonder all over again what the other guys were doing there. Sinful seemed a pretty good trek from New Jersey to take a picture of a dead man.

"I don't suppose you're any closer to catching the killer?" I asked.

"You know I can't tell you that."

"I know. I was just hoping..."

He sighed. "You're worried about Ida Belle. The truth is, I am too. I'm waiting on the lab reports, but if they can prove the poison I took from her shed was the same one used to kill Ted, I'm not going to have a choice in arresting her."

He looked so miserable that I felt the overwhelming urge to hug him, which was somewhat disconcerting in itself. I had never thought myself the overly sympathetic type. "I know. And even though it probably won't make you feel any better, so does Ida Belle."

"Thanks. I notice you didn't include Gertie in your declaration."

"Gertie will not take it well and will likely spend the rest of her life punishing you. Loyalty is a religion with Gertie."

"You've got her pegged."

I shrugged. "She's easy, and there's far worse character flaws."

Ally slid Carter's breakfast in front of him and gave us both a big smile. "Is there anything else I can get you two?"

We both shook our heads and Ally bounced off to another table.

Carter tore into his breakfast with the same gusto I had. "Looks like you're as hungry as I was," I said.

"Haven't had a regular schedule lately. Seems every time I start to eat, something else comes up. No chance to grocery shop in a while and while I love Francine's cooking, sometimes I just don't want to hear the crap that I do when I come here."

I nodded, completely understanding his desire to get away

from people, especially people who were judging your ability to do your job when they really had zero idea what that job entailed.

Maybe it was my guilt at keeping evidence from Carter talking. Or maybe it was simply the fact that I'd only had two cups of coffee. Either way, I found myself unable to stop from saying, "Any time you want to avoid the masses and I'm home, you're welcome to a free meal at my house. With Gertie, Ida Belle, and Ally all testing recipes on me, I've almost always got something worthwhile on tap. If not, then I always have my fallback roast beef sandwiches and chips."

Carter paused for a moment, his fork in midair, a piece of biscuit dangling from it. His expression was a mixture of surprise, satisfaction, and a slight hint of wariness. If he knew the real me, the wariness would have been a lot higher.

"Are you asking me out on a date?" he asked, his lips quivering with the smile that wanted to break through.

I felt a blush start on my neck and prayed it didn't show in the dim light. "I didn't ask you 'out' anywhere and I wouldn't call feeding a hungry friend a date. You're hungry and too busy to shop. You sometimes want to avoid people at all costs and I totally get that. It's just food, Carter."

"So we're friends?"

"Yeah. I mean, unless you think otherwise."

He smiled at my obvious discomfort. "Friends it is then, and I just may take you up on your offer of a free meal. You've got the best cooks in Sinful supplying you."

"Very true."

I frowned, thinking about how easily I'd offered to feed Carter and wondering why he didn't hit up some of the single women in Sinful for a meal. I was sure some existed and if they didn't think Carter was a good catch, then I wasn't sure what they were waiting on to arrive in the middle of the swamp. What the hell? I'd already stepped outside of my own boundaries of getting too personal, so I might as well assuage my curiosity.

"I find it hard to believe that no other women in Sinful have made the same offer," I said.

"Well, the married ones don't dare," Carter said, "and offers from the single ones tend to come with strings attached."

"What kind of strings?"

"The kind with a wedding band tied to the end. So I say a polite 'no thanks.'"

"But you accepted my offer," I pointed out. "I'm single."

"Let's just say I get the impression that you're not looking for a husband."

"God no!" I was just learning how to manage friendship. The thought of having another person constantly in my space and taking his feelings into account every time I made a decision was a level of overwhelming I might never be ready for.

He laughed. "See. I get a good meal out of the deal and don't have to worry about you casting out a marital net."

I shook my head. "Is that the sort of thing guys have to worry about all the time?"

"I guess if a guy is reasonably good-looking, has a decent job, and lives in a town with more single women than men, it's a fairly good chance he spends some time dodging commitment."

I thought about the guys I'd seen roaming around Sinful and decided Carter didn't have much by way of competition, at least that I'd observed. "I probably wouldn't leave my house."

"Ha. That's not really an option. Besides, I'm sure you get your share of unwanted male attention. Bobby hadn't been back in town a day before he locked his sights on you."

"His aim is bad. I'm not interested."

Carter smiled. "Yeah, I kinda got that. If it makes you feel any better, I think Bobby did too."

I shrugged. "Fewer interruptions while eating, I suppose."

Carter cocked his head to the side and studied me. "You have an interesting way of looking at things."

"Not really. I just think simple is best and I tend to see things for what they are. I don't like complications and I don't do drama."

"I see. How's that working out for you, being friends with Ida Belle and Gertie?"

I smiled. "Some people are worth the hassle."

"Yeah. I guess they are."

I WAS HAPPY TO FIND THE GENERAL STORE FREE OF CUSTOMERS when I walked in. The morning had already been entertaining enough. I wanted to quietly get my cat food and get home to prepare for my afternoon tree-climbing adventures. Walter was at the counter with his newspaper and smiled when I walked in.

"If I didn't see you sometime today," he said, "I was going to call."

I slid onto a stool across the counter from him. "Why? What's wrong?"

"Nothing's wrong with me. I wanted to check on Ida Belle."

I frowned. "You haven't talked to her?"

He sighed. "I've left at least ten messages, but she's not returning my calls."

"Oh." He looked a little upset and I instantly felt bad. "I'm sorry. I just assumed..."

"She's shutting me out because she's afraid my being involved will cause me problems."

"Is she right?"

"Of course she's right, but that's not the damned point!"

I stared. I couldn't remember seeing Walter that angry before. Frustrated and irritated, certainly, but this was different. While I understood that Ida Belle wanted to prevent her friend and long-time admirer from unnecessary trouble, I thought she might be making the wrong decision. Walter was a big boy. If he didn't care about trouble, neither should Ida Belle.

"I'm sorry," I said. "I'll talk to her if you want me to."

He waved a hand. "Hell, no. The last thing I need is you interceding on my behalf. That just makes the whole thing even sadder."

I squirmed on my stool. This entire situation was way out of my element. Everything about relationships made me uncomfortable, even if they weren't my own. Or maybe it was that other people's relationship problems forced me to acknowledge my own issues on some level. Whatever. Either way, I wished Ida Belle would just talk to the man.

"Then at least let me tell you how she's doing," I said.

Walter relaxed a bit. "I'd appreciate that."

"Nothing else has happened on the police front, but I just had breakfast with Carter and he's worried about the test results on the poison he took from Ida Belle's shed. He's expecting them anytime."

Shit. A wave of guilt washed over me as I realized I'd just repeated something Carter probably thought he'd told me in confidence.

"But I never said that," I said. "Understand?"

"Don't worry. He'll never hear it from me, but I'm glad you told me. It's always better to be prepared."

I nodded. "Ida Belle is holding up as well as you would expect. Aside from some hang-up calls and that incident with the rock through her window, things have been quiet. She's sticking inside her house most of the time and either Gertie, me, or the Sinful Ladies are usually around...you know, just in case."

"In case she needs an alibi." He shook his head. "I hadn't even thought about that."

"Carter did. He's the one who suggested I stick close by."

"Carter asked you for a favor?"

"I don't know that it was so much a favor as he figured if Ida Belle and I were both closed up inside her house, we couldn't get in the middle of his investigation."

"Probably true."

"Anyway, the spunk is still there and I haven't noticed any decrease in the sarcasm level."

"But?"

I sighed. "But she's worried. She's careful to hide it...mostly, I think because she doesn't want Gertie more stressed than she already is. But it's wearing her down. I can see the cracks around the edges, and you and I both know what it takes for Ida Belle to crack."

Walter rubbed his forehead and blew out a breath. His eyes misted up a bit and I couldn't imagine how difficult it must be for him to know Ida Belle was struggling and not be able to do a thing about it. I may not be thrilled about the things I'd done the last few days or about the things I was about to do, but at least I didn't have to sit in my house with my hands tied, waiting for things to happen.

I reached across the counter and squeezed his hand. "We're working on things...me and Gertie. I don't want to tell you about them because that information might put you in a bad position with Carter, and I don't want that. But I want you to know that I'm doing everything I can."

Walter put his other hand over mine and gave me a grateful look. "I know you are. And something tells me it's all going to turn out all right. I've got a good feeling about it, despite the odds being stacked against you."

"She's going to be fine. I promise you."

I had no idea what made me say that. Maybe it was because I really liked Walter, and his lifelong devotion to a woman who kept turning down his marriage proposals made me a little emotional and girly. Maybe it's because he was the kindly older man that I sometimes wished my father had been. Maybe I needed to say the words out loud so that I believed them myself.

No matter. It worked.

A slow smile started on Walter's face and the resolve that I normally saw in him flooded back. "Damn right she's going to be fine." He shook his head. "Fortune, you've got to be the strangest librarian I've ever come across."

"Then I guess I'm in the right town."

He grinned. "You have a point. Maybe you should consider relocating permanently."

I shook my head. "I'm enjoying my stay—sorta—but my life is back north."

"So get a new life." He winked at me. "Maybe one with your breakfast companion."

"Oh no. No playing matchmaker. You, of all people, ought to know the pitfalls of love. I'm even more hardheaded than Ida Belle. You and Carter would be two old, lonely men, sitting on the front porch and talking about how things would have been different if you'd only fallen for normal women."

He laughed. "Maybe. For someone who came here to settle up an estate, you certainly have proven to be a challenge for some. Still, challenge is what keeps people young. Keeps them alive. You can't run from commitment forever, Fortune. Sooner or later, it's going to catch you in one form or another."

"It already did," I said, feeling a bit smug that I had one up on Walter now. "I have adopted a stray cat and need some food for him."

He raised his eyebrows. "Well, that's a big step. What did he do to get your attention?"

"Made me shoot out two window panes in the guest room. As soon as I get the measurements, I'll need to see about ordering replacement glass as well."

Walter stared at me for a moment, then when he realized I wasn't joking he started laughing again, but this time, so hard his whole body began to shake. "So what I'm getting from this is that if Carter ever got you mad enough to shoot up your own house, you might keep him."

I couldn't help but laugh. Walter was nothing if persistent. "You never know."

"Well, I got a bag of dry cat food right over here." He walked over to a shelf near the counter and picked up a bag. "I suggest you start with a small bag first. One, to make sure he likes it, and two, to make sure you like him."

"What about canned food? I see those commercials."

"I don't recommend it. Feed 'em the canned food and you'll be stuck providing it forever. It's more expensive and doesn't smell all that great. Do you need a cat box?"

"I don't know. What's a cat box?"

"A place where a cat does his business. Litter box, I guess it's called." He waved a hand in dismissal. "Since he's a tomcat, he'll probably prefer to go outside."

"I prefer that as well." As someone who avoided domestics like the plague, that cat box thing didn't sound remotely like something I was interested in. If Gertie hadn't shown up once a week, insisting on cleaning my house, it would probably resemble my apartment back in DC. Or a military barracks. Same difference.

"Then I guess this will do it," he said and put the cat food on the counter. "Is that it?"

"That will do it for now."

He nodded. "I'll just put it on your tab. You can settle up with me the next time you do a beer run."

"Great."

He was still smiling as he grabbed his customer charge book, but when he glanced outside, the smile instantly disappeared. "Oh hell."

I glanced behind me and saw Paulette and her cousin about to pull open the door to the store. Crap! The last thing I wanted was to be in the middle of another downtown scene like the mob in front of the sheriff's department two days before.

CHAPTER NINETEEN

I JUMPED OFF THE STOOL AND SCURRIED BEHIND THE COUNTER, pushing Walter out of the way as I sank down behind it, out of sight. Walter looked startled when I shoved him, but as soon as I sank down on the floor and put my finger over my lips, he caught onto my plan to save us both some grief.

He gave me a nod, then looked up and forced a blank expression. "Can I help you, Mrs. Williams?"

"If there's a God...has my hair spray come in yet?" Paulette asked.

"It's possible. I got a shipment yesterday evening, but I haven't unpacked it yet."

"Well, do you think you can stop reading the paper long enough to do your job?"

I clenched my fists, ready to jump up and punch her dead in the face. A second later, Walter's foot connected with my leg and I was certain it wasn't an accident.

"Let me go check the back," Walter said, with a level of politeness I could never have managed.

"Do you have to be so rude?" Tony asked as soon as Walter entered the back storeroom.

"I'm so sick of these hicks. If I don't get out of this town soon, I'm going to lose it."

"It's just another couple of days. Once the funeral is over, we'll make arrangements and get you back to New Jersey."

"Oh, and that's nothing to worry about."

"What's to worry?"

"How I'm going to live, for one thing. I'm not one of those ball-breaking career women. God made me to look pretty surrounded by expensive fabrics. At least Ted understood that about me."

I cringed. A certain group of men might be attracted to Paulette, but I doubted any of them would find her pretty. And if any of the fabric I'd seen in her house was expensive, then I'd just stick to cheap cotton because wow, talk about ugly.

"Judy is opening a boutique. Only designer label. Maybe you can work there until you find a new situation."

"You want me to stand around taking shit off bitches buying clothes I ought to be buying for myself?"

"It is what it is, Paulette. Until you can find another man, you still gotta eat."

"Whatever."

I shook my head. That Paulette was a piece of work, thinking she was entitled to a life she hadn't lifted a finger to earn. But then, Ted hadn't exactly earned his money in any respectable or laborious way, so I probably shouldn't have any expectation that she'd think she should actually work like normal folk.

"I don't suppose that cop found out anything about those guys who broke in?" Tony asked.

"Please. You think this bunch of hicks can solve a crime? He hasn't found out who killed Ted and it's been days."

"What do you think those guys were looking for? Was...er... Ted doing business here?"

"Probably. He had money sometimes. I never asked where it

came from. I didn't care as long as I got my share and got the hell out of this town for a while."

"Do you think—"

"Got it." Walter walked out of the storeroom holding up a bottle of hair spray.

"At least I can look presentable at the funeral," Paulette said. "Put it on my tab."

Her high heels started clicking on the hardwood floor before Walter even answered. I waited until the bells over the front door jangled, then popped up from behind the counter.

"What a bitch!" I said and repeated what I'd heard, leaving off the part about Ted's local business venture.

Walter shook his head. "I never understood what Ted saw in that woman. She's the kind that will bleed you dry until you're nothing but a chalk line on the floor."

"Looks like someone beat her to it."

———

"I CAN'T QUITE REACH IT," GERTIE SAID.

I put my hand under her rear and shoved it upward into the tree. We'd been at this for thirty minutes already and it was going about as well as I'd expected it to go. The back side of the cemetery was surrounded by swamp and skirted by the bayou. With all the water, no vehicles could get back there, so we'd borrowed Ida Belle's recently repaired boat and tied it off to some cypress stumps.

According to Ida Belle, it should have been a two-minute trek from our docking point to the cemetery, but Gertie, who was still fuddled from her head cracking the night before and sporting a black eye a prizefighter would have been proud of, started us off in the wrong direction. Ten minutes later, we finally arrived at the back edge of the cemetery and started scouting for a good tree, which turned out to be harder than I'd thought it would be.

If we picked a tree at the front of the tree line, we risked being seen by a funeral attendee, and that was not an option. So we had to search for a tree along the second row that had enough coverage to camouflage us but also offered a clear, if narrow, view to the burial site. We'd finally found the perfect location, but getting Gertie into it had proved to be more of a challenge than finding it in the first place.

All the trees at the edge of the swamp were old and thick, the lowest branches a good ten feet off the ground. The height posed no problem for me, but Gertie had a history of being vertically challenged, and now was no exception.

She clutched the lowest limb on the tree as though the drop was a hundred feet straight into hell and kicked her feet, scrambling up my back and the top of my head until she was finally lying across the tree limb.

"Do you need to take a break?" I asked as she leaned over the branch, huffing like an asthmatic.

"Why do you always think I can't handle things?"

"Maybe because of the tennis shoe tread on top of my head?"

She shot me a dirty look, then climbed into a standing position and started pulling herself up onto the next branch. I watched for several seconds, ready to break her fall, but she managed to get onto the branch and into a sitting position.

"They're starting to arrive," she said. "Hurry up!"

I positioned the backpack over my shoulders and jumped up to grab hold of the lowest branch. In one fluid movement, I pulled myself on top of the branch and immediately sprang up onto a branch next to Gertie.

"Show-off," she said as I straddled the branch and pulled the backpack in front of me.

I grinned as I pulled out two sets of binoculars and handed one to her. "Look for the four people on our suspect list first and point them out to me," I reminded her. "I may not be able to pick them out in a crowd from just the photos."

She nodded and put the binoculars to her eyes, wobbling a bit as she leaned forward to see between the branches. I said a silent prayer that she wouldn't fall, at least not before we got what we came for. I lifted my own binoculars in time to see Father Michael leading the group of pallbearers to the grave site. Directly behind them were Paulette and Tony.

Tony wore a shiny black suit that looked like something out of *The Sopranos*. Paulette was wearing black, but it was too tight, too low-cut, too glittery, and too youthful to be appropriate on any level.

"At least she wore black," Gertie said with a sigh.

I smiled. Great minds.

I scanned the rest of the attendees, spotting Celia and Ally, followed by Marie and some of the other Sinful Ladies who were brave enough to venture out and pay their respects. Walter and a couple of the old fishermen trailed behind the women, my "friend" Bobby walking just to the side of them. The rest of the crowd moved forward among the people I knew, but I didn't know any of them by name. Carter was the last in the line of attendees, and I had to admit he looked sharp in a black suit and gray shirt.

Paulette and Tony took seats in front of the coffin along with a couple of the more elderly attendees. The rest of the crowd dispersed in a circle around the grave site, Father Michael standing in the middle next to the coffin.

"There," Gertie said. "On the right in blue jeans and a Dale Earnhardt T-shirt. That's Toby, the boat thief. The guy next to him wearing the bowling shirt is Blaine, the alligator poacher."

I scanned to the right and grimaced. "I thought for a second you were joking about the clothes."

"I wish. Unfortunately, that's probably the best shirts they own. The two unfortunate women off to the left are their wives. Since they arrived separately from their husbands and are dressed appropriately, I'm guessing they prefer not to be seen with them."

"Wouldn't a divorce be easier?" I asked.

"How would I know? I never made the mistake of getting married."

Touché. "Do you see the other two?"

"The adulterer Shelly is standing in the middle, wearing the dress that's baby-poop green."

"Baby poop is green?" I shook my head, wondering again why anyone wanted kids. I scanned to the middle and found a woman wearing a hideous green dress. I recognized the hooked nose and mole on her forehead from the blackmail picture.

"What about Lyle, our dope retailer?" I asked.

"Give me a minute...yep, he's three down from baby poop wearing a blue suit from the 1940s. Probably belonged to his dad. God rest his soul."

I located the ancient blue suit. "Got him. Great." I let the binoculars hang around my neck and pulled two small video cameras from the backpack, happy with the way things were going so far. We could see all of the suspects' faces and since they were grouped in pairs, we could easily capture them on video.

I handed Gertie one of the cameras. "You take baby poop and old suit. I'll get tacky and tackier. How long will this part last?"

"Fifteen minutes. Maybe less. Father Michael is less inclined to get long-winded during summer burials because of the heat and all."

"Gotcha." I lifted my camera and started filming the two idiots in T-shirts, closely watching their expressions as Father Michael did his number, waving his Bible in the air. "I wonder if Ted had gas during the ceremony?"

"Well, he was certainly full of it, so it wouldn't surprise me."

"See anything interesting?"

"Mostly everyone looks bored. If you'd heard one of Father Michael's graveside services, you'd understand."

I focused on my two targets again, but had to agree with

Gertie—all I saw was boredom. "I hope Father Michael is wearing something itchy and this is over soon."

"We should have thought to rub poison ivy in his underwear."

I glanced over at Gertie, then back to my guys. I wasn't even going to ask why that particular idea was right at the forefront of her mind, and was certain I never wanted to know how she would have accessed Father Michael's underwear drawer.

It took another eight minutes of talking and Bible-waving before Father Michael wrapped things up. He motioned to Paulette and Tony, who stood as the casket was lowered into the grave, then each tossed a handful of dirt on it. Paulette covered her face with a Kleenex and leaned against Tony, who put his arm around her as they walked away. Some of the other fifty or so attendees followed Tony and Paulette. Others lined up single file to get their handful of dirt.

Lyle was one of the first to throw the dirt and make his exit. Shelly was toward the end of the line, and I saw her glance around before leaning over to toss the dirt. It seemed a bit odd and I hoped I'd be able to zoom in on it with the camera footage and get a better look. Toby and Blaine, whose wives had long since tossed the dirt and fled the cemetery, were the last to go but instead of trailing off after the rest of the crowd, they stood back, chatting as the gravediggers came over to start filling the hole.

"Keep filming Toby and Blaine," I told Gertie as I reached for my backpack. I slipped my video camera back inside and drew out my binoculars, hoping to get a closer look at the two guys.

"Why are they standing around in the cemetery talking?" Gertie asked. "It's morbid. They should go to a bar or something."

"They're already dressed for it," I agreed.

I shifted the backpack back over my shoulder and lifted the binoculars, taking a second to lock on to my two suspects. They were still standing in the same place chatting and showed no signs of leaving.

I reached for the focus and twisted it a bit to sharpen my view. I had just gotten it perfect when I heard a gunshot. A split second later, the branch above me splintered.

CHAPTER TWENTY

IMMEDIATELY, I TUCKED IN BEHIND THE TRUNK AND DUCKED. "What the hell!"

Gertie had flattened herself on the branch, her legs and arms dangling on each side, one hand still gripping the video camera. "You never know—"

"When someone might start shooting. I know. But why are they shooting at us?"

A second shot rang out, but this one farther away, and a flock of gray birds flew out of the tree, some of them headed straight for us. I ducked as two of the birds zoomed by but Gertie wasn't as fortunate. One of them smacked her right on the head and sent her tumbling backward off the branch.

I lunged for her, but couldn't reach her in time. Gertie's body went into survival mode and her legs locked around the tree, preventing her from falling, but leaving her dangling like a bat, the video camera still clutched in her hand with a death grip.

"Doves," Gertie said. "They're not shooting at us. They're hunting out of season."

A third shot rang out. "Let's talk later," I said as I grabbed Gertie's shirt and pulled her up, praying the fabric held. When she was back on the branch enough to keep from falling, I reached down and grabbed the video camera from her and then tossed it into my backpack.

"Start down and try to stay on the back side of the tree," I said.

I pulled the binoculars from my neck and secured them in the backpack, then glanced down at Gertie, who had managed to get as far as the bottom branch but was now perfectly still and squinting at something in the cemetery. I glanced up and my heart dropped. Carter was running across the cemetery, and at the rate he was moving, would hit the tree line in less than a minute.

"It's Carter," I said. "Go. Go."

I flipped over the branch and swung down to the lower one, releasing the upper branch with perfect timing and grabbing the lower like an Olympic gymnast. But with gunfire. As soon as my hands gripped the lower branch, I dropped straight down and made a perfect ten-point landing on the ground below.

I looked up at Gertie, who was still inching down the last branch. "Hurry up."

Gertie looked down and frowned. "We're not all in our twenties anymore, and that bird shit on me. It's gross."

"Forget the bird shit. Just drop. I'll break your fall." If she didn't get out of that tree in the next ten seconds, Carter would be on top of us, and there was no way we could come up with an explanation for this one that would slide.

I'd expected an argument, or at least hesitation, but the words were no sooner out of my mouth than Gertie let go of the branch and plummeted down like a stone. Before I could brace myself, she slammed into me and we both hit the ground with a thud. I was up before the dirt even had time to land on my clothes and pulling Gertie up behind me.

Carter was only thirty yards away and closing fast. "Run," I hissed and shoved her down the trail. She took off at a clip faster than I thought she had in her and I set out after her. Another shot rang out and I was pleased that it was off to our right. That should draw Carter off of us a bit and give us some time to get to the boat and get away cleanly.

Then Gertie veered to the right and I realized the trail was probably going to put us right on top of the shooters.

We burst into a clearing, and two men wearing camouflage and holding rifles froze and stared. Neither one of us even hesitated. We just ran right by without so much as a glance. A second later, I heard Carter yelling behind us and then the sounds of the men dashing off into the swamp. With any luck, the hunters would make more noise than us and draw Carter off.

We were running so fast, we didn't realize we'd reached the bayou until it was too late. The trees abruptly ended and Gertie launched off the bank and dropped five feet below into the water right next to the boat. I put on the brakes and grabbed hold of a tree to keep from going in right behind her.

I hustled down the cypress roots into the boat and reached over the side to help a sputtering Gertie into the boat. As soon as she had two feet inside, she sprang up and hurried to start the motor. It roared to life with a single pull and I barely had time to stow my backpack in the bottom of the boat before Gertie twisted the throttle.

The boat leaped out of the water and I clutched the sides, praying her addled brain cells could operate at this speed. Her diminished mental capacity and constant refusal to wear glasses combined with the rate at which she whipped the boat down the curvy bayou was enough to make a thrill-seeker take up knitting.

I kept my head down in case Carter made it to the bayou before we got out of sight. I have no idea why. There couldn't possibly be that many combinations of an old woman driving a boat like a bat out of hell and a young woman with a blond ponytail holding on for life in the bow.

I thought we had made it but as we made a hard left about fifty yards from our docking point, Carter leaned over the bank and looked down the bayou. Gertie whipped the boat around the corner so close to the bank that the side of the boat rubbed against the cypress roots as we went.

"Move to the center!" I yelled.

Gertie overshot the middle by a good twenty feet and only managed to move the boat as close to the right bank as she had been to the left. "Did Carter see us?"

"Yes. Right before we turned the corner, but I'm not sure he could make out who we were."

"But he'll suspect."

Oh yeah. He'd suspect all right. "We need to get back to Ida Belle's as soon as possible."

It was the right sentiment, but the wrong thing to say. Gertie twisted the throttle on the boat even harder, roaring past a couple of fishermen headed the other direction. They yelled at her to slow down, but it didn't faze her one bit. By the time we rounded the corner to the boat launch, I was certain I would die in a flat-bottomed aluminum boat on Sinful Bayou.

And that was just all levels of wrong.

Gertie didn't cut the engine until she was only ten feet from the dock. I didn't even bother to try to catch one of the pylons and chose instead to drop down into the bottom of the boat rather than be catapulted out of it when we collided with the pier. The force of the impact sent Gertie sprawling into the bottom of the boat, cussing a blue streak.

"Get the trailer," Gertie yelled as she struggled to get up. "As soon as the boat's on it, take off. Don't worry about the hook. Just get to Ida Belle's before Carter does."

I grabbed the backpack and leaped onto the dock, digging my keys out as I scrambled for my Jeep. I vaulted into the driver's seat and backed the trailer down the boat launch with the skill of a seasoned bass fisherman. Gertie had already backed away from the dock and was circling around to get a straight shot at the trailer.

I wasn't convinced of Gertie's "no hooking" plan but with no time to come up with something better, I put on the parking brake and waved her up.

Time was of the essence. I knew that. But I didn't expect Gertie to launch the boat toward the trailer with quite the gusto she did it with. I knew she'd miscalculated the instant she took off, but with a rattled head and no glasses, I was going to get potluck. I waved my hands and yelled, trying to slow her down, but she was only twenty feet from the trailer before she realized she was going way too fast.

She cut the engine, but the damage was already done. The boat shot straight up the back of the trailer, but didn't stop when it got to the front. Instead, it rode right over the top of the trailer and straight into the back of my Jeep.

I jumped away from the Jeep as the bow of the boat crashed to a stop across the backseat. The back of the boat tipped down into the trailer, wedged between the side rails.

"Go! Go!" Gertie yelled, still perched in the boat.

I jumped back into the Jeep and took off, praying the boat didn't fall off the Jeep. As I pulled out of the boat launch area and onto the street, the boat slid a bit on the back of the Jeep, and the sound of metal grinding on metal made my teeth ache. I cringed and pushed my foot down on the accelerator, going as fast as I thought I could risk.

I could hear the trailer bouncing behind me and I checked the rearview mirror to make sure Gertie was still holding on. The top of her head barely peeked out from the bottom of the boat, so I pressed the gas a little harder.

As I squealed around the corner into the neighborhood, a car started backing out of his driveway and I knew there was no way I could stop in time. I laid on the horn and the car jerked to a stop. By the time I blew past, the middle-aged man driving the car had jumped out and was staring, mouth open. Maybe I'd luck out and he'd be one of those town drunk types that no one believed. I made the four blocks to Ida Belle's house without any more trouble and let out a sigh of relief when I didn't see Carter's truck anywhere.

Ida Belle was standing on the sidewalk in front of her house and waving me toward the garage. Her prized Corvette was parked at the curb. I wasn't sure what she had in mind because the Jeep and the trailer weren't even going to fit in the garage, but I whipped the Jeep around and backed the trailer into the garage, hoping our minor boat problem wouldn't be as noticeable.

Ida Belle ran into the garage to help Gertie out of the back of the boat. I grabbed my backpack, jumped out of the Jeep, and ran into the house after Ida Belle and Gertie. I didn't stop running until I got to the living room, where I collapsed on the couch. Gertie stumbled in after me and slumped in a recliner.

Ida Belle stood in the center of the living room, hands on her hips, glaring at the two of us. "What the hell did you do to my boat?"

"It was her fault." Gertie and I both spoke.

I glared at her. "How could it possibly be my fault?"

"You backed the trailer too far in the water."

"Are you kidding me? I could have been parked in Texas and you still would have driven that boat into my Jeep." I looked at Ida Belle. "No more boats until you teach me how to drive."

"Given that it's probably going to take a crane to get my boat out of your Jeep," Ida Belle said, "you'll get no argument from me." She looked at Gertie. "What exactly is the big rush? All I understood from your phone call was that I needed to open my garage and move my car."

"Two guys started shooting at doves in the trees right next to us," I said. "Almost hit us with the first round."

"It's not dove season," Ida Belle said. "It's not *anything* season."

"That's what Gertie said, which explains why Carter came running straight to our hiding place."

Ida Belle's eyes widened. "Oh! That's not good."

"So we hauled it out of there and made for the boat. He didn't catch us in the swamp, but I'm pretty sure he saw us in the boat before we rounded the corner."

"Crap," Ida Belle said. "Do you think he made you?"

As I opened my mouth to answer, her doorbell rang. Ida Belle rushed to the window and peeked out the blinds. "It's Carter." She looked back at us and shook her head. "I got nothing for this one. I'll have to make it up on the fly."

CHAPTER TWENTY-ONE

IDA BELLE WALKED TO THE DOOR AND OPENED IT. "HELLO, Carter. What can I do for you?"

Carter peered into the living room and frowned when he saw Gertie and me sitting there. "I need to talk to you about your boat."

"You looking to buy a new one?"

I saw his jaw flex. "No, I'm not looking to buy a boat. Your garage. Now!"

Ida Belle glanced back at us as she followed Carter outside. Gertie and I jumped up and hurried out behind them. I had zero idea how to explain the situation, but I needed to come up with something in the next ten footsteps.

Carter walked right to the back of my Jeep and pointed to the boat, still resting halfway in my vehicle. "Anyone care to explain this?"

"We were working on my boat," Ida Belle said. "I don't have a lift, so we improvised."

I held in a smile. Damn, she was good.

He stared at each of us one at a time, his eyes unwavering. But he'd met his match in the three of us. We all looked him straight in the eye and with the most innocent expressions you'd ever seen. Quite frankly, if I wasn't so worried about blowing my cover, it would have been downright scary.

"You expect me to believe that this boat, that is dripping water all over your garage, has been sitting here all afternoon, and that the three of you have been working on it?"

"We were scraping barnacles off of it and giving it a good scrub," Ida Belle said. "How were we supposed to clean it without water?"

Carter shook his head, clearly exasperated. "So if I question your neighbors, they'll tell me they saw you all out here working on this boat? You couldn't possibly have been on Sinful Bayou behind the cemetery."

Ida Belle shrugged. "Most of my neighbors are buttholes, so I have no idea what they'll say. But you're free to ask."

Carter turned around and looked straight at me. "What were you doing in the swamp?"

The guilt was overwhelming and I chastised myself, once again, for letting things get personal. If I hadn't allowed myself to get friendly with Carter, I wouldn't feel bad about lying to him now. I never thought I'd admit it, even to myself, but being a normal person was so much more difficult than being an assassin.

"We weren't in the swamp," I said, working hard to keep my voice level. "We were here all afternoon."

I could tell he was disappointed. Despite the fact that I hadn't given him any tells, he knew I was lying. The evidence was simply stacked against us.

His cell phone signaled that he'd received a text and he pulled it from his pocket and frowned as he looked at the display.

"Fine," he said when he looked back at me. "If that's the way you want it." He turned around without another word and strode back to his truck. Without so much as a backward glance, he drove off.

I felt my heart clench as I watched him drive away. I hated

lying to Carter. And I hated that I hated lying. Why had I let things get so confusing? I needed to get back to basics, and the most basic rule was always "don't get personal." My partner, Harrison, would be the first to point out that every problem I'd had since my arrival in Sinful could have been avoided if I'd just followed rule number 1.

"What was that about?" Gertie asked. "I know he thinks we're lying—"

"Because we are," I pointed out.

"Naturally," Gertie agreed, "but it's hardly the first time we've done so. Hell, Ida Belle and I have been making up tales for local law enforcement since we were teens. Carter has been frustrated with us in the past, but I've never sensed he took it personally until now."

"I don't think his disappointment is because of you and me," Ida Belle said.

Gertie looked confused. "Then why... Oh." She looked at me.

"Why are you looking at me?" I asked. I knew why, of course, but I wasn't about to admit it.

Gertie grinned. "Carter's got a crush on you, and your duplicity is breaking his heart."

"That is better fiction than I saw on television last night," I said.

Gertie shook her head. "Ida Belle's right. Carter's never taken it personally when we've made up stories to cover our shenanigans. Not until now. And the only thing that's changed is you."

I felt a blush creep up my neck. "We barely know each other, and even you have to admit that we haven't exactly had smooth going since I've arrived."

"True," Ida Belle said, "but despite all of that, he's still interested. I may be an old maid, but I know what male interest looks like."

Gertie waved a hand at her. "Walter slipping you a free pack of toilet paper with your grocery order hardly qualifies as the ultimate in male interest. But despite Ida Belle's overblown description of her knowledge of how men think, I think she's right this time."

"Well, it's all a moot point, isn't it?" I said, desperately wanting to bring the discussion to a halt. "I'm not going to stop lying to Carter when it's necessary, and he's not going to be able to stand it. So we're at an impasse. I'm more worried about that text he got. Regardless of what you two think Carter feels, I don't think my lies had anything to do with his abrupt exit."

Gertie sobered and shot a worried look at Ida Belle. "Do you think it's about the tests on the poison?"

I shook my head. For Ida Belle's sake, I hoped not because I didn't think the outcome was going to be in her favor.

"Then we best get this show on the road," Ida Belle said. "Please tell me the cameras didn't go into the bayou with Gertie?"

"How do you know I fell into the bayou?" Gertie asked.

"You stink of it for one thing, and I think I'd remember if you left my house with your hair wet and stuck to the side of your head. Besides, you're dripping all over my garage." Ida Belle rolled her eyes at me and waved us back inside, where she sent Gertie upstairs to dry off and change.

I sat down at the kitchen table and retrieved the cameras from my backpack. Ida Belle connected the first camera to her laptop and pressed play. I watched as the view of the cemetery went from blurry to only slightly blurry and then focused on Shelly and Lyle.

"I hope the picture clears up some," Ida Belle said.

I held in a groan. "I wouldn't count on it. That was Gertie's camera."

Ida Belle glanced over at Gertie, who'd just walked into the kitchen, and sighed.

Gertie threw her arms in the air. "Fine. I'll go get new glasses. Are you happy?"

"Immensely."

"Absolutely."

Ida Belle and I both answered at the same time and Gertie shot us both dirty looks.

I dragged my chair closer to Ida Belle's and leaned forward a bit to get a better look at the monitor. "Unless I missed something, I didn't see much going on while Father Michael was speaking."

"Nothing but people trying to keep from yawning," Gertie agreed as she stood behind Ida Belle's chair and peered over her shoulder.

We watched Shelly and Lyle closely while Father Michael did his thing, but they wore either bland or slightly bored expressions. Nothing to indicate guilt or fear of being discovered. Finally, they began the dirt-tossing part of the ceremony.

I watched closely as Lyle tossed the dirt. "Stop that. Back it up and see if you can pause the video right before he turns to walk off."

It took a couple of attempts, but Ida Belle finally managed to freeze the video at the spot I wanted. I smiled. I'd been right. "He's smirking," I said.

"Does that mean anything?" Gertie asked.

"Maybe," I said. "Start it back up again, Ida Belle."

"Shelly is coming up next," Gertie said.

I watched as Shelly picked up her handful of dirt and leaned over to toss it on the grave. Something about it looked as odd now as it did when I'd seen her in the cemetery. "She's doing something," I said. "Rewind it again."

I leaned forward and watched her body movements as soon as she approached the coffin, the uptick of her head, the glance to her left where the few remaining people were waiting, the slight lean over the grave site, and then the barely imperceptible forward movement of her head.

I sat up straight. "She spit on his grave."

"I didn't see that," Ida Belle said and backed up the footage again.

"Do you think that means she did it?" Gertie asked.

"Unless she's a complete idiot," I said, "I doubt it. More likely she's celebrating that someone else did the dirty work and taking a last shot at Ted since she couldn't while he was alive."

Gertie sighed. "What good is this doing? We still haven't eliminated anyone from our list."

"No," I agreed, "but we may get a better idea where to start taking a harder look." I waved at Ida Belle. "Start it up again."

I focused back on the screen and watched as Toby and Blaine tossed their handfuls of dirt. Nothing untoward with either of them, unless you wanted to count the fact that they stood watching the burial rather than leaving with everyone else.

"What are they doing just standing there?" Ida Belle asked. "It's morbid."

"That's what I said," Gertie piped in.

I inched forward a bit more and squinted at the screen. "Go back again," I said to Ida Belle. "To right after they step away from the coffin."

Ida Belle scanned back. "What do you see?" she asked.

"I'm trying to see what they're saying," I said as I studied their lips, wishing Gertie wasn't so stubborn about wearing glasses. There was just enough blur to prevent me from being certain of the words.

"You can read lips?" Gertie sounded surprised.

"Part of the job description," I said. "Back it up again and I'll translate what I think they're saying."

Ida Belle reversed the footage once more and I started relaying their conversation.

"Do you think...photos?"

"No, or we'd...jail."

"Should we...find...?"

"With the...hanging around?"

"What if...find them?"

"...we're fucked."

"Who...think...killed...?"

"I don't...like...shake...hand."

"I don't know but I'd like to shake his hand," Ida Belle filled in the blanks of the last sentence and gave me an admiring nod. "That was incredible."

Gertie nodded. "And even though you were missing some words, I think we got the gist of it. They are afraid Carter will get the photos but can't look for them again, so now we know they were the two men in Ted's house that night with us."

I nodded. "More importantly, we know they didn't kill Ted."

"That's two off the list," Ida Belle said.

I considered this for a moment. "Is it possible that Toby killed Ted and Blaine doesn't know? Or vice versa?"

"I really don't think so," Ida Belle said. "Those two have been partners in crime since kindergarten. I bet they even share underwear."

I cringed. That was a visual I really didn't need. "Okay, so we put them at the bottom of the list for now. Shelly is second, and I think Lyle is first up for further investigation."

Ida Belle nodded. "I agree."

"Okay. How do we do that?" Gertie asked.

"We watch him and see if he does anything to give himself away," Ida Belle said. "That's what they do on television."

I looked back at the laptop. "Is he dangerous? I mean, other than the fact that he might have killed his blackmailer, which I sorta get on a criminal kind of level."

"He was a pit fighter for a while in New Orleans when he was in his twenties," Ida Belle said. "I never saw him fight, but I hear he was a real terror."

"He served time for assault a handful of times—the last time was a couple of years ago," Gertie said.

"Was this the bar fighting kind of assault?"

"No, some guy whipped in front of him at a gas station and took the pump Lyle had been waiting for. The guy refused to move, so Lyle beat him half to death with the nozzle."

I stared. "That would be a 'yes' on the dangerous question."

Great. I was about to stalk the bayou Mike Tyson.

CHAPTER TWENTY-TWO

AFTER WATCHING ALL THE FOOTAGE ONE MORE TIME FROM start to finish, we headed to the garage to get Ida Belle's boat out of my Jeep. It took some serious muscle, and some ingenuity with tie-downs and an exposed rafter in Ida Belle's garage, but we managed to get the boat back on the trailer and pushed into Ida Belle's backyard. The gaping hole in the front would have to be addressed before it saw water again.

Once my Jeep was free and clear of all boat, we decided to call it a wrap and meet back at Ida Belle's that night to plot our plan to spy on Lyle. I was just walking out Ida Belle's front door when her phone rang.

"Wait!" she yelled. "It's Marie. She says Tony is out on Paulette's front porch, talking on his cell phone and smoking a cigarette."

"So?" Apparently, I'd missed the significance of his actions.

"Hold on a second," Ida Belle said. "Then she saw Paulette come out of her back gate and slink down the side of the fence to the street behind her."

I frowned. "Why would she sneak out of her own house?"

"Sounds like she was trying to ditch Tony," Ida Belle said.

"Why?" Gertie asked.

"I don't know," I said, "but maybe I can find out."

I ran across the street and in between two houses to the next street over, then shifted a bit to the next open passageway between houses and took off again. When I reached the back side of Marie's block, I skirted down several houses before crossing to the next block and slowed to a walk, in case Tony was looking. Someone running in between houses might attract attention, but a slow stroll shouldn't draw his gaze.

When I got to the next block, I didn't move directly to the sidewalk, choosing instead to stay closer to the front of the houses, skirting from hedge to hedge. When I got to the house that backed up to Paulette's, I stopped and peered through the azalea bushes. So far, I hadn't seen any sign of Paulette.

I pulled out my cell phone and called Marie. "Has Paulette returned?" I asked as soon as she answered.

"No. I haven't taken my eyes off of the house. Tony is still outside, but I haven't seen Paulette."

"Thanks." I disconnected and turned the phone on vibrate before slipping it back into my jeans pocket. I peered out once more, but didn't see any movement in the neighborhood, so I slipped around the hedge and started a quick walk across the lawns, trying to keep myself positioned in a way that foliage and vehicles would block my approach from anyone in the distance.

The street was a dead end, with a patch of ground about twenty feet wide that was kept up by the town. Directly beyond that was the swamp. I looked behind me and blew out a breath. She must have gone into a house, but which one? And why would she go to such lengths to hide visiting a resident from her cousin?

I was just about to chalk it up as a loss and leave when I saw a flash and then something moving at the edge of the swamp. I ducked behind a magnolia tree and peered around, trying to see what had gotten my attention. A couple of seconds later, Paulette stepped out of the swamp, her sequined gold top glinting in the sunlight. The flash made total sense now.

What the hell was she doing in the swamp?

Unfortunately, it was a question that would have to wait because she set out straight toward me. I tucked myself in and pressed myself flat against the trunk of the tree. It wasn't long before I heard her footsteps coming toward me. I listened closely to the sound of her steps on the grass and inched around the tree at the exact moment that she passed.

I'd no sooner skirted to the other side of the tree when I saw a man emerge from the swamp from the same place Paulette had exited. I dove for a set of low hedges and crouched behind them, peering through the branches to see if I could get a good look at the man. Even though he was wearing a ball cap pulled low and I only had a limited side view of him, it only took me a couple of seconds to place him.

But what I couldn't do is come up with any plausible reason for Bobby to secretly meet Paulette in the swamp.

———

"BOBBY?" GERTIE ASKED. "YOU'RE SURE?"

I nodded. "I got a good look at the side of him, and I recognize his stride from when I met him at the rally."

"And from when he left Francine's this morning after you blew him off for Carter?" Ida Belle asked.

I shuffled my feet. "Where did you hear that?"

"One of the Sinful Ladies called to tell me about it while you and Gertie were tree-climbing. It's getting around."

I groaned. The last thing I needed was even more people talking about me.

"So why would Bobby meet Paulette?" I asked, trying to shift the subject back to something more comfortable.

Ida Belle and Gertie both shook their heads.

"I'm surprised he even knows her," Ida Belle said. "He left Sinful before Ted and Paulette moved here."

"But he's been back on leave, right?" I said. "Could he have met her then?"

Gertie frowned. "You know, I only recall seeing him once since he left, and I can't remember if that was before or after Ted and Paulette moved here. His mother was complaining that he always had somewhere better to go instead of visiting her."

"His mother is a total nag," Ida Belle said. "Going to hell is a better option than visiting Vera."

"There is that," Gertie acknowledged.

An idea formed in the back of my mind, and even though it was as thin as the edge of a razor blade, I couldn't seem to stop it from taking shape. "What if he met up with Paulette in New Orleans during his leave?"

Gertie's eye widened. "What makes you think that?"

"No solid reason. Probably because he's a flirt and it irritates me. I've only seen him twice and both times, I'm sure he was hitting on me, or getting around to it."

Ida Belle nodded. "He has a reputation of being rather a hound dog."

"Always sniffing around a woman," Gertie agreed.

"Well, Paulette certainly didn't spend any time in the military," I said, "and I can't think of any other reason for him to talk to her. If he wanted to pay condolences, he would have rung the front door bell and been holding a casserole, like everyone else in this town."

"Do you think he could have killed Ted?" Gertie asked.

"Sure, he could have," I said. "Almost anyone could have."

"But you don't think so?" Ida Belle said.

I shook my head. "I had him pegged for a louse, but not a killer. Of course, I've been off a bit since I've been in Sinful. The residents here are not nearly as predictable as terrorists."

"Preach," Gertie said.

"If we follow the line of Bobby having a fling with Paulette during his leave," I said, "then what would make sense is him meeting with her to impress upon her the importance that she didn't tell anyone."

"I get it," Ida Belle said. "Given the timing of his arrival back in Sinful, if people knew he'd been carrying on with Paulette, he'd move to the top of the suspect list."

"Exactly."

"But you don't think he did it?" Gertie asked again.

"No...but I don't know why."

"It's hard to believe anyone would get that worked up over Paulette," Gertie said.

"There's that, and since we now suspect Ted didn't have the money we originally thought he had, if Paulette wanted to be with another man, she could have simply left. Nothing to lose, right?"

Ida Belle sighed. "While it's an interesting piece of information, if it doesn't help our case, then I guess we better shelve it and get back to our original plan of checking out Lyle."

I nodded, but was only half listening. I wasn't being dishonest when I said I didn't think Bobby had killed Ted. Something about him didn't say killer, his military career notwithstanding. But I did think he was a liar. Something about him wasn't genuine, but I couldn't put my finger on it.

I just hoped whatever Bobby was hiding had nothing to do with Ted's murder.

———

AFTER MY BIG REVEAL ABOUT PAULETTE AND BOBBY, I HEADED home for a shower, food, and some thinking about everything we knew so far and a plan for getting the goods on Lyle. Assuming there were some goods to get.

Ida Belle and Gertie couldn't come up with a better explanation than I had for Bobby's clandestine meeting with Paulette, and I had a feeling they weren't going to. From the beginning, I'd had the feeling that Ted's murder was just the surface of everything that was going on. The photos, Ted's hidden past, the two guys taking a picture of Ted's corpse...I knew all of it was important and somehow it all fit together.

But damned if I could figure out how.

I couldn't remember a time when I'd been more frustrated. This must be what CIA analysts felt like when they had so many facts in front of them and were trying to piece them together until they made sense. Considering that an analyst's report might result in a hit on someone, I imagined they were considerably stressed as well as frustrated.

All the times I'd read the files on my targets, I'd never once stopped to consider what someone went through to gather all that information, then put it together in a way that not only made sense, but created a call to action. As soon as I got back to DC, I was buying every one of the analysts an expensive bottle of wine.

Carter has to do this every day as well.

The thought ripped through my mind as I pulled into my garage and instantly, a wave of guilt washed over me. Carter was the one who was ultimately responsible for piecing all of this together, and he was working with half the information we were. Once again, I tried to think of a way to get him the information without implicating myself and Gertie, not to mention making things even worse for Ida Belle. But by lying to begin with, we'd gone past the point of no return.

If we fessed up now, then we'd be guilty of interfering with a police investigation. And since one of the culprits was currently the prime suspect, I figured that would be very, very bad when the prosecutor found out. Carter had been lenient in checking my background. So far, he'd only given it a cursory look, which wouldn't yield anything suspicious. But if the state prosecutor got even a whiff of an idea that I was hiding something, he would tear my cover apart one layer at a time.

I walked into the kitchen and threw my keys on the counter. "You really stepped in it this time, Redding," I said to the cabinets.

A loud meow sounded below me and I looked down to see Merlin, who began his leg-rubbing routine. I reached down to scratch him behind the ears, then remembered he hadn't eaten since last night when I'd given him leftovers. Of course, when I left the house for my funeral fun, he still hadn't moved from his spot on my bed, so I didn't exactly feel sorry for him.

I reached for the cat food and dumped some in a bowl. Merlin's meows got louder and more insistent. "Give me a second, you infernal beast. How much of an appetite could you possibly have worked up sleeping?"

I put the bowl of food on the floor and Merlin leaned over to delicately pick up a single piece of the food before sitting down to crunch it. Cats certainly had more table manners than dogs. Bones always managed to spread more food across the kitchen floor than he actually got into his stomach. Of course, Bones was a hundred years old and had three teeth left. Maybe when Merlin was older he'd be as messy.

Which then made me wonder how old the cat was. He didn't look like a baby, but I had no idea how one gauged a cat's age. As soon as this entire mess with Ida Belle was over, I needed to take him to a vet. They could probably tell me if I was shacking up with a teenager or an older man.

Now that the noise level in the kitchen had subsided, I pulled sliced roast beef from the refrigerator and made myself a sandwich. I managed to eat half of it with no interruption, but I'd no sooner taken a bite out of the second half when my cell phone rang. I glanced down at the display and saw Walter's number.

I chugged some soda and answered.

"It's about to happen," Walter said, his voice shaking.

"What's about to happen? Are you all right?"

"I went to the sheriff's department to talk to Carter. I don't care if it's his job. He needs to be reminded that Ida Belle couldn't possibly kill someone."

"Hmm," I said. Ida Belle had actually killed someone last week, but since that person was about to kill me, I supposed that didn't count in Walter's tally.

"The front office was empty when I walked in, so I started back to Carter's office and that's when I heard him on the phone."

I heard him take a deep breath and blow it out.

"I know I shouldn't have been listening," he said, "but damn it, I did anyway."

Since I'd first heard Walter's voice, I'd been on edge, knowing something was very wrong, and I knew with certainty that I didn't want to hear what he was going to say.

"The lab results came in," Walter said. "Ida Belle's gopher poison is a match."

My lower back tightened so hard and so fast, it made my head and neck ache. "Do you think he's going to arrest her?"

"Once the prosecutor gets that information, I don't think he's going to have a choice."

I checked my watch. It was almost five o'clock. With any luck, Carter wouldn't be able to get the information to the prosecutor until tomorrow. That bought us until tomorrow morning before Ida Belle was behind bars and things got infinitely dire. Which meant we had a little over half a day to solve a murder, get the information to Carter without implicating ourselves, and clear Ida Belle's name.

I could do this. I'd single-handedly overturned militias with less effort.

How bad could it be?

CHAPTER TWENTY-THREE

FAMOUS LAST WORDS.

It was 11:00 p.m. and I was lying flat on the ground, under a hedge, staring across the street at Lyle Cox's house, praying that he did something a murderer might do. So far, he'd sat in his recliner in the living room, drunk beer, and watched two hours of sports television, which looked pretty darn nice from where I sat. Or lay.

Due to my training, my body could take hours of immobility, so my muscles hadn't started to cramp, but my mind was ready to leak out my ear and go do something of interest. Anything but sit here another two hours getting eaten alive by the biggest mosquitoes God had ever created. Seriously, I'd been in aircraft that was smaller.

Ida Belle and Gertie were faring worse than me. Ancient bones didn't like being cramped on the ground under a bush, and since Ida Belle was the only one who exercised with any regularity, my guess was Gertie would be walking like the Hunchback for days to come. Still, I had to give them points for not complaining. I'd worked with CIA agents who weren't as durable as the two senior citizens beside me.

"If he's not going to do anything worth watching, I wish he'd pass out or something," Ida Belle said.

"It's probably our luck he's a night owl," I said.

"Or a vampire," Gertie said.

A vampire wouldn't be the oddest thing I'd seen in Sinful, so I left the possibility open. I saw movement through the window and got more excited than the situation truly warranted. "Look. He's moving."

All three of us stared at the window like children looking through the glass storefront of a candy shop. Lyle, who'd finally risen from his recliner, now stretched, then headed out of the living room and out of our view.

"He's probably just going to pee," Gertie said. "He's drunk a six-pack at least."

Given that he hadn't turned off the television or the living room lights, I figured she was right, but a girl could still dream. After several minutes, my dreams began to fade back into reality.

"Good Lord," Ida Belle said. "How long is he going to be in the bathroom?"

"A six-pack worth?" Gertie suggested.

I said a silent prayer that he hadn't fallen asleep on the john or passed out on the bathroom floor. Otherwise, it was going to be a long night of nothing.

I'd convinced Walter to keep the tidbit about the lab tests to himself, then I sweated the rest of the evening, worried that Carter would show up at Ida Belle's house to arrest her. My rationale was that if Gertie and Ida Belle knew how close Ida Belle was to the clink, their stress level would go up significantly. And stress led to mistakes.

Walter hadn't been happy at all as he saw our silence as basically colluding to lie by omission. I told him I had a really good reason for my request and that if I told him why, he'd then become a party to something illegal. I'm not sure which part he was unhappier about, but he said he'd trust me this time. The unspoken understanding was that if I blew it, I was in the negative with Walter when it came to trust.

No pressure, right?

I was just about to decide that Lyle had gotten the munchies and was in the kitchen fixing a casserole, or maybe an entire Thanksgiving spread, when a light went on upstairs. I grabbed Ida Belle's sleeve and pointed.

"Maybe he's going to bed," I suggested.

"With all the lights and the television on downstairs?" Gertie asked. "That's such a waste of electricity."

"He just drank half a bar," Ida Belle said. "I don't think he's thinking about his electrical consumption. The room with the light is the master bedroom."

"Should I even ask how you know that?" I asked.

"Don't be ridiculous," Ida Belle said. "If I won't marry Walter, why would I have sex with Lyle?"

"Good point."

"He inherited the house from his mother," Ida Belle said. "She passed a year ago. Do you really think he cultivated those roses or painted the shutters purple? He's let the place go to pot, but the bones of something beautiful are still there."

"If she can see how ratty her roses have gotten," Gertie said, "Martha is probably turning over in her grave."

Ida Belle nodded her agreement.

We waited what seemed like forever, but was probably only a couple of minutes, and the light upstairs went off. I watched the downstairs closely, but didn't see movement again.

"I think he may be wasting electricity," I said.

"He hasn't come back downstairs," Ida Belle agreed.

"We didn't see anything at all that will help," Gertie said, her voice a bit strained. "I feel like we ought to do something besides go home."

I did too, but I'd been hoping Lyle would be gone when we arrived at his house. My idea was much riskier with him in residence, especially as he had the look of a man who wouldn't think twice about shooting a trespasser, but we were running out of time and options.

"Does he have a shed out back like you, Ida Belle?"

"Sure, most people do. Not like anyone wants a lawn mower in their living room, and these one-car garages don't hold much else but one car."

"I think we should look in his shed and see if there's something in there with the same chemical makeup as the poison taken from your shed."

Ida Belle frowned. "That's a bit of a long shot, isn't it? And risky, even by our standards. Lyle will shoot first and ask questions later if he catches us in his backyard."

I squirmed a bit, trying to come up with a valid reason for taking such a risk that wasn't the real reason I was willing to take the risk. "I'm just hoping to find a way to pin something on one of the other suspects, and Lyle is the most likely at this point. Even if we can throw suspicion on someone else, that will make a case against you weaker."

Ida Belle narrowed her eyes at me. Crap. I'd said too much and Ida Belle was too shrewd to miss the implication.

"The lab tests came back, didn't they?" she asked.

Gertie sucked in a breath. "No. Fortune wouldn't keep something like that from us." Then her expression wavered and a bit of doubt crept in. "Would you?"

Damn it.

I blew out a breath. "Yes, the lab test came back. And the poison Carter took from Ida Belle's is a match."

"How did you find out?" Ida Belle asked.

"And why didn't you tell us?" Gertie chimed in.

"How I found out is irrelevant, and I didn't tell you because I didn't want you even more stressed when we were out here tonight. Stress leads to a clouded mind, which leads to mistakes."

They both stared at me, completely silent.

"I promise I was going to tell you as soon as we were done spying on Lyle."

Finally, Ida Belle sighed. "I get it, and it's sorta sweet how you're trying to protect me and Gertie, but it's not necessary. We're two tough old birds. We can handle this. I promise you."

"Okay," I said. "Then the bottom line is, my guess is that unless we can give him another option to muddy the waters, Carter will arrest you tomorrow. Once the prosecutor sets his sights on you, it's going to be twice as hard to get him to look elsewhere."

"Crap," Gertie said.

"Exactly," I agreed. "So if we can find another match for the poison, it would be great."

"And if we can't?" Ida Belle asked. "The reality is, anyone in Sinful could have walked into my backyard and taken the poison."

"True, but it's worth a look."

"And if we don't find anything and Carter arrests Ida Belle?" Gertie asked.

I blew out a breath. "Then I gather up everything we have—Ted's true identity, the pictures—and I take it all to Carter and fess up."

Ida Belle shook her head. "I can't allow you to do that. You'll blow your cover."

"Then I'll do it," Gertie said.

I knew Carter would never buy that Gertie did all the things we'd done alone. He'd know I was involved regardless of who knocked on his door and handed him a bag of evidence, but I didn't see the point in drawing out a losing conversation any longer.

"That might work," I said.

Ida Belle cut her eyes at me and I knew I hadn't fooled her at all, but Gertie looked temporarily mollified, so I left it at that.

"So it's settled," I said. "I take a peek in his shed."

"You're not going alone," Ida Belle said. "You don't even know what you're looking for."

"If she's going, I'm going," Gertie said. "You can't make me stay."

I hated to agree with Ida Belle, but she was right. I wasn't an expert on homeowner poisons.

"Fine, but if he starts shooting, we get the hell out."

"That's a given," Ida Belle agreed.

"You never know——" Gertie started.

I held up a hand to stop her. "I know. I don't need a reminder. I think we should skirt down the back side of this hedge and cross the street two houses down from Lyle's. It's darker there and gives us more cover."

They both nodded so I backed out from under the bushes and started down the back side of them until I reached the next yard. Ida Belle and Gertie were right behind me, so I continued my progress down the street, then across, then back toward Lyle's house, until we'd finally slipped around the corner and down the side of his house toward his backyard gate.

I checked to make sure Ida Belle and Gertie were in position behind me, then pushed open his gate just enough for us to slip through, then eased myself inside. The back porch light cast a dim glow over the backyard, and I was pleased to have enough light to work with but not a spotlight that illuminated the entire lawn.

Ida Belle pointed to the storage shed in the back right corner of the yard and we skirted the yard, keeping close to the fence and outside of the glow of the porch light. When we reached the shed, I was pleased to find it wasn't locked. Which seemed stupid, given the situation Ida Belle was in, which then reminded me that my own shed wasn't locked, and it's something I needed to address first thing in the morning. Given that she had a hidden arsenal inside the house, God only knew what Marge had tucked away in the shed.

I opened the shed door enough to get my arm around and click on my penlight. I peered inside and shone the light around the shed. It didn't have a window, which definitely helped us avoid detection, but given the somewhat haphazard state of the shed, I wasn't comfortable breaking out a bigger light. Cracks revealed lighting inside an enclosure just as easily as a window did.

I crept inside, careful not to upset any of the cans, tools, and other items stacked randomly throughout the shed. I looked back at the door as Ida Belle poked her head in and motioned to her to join me.

"Take a look around and see if you see anything you think may have the same chemical makeup as the poison in your shed."

Ida Belle nodded and clicked on her penlight, scanning the stacks of cans, bottles, and bags. Gertie slipped through the door and joined her, squinting in the dim light. Since she still wasn't wearing her glasses, I had doubts she could see anything much beyond shapes, but apparently, Gertie's promises to comply with corrective vision were fictional.

"What is that brown bag over there?" Ida Belle said and pointed to a bag to the left of me.

I shone my light on it. "Ant poison?"

Ida Belle shook her head. "Not the same chemical makeup."

"What about over here?" Gertie asked, and pointed to the right side of the building about five feet back from where she was standing.

Ida Belle shone her light to where Gertie pointed and that's when all hell broke loose. The snake that had been draped on a beam at the top of the shed was apparently tired of our noise and lights and dropped straight down on Gertie.

CHAPTER TWENTY-FOUR

GERTIE LET OUT A SCREAM THAT WOULD HAVE MADE A HORROR movie producer celebrate. The instant the first echo of sound left her mouth, I knew things were about to get really bad, but by the same token, I couldn't blame her. The thing was as big as an anaconda.

Before I could even react, Gertie leaned forward, flinging the snake off her shoulders, and bolted out of the shed, shoving the door so hard it hit the side of the shed with a bang that was probably heard blocks away.

Ida Belle bolted out of the shed behind her and I wasn't even an inch off her as we barreled out of the shed. The second my feet hit grass, I heard a racket at Lyle's back door and a second later, an enormous Doberman ran through a doggy door and straight for us, completely cutting off our path to the gate.

"Back fence!" I yelled and we all spun to the right and sprinted for the back fence. I glanced back and saw the dog closing rapidly. We were going to be cutting it very close.

I turned on the afterburners, knowing I would have to help Gertie over the six-foot structure, and that's when she face-planted, just like she had in the swamp two nights before. To keep from running right over her, I dove, completing a somersault as soon as I hit the ground.

In an instant, I sprang back up and turned around to grab Gertie. "Go," I said to Ida Belle.

"My ankle," Gertie said as I pulled her up.

I grabbed her around the waist and practically dragged her to the fence. I leaned over to make a step with my hands. "Put your good foot in and be ready. I'm going to launch you over."

It wasn't the best idea, but at the moment, it was either throw a senior citizen over a fence or be eaten by an angry dog. Gertie stepped into my hands and I pushed up with all my might. Unfortunately, it was more than either of us anticipated.

Gertie flew over the fence, barely grazing the top, and I heard a whoosh of air and a thud, then the sound of heavy objects hitting the turf. I leaped for the top of the fence just as the dog reached me, and could see Ida Belle and Gertie in a tangled heap on the other side. Before I could scramble over, the dog grabbed my shoe and started shaking my leg like a rag. I yanked as hard as I could, but he had a grip that I couldn't shake.

I started to reach for my pistol, then hesitated. The dog was just doing his job. A warning shot might get rid of him, but it would also attract the attention of everyone else in a mile radius. Seeing no other option, I looped my left arm over the fence so that I could reach for my pistol with my right, and at that moment, the back door of the house burst open and Lyle started shooting.

Being shot at...again...must have given me some extra strength in my leg, because when I pulled this time, the shoe popped right off my foot, likely permanently lodged in the dog's mouth, and I launched over the fence with a force I hadn't planned for. I crashed into the ground and immediately leaped up.

Ida Belle and Gertie were standing—Gertie on one leg with Ida Belle holding her upright. A bullet tore through the fence and whizzed by my ear, so I shoved my arm under Gertie's shoulder and ran. I had my doubts that Ida Belle could keep my pace, but either I was moving slower than normal or gunfire prompted a whole other level of ability in her as it did in me.

Either way, we ran through a vacant lot to the next block, then turned and started across front lawns, putting as much distance as we could between us and Lyle. We made it a block before slowing to a stop. We sat Gertie on a boulder in a flower bed and Ida Belle and I leaned over, both panting.

"It's a good five blocks to my house," Ida Belle wheezed.

"I can go get my Jeep and come back to pick you up."

Ida Belle shook her head and pulled out her cell phone. "It would take too long, and Lyle might come looking for us. Besides, as soon as someone reports shots fired to Carter—and you know someone will—he'll come looking for you."

Crap.

Ida Belle lifted the cell phone to her ear. "Marie, we need you to come pick us up right now. We're in Stumpy Pitre's lawn on the side of the house with the boulder. Don't even take the time to dress—just haul ass."

She disconnected and slipped the phone back in her pants pocket.

"Do you think Marie will move that quickly?" I asked, still deliberating hauling it to Ida Belle's for my Jeep.

"Oh yeah," Ida Belle said confidently. "Marie panics and worries, but she's also not much of a thinker. When you tell her to do something right now, she launches into response without even thinking. Probably dangerous for her, but it's come in handy for Gertie and me."

I understood the concept, kinda. Soldiers were trained to react rather than to question, but I wasn't convinced that a bit-past-middle-age woman who rarely left Louisiana was the best candidate for that sort of conditioning. As it turned out, my limited faith in Marie's abilities was unfounded.

Barely a minute had passed when Marie screeched to a stop in her car. Ida Belle and I got Gertie into the front seat before jumping into the back. Marie took off like a NASCAR driver and didn't bother slowing for stop signs or corners. I clutched the door handle and looked over at Ida Belle, who winked.

At the speed she raced up Ida Belle's driveway, I was afraid Marie would launch her car straight through Ida Belle's garage door, but she slammed on the brakes and the car slid to a stop just inches before the door. Ida Belle and I jumped out and grabbed Gertie out of the passenger's seat, then hauled her around the car. We'd barely cleared the taillights when Ida Belle gave Marie a wave. She threw the car in reverse, flew out of the driveway, and disappeared around the block as quickly as she'd arrived.

"She's good," I said as we hauled Gertie into the house and sat her in the recliner.

Ida Belle nodded. "Told you. Granted, when the adrenaline stops about ten minutes from now, she'll be so stressed she'll knit an entire blanket and probably bake at least two pies before calming down. But I could use a new blanket and Marie's work is the best, so it all works out."

"I could use pie," Gertie piped up as Ida Belle untied her tennis shoe and began to ease it off her foot.

"You could use a walker," I said. "What is up with you and all the tripping? Maybe that foot is worse than you thought. You should have it checked out."

"I didn't trip," Gertie said, somewhat indignant.

"Then what the hell did this?" Ida Belle said and pointed to her ankle.

It was already swollen to double normal size and by tomorrow morning, I had no doubt it would be black and purple. "Is it broken?" I asked.

Ida Belle pressed gently on the sides and shook her head. "Can't tell for sure, but I think it's only sprained. Still, she should have an X-ray tomorrow."

Gertie leaned forward to study her ankle and sighed. "That's my driving foot."

"The only thing you need to be driving is one of those motorized wheelchairs," Ida Belle said.

"I don't know," I said. "Have you seen how fast some of them go?"

"True," Ida Belle admitted, then looked at Gertie. "As soon as this is healed, you have got to start doing yoga with me. You may have moments of brilliance, but overall, your flexibility and balance have gone to hell in a handbasket."

Gertie crossed her arms in front of her chest. "It's not that bad."

I stared. "Seriously? You've injured that same foot three times this week alone."

Ida Belle shook her head. "Yes, it's that bad, and furthermore, we're too old to risk these kind of injuries. It's going to take you ten times longer to recover than it did when we were serving in Vietnam. I hate it as much as you do, but the reality is we're not in any shape to keep up with Fortune and we never will be again."

Gertie sighed. "I'm not sure we ever were in any shape to keep up with Fortune, although she appears to have lost some of her garments in this exchange."

Ida Belle looked down at my foot where Gertie pointed and raised her eyebrows. "I didn't even notice. I'm losing my touch."

"The dog was hungry," I explained. "It was either the shoe or my foot. When Lyle started shooting, the shoe seemed the better option."

Suddenly, it registered that Lyle had my shoe, and no doubt some nosy neighbor had already called in the shots fired. I groaned. "When Lyle gives that shoe to Carter, he's going to know it's mine. I was wearing them this morning because I jogged to the café."

"More than one person can have the same tennis shoe," Gertie argued.

"Yeah, but my DNA is in this one," I said.

Ida Belle waved a hand in dismissal. "Carter's not going to do a DNA test on a tennis shoe on a trespassing charge. Besides, Lyle's not going to give him the shoe in the first place, or he'll have to admit he was the one shooting."

"Those big holes in his fence are sorta a dead giveaway," I pointed out.

Gertie relaxed a bit. "Carter can't prove it happened tonight, and Ida Belle's right. Lyle avoids the cops like the plague. I guess thanks to Ted we know why."

Everything Ida Belle said made sense, so I relaxed a little. Unless Lyle had seen me jogging and normally spent time memorizing ladies' tennis shoes, he wouldn't be able to place the shoe. I threw a log in Ida Belle's fireplace and fired it up to burn the incriminating remaining shoe before taking a seat on the brick hearth. Sinful was hell on clothing.

"I'm going to get some ice for that ankle," Ida Belle said and headed to the kitchen. A minute later, she was back with a dishrag full of ice that she tied in a knot and put on Gertie's ankle. "Why in the world did you scream, anyway? It was just a chicken snake."

"I don't care if it was a two-turtledoves snake," Gertie said. "I don't like snakes to begin with and I certainly don't like them attacking me from rafters."

"I know it's a totally girly standpoint," I said, "and likely to lower my stock considerably, but I gotta say I'm with Gertie on this one. I may not have screamed, but I'd probably still be running."

Ida Belle shook her head and sat on the end of the coffee table. "That snake was no risk, especially compared to that dog or Lyle shooting. And when did Lyle get a dog?"

Gertie shook her head. "No idea."

"No matter," Ida Belle continued. "My point still is, all the screaming precipitated the running, which led to the tripping, which results in this." She pointed to Gertie's ankle.

"I didn't trip!" Gertie insisted again.

"I saw you fall," I said. "And I didn't push you."

Gertie rolled her eyes. "I never said anyone pushed me. I just said I didn't trip. The ground swallowed up my foot."

"Lord, help us," Ida Belle said, looking upward, then looked back down at Gertie. "Stepping in a hole and falling *is* tripping."

"But that's just it," Gertie said. "The hole wasn't there when I stepped on it. It's like the ground started disappearing below me and it closed in on my foot. Like it was being pulled down by Mother Earth herself."

Ida Belle's eyes widened and she jumped up. I thought it was a bit of an overreaction to Gertie's dramatic portrayal of clumsiness, but emotions were high, so I figured I'd give her a pass.

"That's it!" Ida Belle said and clapped.

She grinned at both of us. I just stared, not understanding why Gertie's tripping was so exciting all of a sudden. Gertie frowned and stared at Ida Belle for several seconds, then sucked in a breath.

"A gopher hole," Gertie said. "I stepped in a gopher hole."

Ida Belle grinned. "We got him."

CHAPTER TWENTY-FIVE

I WOKE UP BRIGHT AND EARLY THE NEXT MORNING, EAGER TO get started on my tasks for the day, and that was a welcome change. We'd spent hours the night before tossing around ideas of how to get Carter to investigate Lyle, while trying to avoid implicating ourselves in anything, when finally my muddled mind had cleared and the answer seemed so obvious.

Walter.

First, I'd head to Francine's for breakfast and any gossip Ally had that might prove useful. Then as soon as Walter's shop opened, I'd be inside, asking him to check his records and see if Lyle had ever ordered gopher poison. We all knew there was a chance he hadn't gotten poison through Walter, but for whatever reason, we all chose to believe that this was going to be the answer—the thing that created reasonable doubt for Ida Belle.

Francine's was only half-full, but then, I was early compared to most of the retirees who wandered in later in the morning. Ally gave me a wave as soon as I walked in and motioned to my usual two-top in the corner. I was pleased to see that none of the other patrons were seated close by. That gave Ally an opportunity to spill without being overheard.

She delivered the breakfast to a table across the café, then poured a cup of coffee and hurried over to my table. "I was hoping you'd come in," she said as she put the cup down and pulled out her pad, so that it looked like she was taking my order.

"What's up?" I asked.

"Aunt Celia called me last night and said Paulette left for New Jersey last night."

"What? That's rather abrupt since her husband's barely in the ground."

Ally nodded. "Aunt Celia thought it was crass, but then everything about Paulette was, so I don't know why people thought she'd be any different over this."

"But Celia's sure she's gone?"

"Yep. She dropped by late yesterday evening to take a potpie and some coffee cake, and her cousin Tony answered the door. He said Paulette needed to get away from all of this for a bit. She was able to catch a flight last night, so she packed a bag and hauled butt."

I frowned. "Why didn't Tony go?"

"Celia asked that too, but he said there was only one seat left. He said he'd be leaving as soon as he could catch a flight today. Paulette will be back later to settle up things in the house."

"I assume Carter knows she left," I said, rolling this information around in my mind.

Ally's eyes widened. "I didn't even think of that. I thought only suspects couldn't leave."

"Usually, but with the break-in at her house and then the church, I figure Carter probably would prefer her to stick around, especially since her house won't be occupied after Tony leaves, but everything's still inside."

"You think someone will break in again?"

"If you were the thief and you didn't get what you were looking for the first time, then you found out the house was empty, would you break in again?"

Ally blew out a breath. "I guess so. God, what a complicated mess. That woman has been a pain in the butt since her arrival in Sinful. She could have stayed another week—getting served fantastic food by all the locals, I might add—and let Carter do his job. But no, leave it to Paulette to make everything harder."

I smiled. "Why Ally, are you talking bad about a poor widow?"

Ally rolled her eyes. "If I thought for one moment Paulette gave a hoot about anyone but herself, I might feel a twinge of guilt. But since I'm certain Paulette only cares about the size of a man's wallet, then I'm not inclined to extend any sympathy."

I grinned, then looked over as the bells jangled above the café door. I barely held my smile in place as Bobby walked in. Ally glanced at the door, then back at me and frowned.

"He's such a flirt," she said. "And twenty bucks says he's going to head over here as soon as I walk away, so let me put in your order so you can get out."

I nodded. "The special, over easy."

"Got it," Ally said and hurried off to the kitchen.

Bobby, true to Ally's word, scanned the café, locked in on me, and ambled over, a big smile on his face. "Are you expecting Carter again this morning, or can I have this seat?" he asked.

"I'm not expecting anyone," I said. "But sometimes, people turn up."

"So what you're saying is if Carter turns up, you want me to make myself scarce?"

I wanted to lean across the table and choke him with my napkin, but the last thing I needed was people gossiping about Carter and me and the relationship we did *not* have.

"I don't really care what you *or* Carter do," I said. "I'm not a breakfast prize."

He grinned. "Fair enough. So what brings you out this early?"

"I'm a morning person."

"Me, too. I usually jog but I wasn't feeling it this morning. Maybe I'll do a late-night run."

I didn't have anything to add to the conversation, and small talk about mundane things was so not my strength, so we settled into an uncomfortable silence. Finally, Ally saved me by shoving a plate of food in front of me and taking Bobby's order.

"Go ahead," he said and motioned to my plate.

I reached for the salt and pepper and held in a sigh. Like I was going to wait. My table manners didn't extend to people who invited themselves to a meal. I spent a bit concentrating on seasoning my eggs and spreading homemade jam on my toast, then dug in.

"I hear you're Marge Boudreaux's niece," Bobby said, clearly not wanting to let the conversation die a polite death.

I took a bite of toast and nodded.

"You just here for the summer?" he asked.

"I'll leave as soon as the estate is settled," I replied.

"Hopefully, it won't be much of a trial. Some of the seniors in Sinful belong on an episode of *Hoarders*, but Marge didn't seem the type."

"She wasn't," I agreed. "Her house is very functional and has few dust collectors. It will probably take longest to catalog her books. That's where I started."

"That makes sense, you being a librarian and all."

I stared at him. "You checking up on me?"

"Just curious. A beautiful woman with your attitude doesn't exactly fit in Sinful. It made me wonder why you were here, so I asked."

"Well, now you know."

"So I can leave you alone?"

I sat my fork down and sighed. "What do you want, Bobby? I'm not interested in dating. Not you, Carter, or any other overly alpha male in this town who thinks this little woman needs rescuing. When I'm done with the legal requirements for my aunt's estate, I'm going home, which is north. Everything here is temporary and relationships shouldn't be."

He gave me a nod. "Fair enough. But you can't blame a guy for trying."

"Fine. You tried. It didn't work. Anything beyond now is stalking."

He rose from the table. "Then I guess I'll take my breakfast to go."

He gave me a smile and a wink as he sauntered across the café toward the kitchen and I held in a sigh. Guys like Bobby never, ever believed that women weren't dying to be with him. I don't know why I wasted valuable energy spelling it out. With any luck, Bobby would decide what he wanted to be "if" he ever grew up and head right back out of Sinful as quickly as he blew in, just like Carter predicted.

In the meantime, I supposed I would have to start considering breakfast at home if I planned on enjoying the meal in peace.

As soon as I saw Walter's truck pass by the café, I wrapped up breakfast and hurried across the street. The store wouldn't be open this early, but I wanted to speak to Walter without the fear of interruption. I knocked on the front door and saw Walter's eyes widen when he saw me standing there. He hurried to the door to unlock it and let me in.

"Did your uh...plan work?" he asked, trying to avoid any mention of the illegal activities he figured we were up to.

"I hope so. That's why I'm here."

"Sure. Take a seat. What do you need? Do you want coffee?"

He was so nervous it made my heart clench a bit. If something bad happened to Ida Belle, Walter would never be the same. "I just had breakfast, so I'm good. What I need is information."

"Okay."

"I need to know if Lyle Cox ever bought gopher poison from your store. Do you remember if he did?"

His eyes widened and he stared at me for several seconds with an expectant look, then as more time passed, his face fell and he shook his head. "I can't ever remember him ordering it, and it's not something I keep in stock."

My heart dropped into my feet. Had last night been a waste of time and a perfectly good ankle? Were we all so desperate for the answer that we were pinning our hopes on a ridiculous long shot?

"But let me check," he said and pulled a book out from under the counter. "This is my special orders book."

"You keep a record of all the special orders?"

He nodded. "Only way to keep up with what's come in and who's picked up their items. I know I should have it all on a computer, but I just don't feel energetic enough to learn."

I took a peek at the book, making note of the cramped handwriting that filled each row. This could take hours. "Do you have more order books?" I asked. "I can start looking through them if you show me what to look for."

Walter nodded and pulled a stack of ten books from under the counter. I felt my anticipation drop a bit.

"These are for the past two years," he said. "I have more in the back."

He opened a book and turned it my direction. "You just want to look for a note in the last column. That's where I record the order of all hazardous items."

My mood improved tenfold. Scanning the last column wouldn't take long at all, even with ten books. I opened to the first page and traced down the last column with my finger, then repeated the process over and over again, until I'd finished reviewing three books. Walter did the same—both of us tracing invisible lines down the book in studied silence.

On the fifth book, I found a note for gopher poison and my pulse ticked up. I traced my finger over to the left to see the name.

Ida Belle.

Damn it. All I'd found was more evidence to incriminate her.

Disgusted, I flipped the page and continued on, trying not to let my diminishing hope vanish into nothing.

"Here!" Walter yelled, startling me so badly, I almost fell off the stool.

"What?" I asked as I raced around the counter to look at the book.

He pointed to the entry for gopher poison, then slid his finger over to the left.

Lyle Cox.

Gotcha.

CHAPTER TWENTY-SIX

"IT WASN'T ME THAT PLACED THE ORDER," WALTER SAID. "I WAS visiting my cousin in Omaha that week. My buddy Jerry was watching the store for me."

"You're sure?" I asked.

He nodded. "I'd know Jerry's lousy handwriting anywhere. Is this enough to clear Ida Belle?"

"It's not enough to clear her, but if Lyle still has some of this poison, it's enough to create reasonable doubt." It was a whole hell of a lot more than that, but I wasn't about to tell Walter about the blackmail end of things. The fewer people who knew, the better.

"Why didn't I think of this before?" Walter asked. "I'm so stupid. Here I was with the answer and it took you to point it out."

"We don't know how much it answers yet," I said, not wanting Walter to get his hopes too high. This entire mess was still a bit of a stretch to pitch to law enforcement.

"Should I take this to Carter?" Walter asked, his excitement clearly not abating.

"Actually, do you mind if I do instead? There's something else

I need to tell him...something I don't want you implicated in."

He smiled. "I trusted you before and you came up with this. You seem like a pretty good bet, so I'm going to trust you again."

He picked the book up and handed it to me. "Let me know what Carter says and if me or Jerry need to do anything. I'm sure Jerry will be happy to verify his handwriting."

"Thanks, Walter. I'm going to call Carter now and see if he can meet me at the sheriff's office."

"You don't have to. I saw his boat parked at the dock when I came in the door."

"Great!" I grabbed the book from the counter and hurried out the store. With any luck, Carter and the dispatcher would be the only people in the office. Less chance of being interrupted that way.

After our last interaction, I knew he wasn't going to be happy to see me. And he was going to be downright angry after I told him what we'd done the night before.

But none of that mattered. All that mattered was keeping Ida Belle out of jail.

———

"You what?" Carter jumped up from his desk, glaring down at me, his face growing red. "Do you realize you could have been shot? I counted three big holes in the back of Lyle's fence, all made with a .45-caliber pistol. If just one shot had connected—"

"Sinful would have been attending another funeral," I interrupted his rant. "I know, and it was stupid. Can we agree on that part and move on to what's important?"

He threw his hands in the air and flopped back down in his chair. "Sure. Fine. Whatever."

"So after we got back to Ida Belle's, she was griping at Gertie for tripping."

"Like that's the worst thing you did," Carter muttered.

"And Gertie kept insisting she didn't trip," I said, completely ignoring his comment. "Then when she described how the ground sucked her foot in, Ida Belle knew she'd stepped in a gopher hole."

I opened the book and pushed it across the desk to Carter. "So I talked to Walter this morning, and here's the record where Lyle bought the same poison Ida Belle had."

Carter leaned forward and studied the entry, then looked at me. "So I'm to believe that out of all the people in Sinful, you just happened to pick the one other person who bought gopher poison and broke in his shed looking for it?"

"Not exactly."

"Uh-huh."

I'd known this question was coming, so we'd brainstormed a lie last night. I only hoped it was good enough to pass muster.

"We heard through the grapevine that Lyle and Ted got into it a couple of weeks ago."

"What grapevine, exactly?"

I shook my head. "When Ida Belle tried to narrow it down, it just ran in a circle—Sue heard it from Mary who heard it from Jane who heard it from Sue. She couldn't find the original source, but everyone appeared to agree on the content."

"And that's it? Ted and Lyle got into a fight, like human beings tend to do a lot of times, and the three of you leaped right to murder?"

"Not exactly. See, whoever heard the fight said Lyle told Ted he was going to the police himself. So we figured whatever they fought about was something illegal."

"So an undocumented source might have heard Ted and Lyle argue about a crime one of them might be committing with a threat to possibly talk to the police?"

I nodded.

"And that was good enough for you to risk being shot?"

I shrugged. "When you put it like that, it sounds stupid."

"It doesn't just *sound* stupid."

"But we didn't have anything else to go on, and we know it will be harder to clear Ida Belle once the prosecutor sets his sights on her. So we rolled the dice. Yes, it was stupid. And clearly, it was an absurd long shot." I tapped Walter's order book. "But you can't argue with the results."

Carter leaned back in his chair and blew out a breath.

"Look," I continued. "I know you're mad at me...disappointed, whatever. And I don't blame you. But none of this is about me or you, for that matter. It's only about Ida Belle. And if I have to piss off the pope to clear her name, then that's exactly what I'm going to do."

Carter stared at me for several seconds, then the edges of his lips turned up a tiny bit. "I wouldn't give the pope two minutes with you before he prayed for God to take him home."

"So is this enough to get a search warrant?"

Carter nodded. "I think so, and I'm sure Judge Aubry will as well, especially as he keeps putting Lyle in jail and they keep letting him out early. Besides which, he wasn't thrilled about the search warrant he issued for Ida Belle's house, but it's still his job."

"I know. Just like it's yours to arrest her if you get that call."

"Let's hope that doesn't happen," he said but I saw the worry flicker across his face before he masked it. Carter knew better than anyone that he was on borrowed time. "How is Gertie's ankle?"

"Pretty swollen last night and I bet it's black and blue this morning—probably a good match for her eye. Marie is going to take her to the hospital for an X-ray of her foot and head. We figured it better if Ida Belle stuck around..."

As he opened his mouth to reply, his phone rang. He looked at the caller ID and froze. When he answered, his voice was stiff and professional.

"Yes, sir," Carter said. "Are you sure? I have some new information to give you...no, I understand. No, sir. I have no problem doing my job. I'll inform you when she's in custody."

My heart sank into my feet as the last words left his lips. Carter slammed the phone down so hard it made me jump. He bolted up from his chair and cursed.

"You have to arrest Ida Belle," I said.

He gave me a single nod and I noticed he couldn't even look straight at me. His agony was so clear that it made me hurt for him. I couldn't begin to imagine how bad he felt.

I rose from my chair and placed my hand on his arm. "She understands. So do I. There's no conflict from where we sit. No judgment and no expectation of special treatment. If you don't handle this by the book, it could do even more harm to her case if this goes to trial."

"Knowing you're right doesn't do anything to diminish how pissed I am to be in this situation in the first place."

"I know, and I'm sorry. It sucks."

"It's just that I know Ida Belle didn't kill that man, and the prosecutor is forcing me to waste time on an avenue that's going to yield nothing. In the meantime, there's a killer walking around Sinful, smiling and thinking he got away with it. And that pisses me off the most."

"So catch him. Go arrest Ida Belle because you have to, then spend every moment you've got catching the real killer. Everything will turn out all right."

"You really believe that?"

"I have to."

———

I ARGUED WITH MYSELF THE ENTIRE WALK BACK TO THE General Store, second-guessing whether I should have spilled the beans about everything right then, but something told me it would only have muddied the waters. I had no doubt Carter would follow up on Lyle at first opportunity and with any luck, another bag of matching poison would be enough to get the prosecutor off Ida Belle's trail.

For years, I'd been trained to guard information because my life literally depended on it, and for years, I'd done so without so much as a single thought given to who could have also used the information I had and for what purposes. Information dissemination wasn't my call, and I'd never questioned it.

So why was it so hard to keep this information to myself? Information that could blow my cover wide open, which definitely put my life in danger? Why was I struggling so much to keep quiet? Why did I feel this overwhelming sense of guilt?

Because you let things get personal.

I sighed. I really hated it when my father was right.

"SURELY THERE'S SOMETHING WE CAN DO," GERTIE SAID FOR the hundredth time.

I glanced over at Marie, who had been wringing her hands for the five excruciating hours we'd been camped out in her kitchen. Gertie sat in one of the kitchen chairs with her foot propped in a chair, encased in one of those boots that are made to keep your ankle immobile and look like you're about to go skiing, albeit on one leg.

I sat in the chair across from her, absently petting Bones, who had fallen asleep sitting up with his head on my leg.

"Do you need another painkiller?" Marie asked.

"I just had one thirty minutes ago," Gertie said. "Are you trying to sedate me or kill me?"

Our only lucky break of the week had turned out to be a nonbreak. Gertie's ankle was only sprained, but it was a bad one. Not that there was a good sprain, but when you're as old as Jesus, a bad sprain may as well be a missing limb as far as recovery went.

Her head had also checked out okay, although Marie and I still had our doubts.

"I'm sorry," Marie said and reached for a mixing bowl. "I just can't stand all this waiting. What's taking so long?"

"Carter said he was going to push the prosecutor to talk to the judge and try to get bail set," I repeated for at least the tenth time. "He promised Walter he'd play up Ida Belle's age so he could get her out of jail and back home. Walter has already said he's putting up whatever money is required, but all of that is bound to take a long time, especially if the prosecutor argues for no bail."

"Why would he do that?" Gertie asked. "Ida Belle's no killer."

"The prosecutor just looks at the evidence, not the person."

"So you're saying it's not his fault he's a douche bag?"

"Something like that. Anyway. All we can do is wait."

Gertie sighed and reached for her glass of soda. "Are we going to tell Carter everything?"

"If he doesn't find the same poison at Lyle's house, then we'll tell him everything before this goes any further."

I could tell Gertie was gearing up for another question when her cell phone rang. She looked at the display and frowned. "It's Celia. She probably just wants the gossip. I'm not going to answer."

The phone went silent after another couple of rings and then my cell phone sounded off. It was Celia.

"I don't think she's calling me for gossip," I said and answered the call.

"Have you heard?" Celia shouted as soon as I answered.

"Yes. Ida Belle has been arrested. We're waiting for news."

"Jesus Christ, I knew that a hundred moons ago. Do you take me for an amateur?"

She didn't pause after the question, so I assumed it didn't require an answer.

"A couple of fishermen pulled Paulette's body out of the bayou about an hour ago."

CHAPTER TWENTY-SEVEN

I BOLTED UPRIGHT. "HOLY SHIT! HOLD ON A SEC." I PRESSED the speaker button and waved at Gertie and Marie to listen. "I'm here with Gertie and Marie. Could you please repeat that, Celia?"

"I got a call from Babs and she was in a panic. Her husband and his buddy were fishing over around Little Bayou when their anchor got hooked on a log...at least, that's what they thought it was. They pulled on it a bit and managed to get it dislodged, but it weren't no log they pulled up. It was Paulette, dead as a doornail."

Marie dropped into a chair, all of the color draining from her face. Gertie appeared struck silent for the first time since I'd known her.

"I take it she didn't drown?" I asked.

"Hell, no. There was a bullet hole right through her forehead. They pulled the body into their boat and covered it with a tarp. Peter called Babs on the way to the sheriff's department and told her what happened."

"And you're sure it was Paulette?"

"Positive. The face wasn't damaged and besides, she was wearing a gold sequined blouse. No one else in Sinful dresses like a hooker except her. What the hell is going on, Fortune? That cousin of hers told me she'd gone home to New Jersey. Do you think he killed her?"

"I honestly have no idea," I said. "I'll do some checking and let you know if I find something out."

"And I'll keep my ear to the ground over here. I don't know what's going on in my town, but I've gone from worried to downright pissed. I want this settled."

"So do I. Thanks, Celia."

I hung up the phone and stared at Gertie and Marie, trying to make sense of it all. "Who killed Paulette and why?"

"Not anyone from Sinful," Gertie said. "They would have known better than to drop a body in a prime fishing location. There's plenty of places around here a body would probably never surface."

I shook my head. "That only leaves Tony or the guys from the church."

Gertie sucked in a breath. "I hadn't even thought about them. I figured they left after they got their picture. We haven't seen them hanging around."

"No, but they'd stick out in a place like Sinful. If they're still in Louisiana, they would be lying low."

I rose from the table and walked into Marie's living room so that I could peek out her front window across the street to Paulette's house. Marie trailed behind me. "Have you seen Tony today?" I asked.

"No, but I've spent most of the day in the kitchen. I bake when I'm nervous. I think I've got more cookies in my kitchen than Keebler."

I peered at the house, looking for any sign of movement. Tony's car wasn't in the driveway and nothing seemed out of place, but clearly something was very wrong. I was just about to step away when I saw the blinds in the front window of Paulette's house lift up, then drop back down.

"There's someone inside," I said.

"Who?" Marie asked.

"I couldn't see him, but I saw the blinds lift up."

"Maybe Tony's car is in the garage," Marie said.

"He told Celia he was leaving today."

Marie shook her head. "I wish I would have sat here all day and paid attention. I just never thought..."

Gertie hobbled into the living room using the crutches she'd gotten at the hospital. "You couldn't have known," Gertie agreed. "I wouldn't have been watching all day either."

I nodded. "Trust me. None of us saw this one coming."

And I had no idea what to do about it. The logical part of me said to let the police handle it. If a couple of fishermen had delivered Paulette's body to the sheriff's department in the past hour, surely someone would head to the house to secure it as a potential crime scene.

But with Carter at least an hour's drive away and tied up with the judge and the prosecutor, who was left? It was a little after 5:00 p.m., which meant that Sheriff Lee was probably already in bed for the night and besides which, he couldn't properly secure his ancient horse, much less a crime scene. Deputy Breaux seemed nice enough, but I couldn't imagine him making a decision anytime soon on how to store Paulette's body, much less secure her house.

I looked out the blinds again and bit my lip. By the time Carter got done wrangling with the prosecutor, whoever was inside the house might be gone, which meant whoever killed Ted and Paulette might be gone because the chances of anyone having a legitimate purpose to be inside their house was slim to none.

"I'm going over there to try to see something," I said.

"No!" Marie's said. "What if it's the killer that's in there?"

Since I hoped that was the case, I didn't answer immediately. "If I can see who's in there, it might help Ida Belle."

"You're talking about sneaking up on murderers," Marie said.

"All part of the job," I said.

Marie stared. "You're a librarian, Fortune. Not a soldier."

Crap. I'd completely forgotten I was talking to Marie, who had no idea of my true identity.

"I mean it's part of the being-a-friend job," I said, trying to cover my faux pas.

Marie shook her head. "It's too dangerous. Ida Belle wouldn't want you to take such a chance."

"She's right," Gertie agreed.

"Maybe," I said, "but if the situation were reversed, would Ida Belle take the chance?"

Gertie glanced at Marie, then at the floor. Marie stared over my shoulder at the window.

"That's what I thought," I said. "Then it's settled. I'll go through Marie's backyard and over the fence, then skirt around and enter Paulette's backyard like Gertie and I did the other night. You two stay glued to this window. If anything looks suspicious, one of you call me and the other call the police."

Neither of them looked pleased, but they didn't argue.

Before I could change my mind, I headed out Marie's back door.

———

I PAUSED LONG ENOUGH TO SEND MARIE AND GERTIE A TEXT TO let them know where I was before sidling down the fence and entering Paulette's backyard. I was fairly certain they were both glued to the window, but it never hurt to hedge your bets. I inched across the back of the house and ducked behind the bush directly below the living room window. I peered up and saw that the window was cracked open an inch or so.

I was easing up to peer inside when I heard a man's voice.

"What's your problem?" the man asked.

I knew the voice sounded familiar, but it took me a couple seconds to place it as the ringleader from the church.

"You're my problem, Ritchie."

I recognized the second voice as Tony, who apparently hadn't left town as he'd told Celia he would, but then neither had Paulette.

"You got some nerve, coming at me with that attitude," Ritchie said.

"You haven't even seen attitude. What the hell were you thinking? I told you I had this under control," Tony raged. "If I hadn't bugged the sheriff's department when I was there with Paulette the other day, we wouldn't even know someone found the body. We'd be sitting ducks."

"But you did your job, for a change, and we're not. So what's the problem?"

"*For a change?* I had this entire situation under control."

"The boss didn't think so. He thought you were taking too long."

"Look, I respect the boss, but he has no idea how these small towns operate. You can't just murder people and expect that it will blow over like in New Jersey. People actually give a shit around here. Another couple of days and I would have brought Paulette back home to be dealt with."

"The boss said she wasn't allowed to step on New Jersey soil again. Said she didn't deserve it."

"So I could have killed her in New York," Tony argued. "Either way, it didn't have to happen here or now."

"You think it didn't have to happen now? You know she's been talking to that FBI agent, right?"

"What?" Tony's voice inched up a couple of octaves, and I could tell this was unwelcome news to him. "When?"

I froze, trying to make sense of what I'd just heard. What FBI agent? And why would Paulette talk to one? Blackmail was illegal but the small-town stuff Ted had pulled was hardly the sort of crime that interested the FBI.

"She did it the other day, when you weren't looking," Ritchie said, sounding smug. "Point is, you didn't have control over the situation and the boss asked us to make that right. So we did. Maybe it was messier than you like, but if you'd been doing your job and kept Paulette under wraps, you wouldn't be in this position."

"Jesus Christ," Tony said, sounding a lot less cocky than before. "Couldn't you at least have gotten rid of the body in a way that it wasn't discovered? I had people convinced she'd returned home."

"How were we supposed to know she'd be a floater? We weighed her down."

"You weighed her down in someone's favorite fishing hole. She didn't float—they pulled her up on an anchor. And even if the fishermen hadn't found her, that bayou has a huge current that churns the water like a tornado."

"It's a little late for an environmental lesson, isn't it? Look, no one here can track you, right? You did everything under your alias, so hop in your stolen rental car and disappear. How are they going to find you? Mikey and I are out of here as soon as we finish tearing this place apart."

I slipped my hand in my pocket to retrieve my cell phone. I still hadn't figured out what was going on, but I was certain that the men who'd killed Paulette were inside and that was enough for me to call for backup. I had just started my text to Gertie and Marie when I heard a creak above me.

Before I could react, I heard a voice above me.

"Don't move, bitch, or I blow your head off."

CHAPTER TWENTY-EIGHT

I LOOKED UP ENOUGH TO SEE THE SECOND MAN FROM THE church, Mikey, aka The Screamer, leaning out of the upstairs window, his nine-millimeter leveled at my head. "Yo, Ritchie!" he yelled. "We got a problem out back."

A couple of seconds later, the back door flew open and Ritchie and Tony stormed out onto the porch, guns drawn. They both drew up short when they saw me.

"Who the fuck are you?" Ritchie asked.

"That's the bitch that was following us the other day," Mikey said. "I told you someone was following us."

I was certain I hadn't followed Ritchie and Mikey anywhere, but I was pretty sure they wouldn't believe me.

"Well, she's done following now," Ritchie said and waved his gun at me. "Throw that cell phone onto the porch and get inside. No sudden moves or I kill you right here."

I was positive he planned on killing me anyway, but right now it was three weapons on me and no way could I drop my cell phone, draw my nine, and shoot all three of them before one of them tagged me. At this point, going inside and waiting until I had a better advantage was the better option. These guys were thugs, but I was a trained assassin. If I stayed cool, I'd find an opportunity to escape.

I tossed the cell phone on the porch, lifted my hands, and walked up the porch and into the living room. Tony picked up the phone and followed us inside. Mikey ran downstairs as Ritchie closed and locked the back door, then pushed the window down and closed the blinds.

"Anything?" Ritchie asked Tony.

Tony shook his head. "Only a couple of numbers stored. All the texts have been deleted."

"Keep your hands up," Ritchie said and motioned to Mikey to search me.

"What do we have here?" Mikey asked as he pulled my pistol from my waistband.

"What agency are you?" Ritchie asked.

"I have no idea what you're talking about," I said. "I'm a librarian. I'm just visiting for the summer. You can ask anyone."

Ritchie glared. "You want us to believe librarians run around with that kind of piece tucked in their pants?"

"Librarians who live in Sinful do."

"This is a waste of time," Mikey said. "She's not going to talk. None of them do."

"What the hell are we going to do with her?" Tony asked. "This is getting out of control."

"Throw her in the pantry with the other one," Ritchie said. "We'll deal with them when we're ready to leave."

"And that will be?" Tony asked. "We've got to get out of here before the cops get here."

"Another couple minutes to finish tossing upstairs and we're out of here," Ritchie said.

"I hope you know what you're doing," Tony said. "For all you know, the feds could be on their way."

"Well, if they are, she didn't call for them," Ritchie pointed out. "You said the phone is clean."

"Yeah, but who's saying she works alone?"

Ritchie's jaw twitched and I could tell he was getting annoyed with Tony's completely logical arguments. "Finish up the toss, Mikey. I'm not leaving this house without doing the job. I care what the boss thinks." He stared at Tony, his expression clearly indicating his opinion of Tony's dedication to his job.

Tony grabbed me by the arm and shoved me into the kitchen. A chair was wedged under the pantry doorknob and he tugged it away, then pushed me inside. I tripped over something large on the floor, and clutched the shelves to keep myself from falling. I felt the walls for a light switch and was about to decide there wasn't one when I felt a tickle on my neck. I reached up for the string and pulled, illuminating the small walk-in pantry.

Then I stared in amazement at what I'd tripped on.

Bobby lay in a heap on the floor, partially leaned against the back wall. I dropped down and checked his pulse. It was steady, but his breathing was shallow. I pulled him forward a bit and felt the back of his head, easily detecting the huge knot. Someone had clocked him good. He was alive but unconscious.

As I leaned him back against the wall, I saw the edge of something peeking out of his shirt pocket. I reached inside and pulled out a thin leather wallet. I already had an idea what I would find when I opened it, but it was still a tiny bit surprising to see the identification.

Bobby Morel. Federal Bureau of Investigation.

Suddenly, everything made sense. Ted hadn't left New Jersey to escape his trial for extortion. He'd made a deal with the prosecutor to testify against bigger fish, and the FBI had tucked him away in Sinful, thinking no one would ever find him. How the FBI had selected Sinful in the first place was still a mystery as Bobby was in the military when Ted and Paulette were ensconced here, but it was no mystery to me that the agency had sent Bobby to check on things now. He was the perfect choice.

But the big question remained—had the family killed Ted? Or

had Lyle done the deed and they'd found out after the fact and come to Sinful to confirm?

I blew out a breath. None of it mattered at the moment. The only thing that mattered was getting out of this pantry alive and conveying everything to Carter. I felt Bobby's waist, but his holster was empty. I figured as much. Then I moved to his legs and could hardly control my excitement when I found his backup weapon still strapped to his ankle.

I pulled the pistol out and checked the clip. It was full, but I was still at a huge disadvantage with three of them and only one of me. I could easily take out whoever opened the pantry door, but with no way of knowing the position of the others in the house, I would be completely open to attack from the remaining two men.

Ted and Paulette's kitchen had an island that separated the kitchen from the living room. If the other two men weren't in the kitchen, I should be able to dive behind that island and use it for concealment, but it wouldn't offer much in the way of cover. A bullet would probably tear right through the wood, but I could only hope the contents eliminated or slowed down an exit.

And then there was the problem of Bobby. His body was centered directly on the back wall of the pantry. If whoever opened the door shot low, they hit him center mass, but the shelves and contents prevented me from moving him to the side. Finally, I settled on pushing him over and dragging him down more until he was only elevated a foot or so. That was the best I could do.

I crouched at the edge of the doorframe, as far back from the opening as the shelves would allow, and listened, trying to determine where the men were. Footsteps echoed overhead, so I figured Mikey was still up there finishing up. At first, I couldn't hear Tony or Ritchie, but then I heard a door creak close by in the kitchen and heard muffled voices. My best guess was they were in the garage, preparing their vehicles for getaway.

A minute later, the door opened again and I could hear them clearly.

"What about the agents?" Tony asked. "Do we take them with us?"

"Since the locals have Paulette's body, I don't see the point in hiding anything. I say we take care of them here. That way, we don't have to make any stops on the way back."

"Do you have a suppressor?"

"No, use a pillow or something. I'm going up to get Mikey. If he hasn't found anything by now, no one else will either."

I felt something move near my foot and felt my pulse spike a bit before realizing it was Bobby starting to stir. I glanced down and saw his eyelids flutter a couple of times, then close again. I hoped he didn't pick the middle of the fray to sit up and try to get his bearings, but there was nothing I could do about it.

I tightened my grip on the pistol and slowly let out a breath, focusing every ounce of attention on listening for Tony. Timing was the difference between living or dying, and I sure as hell wasn't planning on the second option.

I heard footsteps on the stairwell and assumed Ritchie was headed upstairs to round up Mikey. Then I heard the light steps on the kitchen floor and the scraping of the chair being pulled out from under the doorknob. I said a silent prayer and leveled my pistol at the door.

A second later, the door flew open and I fired.

The element of surprise was definitely on my side. Tony stumbled back, clutching his chest where my deadly shot had entered. He lifted his arm to fire, but I put another bullet in his head and he dropped like a stone, firing off a shot as he dropped. The shot whizzed by, missing me, but I heard a cry behind me and figured Bobby had gotten the worst of it. With no time to worry about Bobby, I scrambled for the island, grabbing Tony's weapon as I went by.

Footsteps thundered down the stairs and I slipped to the far corner. The stairs weren't in my line of sight and there were two entrances to the kitchen—one down the hallway and one through the dining room. I could see into the dining room, but I couldn't get a clear view of the hall without exposing myself.

I slipped to the edge of the island, figuring they'd split up and come at me from both sides. I'd pick off whoever came at me through the dining room, then hope I could get the jump on the man in the hallway.

The house went eerily quiet, but I knew they were inching toward me. The occasional creak of the hardwood floor gave me a progress report, and I knew it wouldn't be long before I launched.

One second. Two.

A shadow appeared in the doorway between the kitchen and dining room and I leveled my pistol at the door. When Mikey peered around the opening, I fired off a round. He cursed and ducked back around the corner.

Damn it!

I'd just winged him. The threat still remained.

I could feel my heartbeat in my chest and worked to better control my breathing. Something as small as your own heartbeat could easily drown out the sound of your target approaching.

I heard the floor creak at the end of the hall and a bullet ripped through the island, coming only inches from me. I put my pistol around the corner of the island and fired back, but with no way to sight my target, I knew I didn't have much chance of landing a shot.

Before I could plan a second shot, I heard a crash behind me and whirled around in time to see Bobby, on his knees with blood streaming out of his shoulder, slam the kitchen chair that had been propped under the doorknob directly into Mikey's crotch. Mikey doubled over, dropping his gun, which slid across the kitchen away from Mikey. I whistled and as soon as Bobby glanced my way, I slid Tony's pistol across the floor to him. He grabbed the gun and leveled it at Mikey.

I heard Ritchie running down the hallway and it only took a second to realize the footsteps were moving away from me, not toward. I jumped out of my hiding spot and took off down the hall. No way was I letting him get away.

I'd just reached the front door when a gunshot blast brought me up short. I heard Ritchie yell and peered out to see him laid out in the front lawn, clutching his rear, his weapon several feet from his reach. I looked up and saw Gertie hobbling across the street, a shotgun leveled at Ritchie's head. A second later, police sirens sounded in the distance.

I dashed back inside to make sure Mikey was secure and found Bobby standing over him in the kitchen, clutching Tony's pistol in one hand and holding a dishrag to his shoulder with the other. Mikey was slumped unconscious against the dining room wall, clutching his side, blood pouring through his hands.

"I don't think he's going anywhere," Bobby said.

I grabbed another dishrag from the cabinet and pressed it into Bobby's wound, then handed him his pistol. "I borrowed this. I hope you don't mind."

He put Tony's gun on the counter and took his own from me.

"Given how things turned out compared to where they were headed," he said, "it's hard to complain." He narrowed his eyes at me. "But I hope you're not planning on continuing to lie about that librarian thing. I came to in time to see you in action. You've had extensive training. So who the hell are you?"

I shook my head. "I'm someone like you who needs to lie low. I know you don't have any reason to trust me or to lie for me, but I'm about to ask you to. If Carter finds out what I did here, he'll look too hard."

Bobby stared at me for a long time then sighed. "It goes against all logic and damn sure against procedure, but I believe you. And since you saved my life, it's hard to be a dick about it. Whoever you really are, your secret is safe with me."

"Thanks. I promise you, it's for a really good cause. My life, in fact."

He nodded. "The cops will be here any minute. How do you want to play this?"

"You take all the credit," I said. "I stayed in the pantry cowering."

He smiled. "You're actually going to try to pull off cowering? When I just saw you outsmart three of the deadliest men in the Maselli family? It's ballsy. I'll give you that."

"I don't have a choice. Make up whatever story you need to. If you play up your head injury, no one will think twice if things don't add completely up."

He nodded. "So play up the fuzzy memory. Smart. What about the shot outside?"

"It's not a problem. She's a friend."

"A good friend to have, apparently."

He extended his hand to me. "It seems wrong, but this is the only thanks you're going to get for saving my life."

I smiled and shook his hand, deciding that in the big scheme of things, Bobby wasn't so bad after all.

CHAPTER TWENTY-NINE

"Quite a week," Gertie said as she readjusted her booted foot on top of the ice chest on my back porch where we all sat, drinking sweet tea and eating truly incredible chocolate chunk cookies. Merlin stretched out in the sunlight at the end of the porch, completely converted to domestic life.

"That's an understatement," I said as I leaned over to slide a pillow under Gertie's foot. "It's not high enough."

"The two of you fuss like old women," Gertie griped.

Ida Belle raised one eyebrow. "Well, if you didn't go barreling into streets with shotguns, then get hit by the ice cream truck, we wouldn't have to fuss."

Gertie threw her hands in the air. "That man is a menace, driving without glasses."

I grinned. "Poor Deputy Breaux didn't know whether to arrest Ritchie or the ice cream man or help you out of the street."

"Have you heard anything from Bobby?" Ida Belle asked.

"Yeah," I replied. "Ritchie's still claiming self-defense on the shootings at Paulette's house. The prosecutor in New Jersey wanted him moved, but it got nixed. He'll be tried in Louisiana. I don't think he's going to like the result."

Ida Belle shook her head. "I'm sure not."

I stared out at the bayou, marveling over the way things had unfolded the past couple of days. I'd been dead-on with my assumption that Ted had turned state's evidence on the family and he and Paulette were in witness protection. A former commander of Bobby's had headed for the FBI a couple of years before and had discussed potential locations for witnesses with him.

Bobby had suggested Sinful as a good place to go undiscovered, and when his buddy had to find a place for Ted and Paulette, he'd sent them south. Bobby had stepped directly out of the military and into the FBI, but it had all been kept very hush-hush, making him the perfect person to head to Sinful and make sure Ted was safe and sound and preparing for trial.

When Ted's true identity came out, people in Sinful were blown away by the fact that they'd had a real-life mobster in their midst and hadn't even known. Ida Belle, Gertie, and I had feigned shock when Carter filled us in, but we hadn't had to fake a thing when we found out who'd killed Ted.

After the big showdown, we hadn't given it another thought, assuming Tony, Ritchie, or Mikey had done the deed. But when all of them were placed in New Jersey the night Ted died, we figured it was Lyle or one of the other Sinful blackmail victims.

None of us figured Paulette for the deal.

Ultimately, it was Ritchie who told. With Tony and Mikey dead, Paulette's murder was already sitting squarely on his shoulders. Apparently, he wasn't interested in fighting a double homicide rap. According to Ritchie, with Ted almost broke, Paulette was no longer willing to wait around and see what happened. Without the support and the money being in the family brought, Paulette wasn't interested in sticking around.

She'd contacted the family and offered to kill Ted in exchange for the information he had and for the price on her head to be lifted. When everything had blown over, Paulette thought she was going back to New Jersey and finding another man to support her, which was supported in part by the conversation I'd overheard in the General Store between Tony and Paulette. Based on the conversation I heard between Tony and Ritchie, I had no doubt the boss never intended for her to make it out of Louisiana alive.

Ritchie said Paulette figured the election was the perfect backdrop for the murder, but she'd seriously miscalculated the relevance of small-town politics. Election murders in New York or New Jersey might happen, but it was far less likely for someone in Sinful to murder over a mayor's seat that paid practically nothing and didn't come with kickbacks. She'd stolen the poison from Ida Belle's shed and doctored a glass of milk she took Ted before bed. She'd added the poison to the cough syrup afterward.

Thinking back to Walter's comments about Ted's bad luck with his truck and boat, it made me wonder if it wasn't so much bad luck but two early—and unsuccessful—attempts by Paulette to make his death look like an accident. If so, that was one secret Paulette was taking to the grave.

The prosecutor, being a smart man, had dropped everything against Ida Belle and was pursuing Ritchie with a conviction that was darn near frightening. The three of us had done some deliberating and finally decided to destroy the photos I'd taken from Ted's house. Ida Belle promised to feed Carter seemingly random gossip on the illegal activities we'd seen captured on film, but we saw no reason to unleash a whole other shitstorm on ourselves by coughing up the photos.

"Did Carter question you again?" Gertie asked me.

"Yeah, but Bobby covered everything pretty well. I just stuck to my story about getting caught spying and huddling in the pantry."

Ida Belle laughed. "I can't even make the stretch to imagine you as a huddled, shivering mass."

"It wasn't the easiest thing to pull off," I agreed, "but with Bobby being FBI and him and Carter knowing each other all their lives, I don't think he picked as hard as he would have someone he didn't know."

Ida Belle nodded. "I'm sure you're right."

"He gave me a butt-chewing of biblical proportion, though. I'm still smarting from it."

"He cares about you," Gertie said, "and from where Carter sits, it was the dumbest thing in the world for you to do."

Librarians have no business trying to apprehend dangerous criminals! What part of "call the police" do you refuse to understand?

The words Carter was sure to say echoed through my mind and I sighed. That was it—the bottom line. As far as Carter was concerned, I was a harmless civilian making stupid choices to help a friend. It was somewhat hurtful and insulting to be considered harmless or stupid, but I didn't really have a choice.

And there were worse things.

"Uh-oh."

I heard Carter's voice and looked up to see him rounding the corner of the house.

"When the three of you are together," he said, "it always seems to be cause for worry."

"The only crime here," Gertie said, giving her tea a wistful glance, "is that these glasses contain no alcohol."

Ida Belle and I laughed, but we'd already had a round the night before of Gertie on painkillers and drinking. Until further notice, we were limiting her to one option or the other.

"I think it's about time to head home for your nap, Gertie." Ida Belle rose from her chair to help Gertie up. She'd insisted Gertie stay with her until she could get around better, and I could only imagine the bitching Ida Belle had endured.

"I don't need a nap," Gertie complained.

"Yes, you do," Ida Belle said, giving her a pointed look. "You need to get that foot above your head and you can't do that sitting in a chair. It won't kill you to sleep a little, and if you don't mind, I'm going to do the same."

Gertie studied Ida Belle for a moment, then glanced at Carter and me and her eyes widened just a bit. "Fine. I'll sleep. But I'm not listening to that relaxation music you played yesterday. That crap makes me want to scream. Put on some George Strait and stop trying to be fancy."

Ida Belle helped Gertie to her feet and grinned. "George Strait it is. I'll give you a call later, Fortune."

As they went inside the house, I motioned to Ida Belle's vacated chair. "Have a seat. Do you want some iced tea?"

Carter took a seat. "Is it sweet tea?"

"Is there any other kind in Sinful?"

He laughed. "Yeah, I'd love a glass."

I headed into the kitchen to pour a big glass of sweet tea and refill the cookie plate. I sat both of them on the tiny table in between our chairs. As he reached for a cookie, I put my hand over them to block him.

"Are you going to yell at me again?" I asked. "Because if you are, you can't have a cookie."

He cringed. "Considering I've already seen the offering, that's pretty harsh."

"Yes."

He studied me for a couple of seconds then smiled. "No, I'm not going to yell at you again. I probably shouldn't have in the first place, but when I think about what could have happened..."

I nodded and removed my hand from the cookies. Even though I had an edge so much bigger than what Carter could ever imagine, the situation could have gone down completely different than it did. Training and intelligence couldn't buy your way out of everything. The bottom line was, sometimes you also had to get lucky.

And I'd gotten very lucky.

"So you're not mad at me anymore?" I asked as he picked up a cookie.

"I wasn't mad, really...okay, I was mad." He frowned for a

couple of seconds and stared across the backyard, then he looked back at me. "The thing that aggravates me the most is that even though I think it was the dumbest thing in the world, I respect you for trying to help your friend."

I stared at him. His statement had been so unexpected, I wasn't sure how to respond.

"However, in the future," he continued, "I would prefer that you leave the bad guys to law enforcement. You're supposed to be here settling your aunt's estate, not figuring out a way to follow her to the grave."

I smiled. "I will do my best to stay out of law enforcement business."

"Your best, huh? That's all you're going to give me?"

"Anything more would require me ending my friendship with Ida Belle and Gertie or potentially being a liar."

He laughed. "Fair enough."

He took a bite of the cookie and settled back in his chair. I felt silly that I had an edgy feeling, sitting there with him, but with everything that had happened, it was almost an automatic reaction.

"So did you need anything in particular?" I finally asked, figuring I may as well get the real reason for his visit out in the open.

He looked over at me and raised one eyebrow. "Do I have to need something in particular to have iced tea and cookies with a friend? You did say we're friends, right?"

I sighed. "Yeah, we're friends. And no, you don't need a reason to be here. It's just that you usually have one other than relaxing."

He put his cookie down on the table. "You caught me. I have another reason."

I felt my pulse tick up a notch. Had he looked into me despite Bobby's story? Had he figured out we knew about Ted's true identity and hadn't told him?

"If you're not busy Friday night," he said. "I'd like to take you to dinner."

My heart began to pound and I stopped breathing.

No!

Logic screamed at me to avoid any further pursuit into the personal, but my mouth had ideas of its own.

"Okay," I said, then immediately began cursing myself for my lapse in judgment.

"Great," he said and rose from the chair. "I'll give you a call tomorrow to let you know the particulars."

I nodded as he headed down the porch steps and started across the lawn.

"Carter?"

He stopped and turned around to look at me. "Yeah?"

"This is a friends kind of dinner, right?"

"If you say so." And with a wink, he rounded the corner of the house and slipped out of sight.

For more adventures with Fortune and the girls, check out Swamp Team 3.

For information on new releases, please sign up for my newsletter on my website janadeleon.com.

Made in the USA
Middletown, DE
13 August 2023

36672229R00149